DIAMOND HILL

KIT FAN

鑽
石
山

dialogue
books

DIALOGUE BOOKS

First published in Great Britain in 2021 by Dialogue Books
This paperback edition published in 2022 by Dialogue Books

10 9 8 7 6 5 4 3 2 1

A CIP catalogue record for this book is available from the British Library.

ISBN 978-0-349-70168-4

Typeset in Berling by M Rules
Printed and bound in Great Britain by Clays Ltd, Elcograf S.p.A.

Papers used by Dialogue Books are from well-managed forests
and other responsible sources.

Dialogue Books
An imprint of
Little, Brown Book Group
Carmelite House
50 Victoria Embankment
London EC4Y 0DZ

An Hachette UK Company
www.hachette.co.uk

www.littlebrown.co.uk

*For those who were and are unhoused
and in temporary accommodation*

The hermit crab prefers a little shell for
his home. He knows what the world holds.
The osprey chooses the wild shoreline, and
this is because he fears mankind. And I too
am the same.

Kamo no Chōmei, *Hōjōki*

From the entry into force of the Joint
Declaration until 30 June 1997, premium
income obtained by the British Hong Kong
Government from land transactions shall,
after deduction of the average cost of land
production, be shared equally between the
British Hong Kong Government and the
future Hong Kong Special Administrative
Region Government.

Clause 7 of Annex III 'Land Leases'
in the *Joint Declaration of the
Government of the United Kingdom of
Great Britain and Northern Ireland
and the Government of the People's
Republic of China on the Question of
Hong Kong*, signed in Beijing on 19
December 1984

The mind, that ocean where each kind
Does straight its own resemblance find;
Yet it creates, transcending these,
Far other worlds, and other seas;
Annihilating all that's made
To a green thought in a green shade.

Andrew Marvell, 'The Garden'

The boys would be able to draw the Buddha
with their fingernails ... It is done by the high
eyebrow, soaring outwards, by the long slit eye,
almost shut in meditation, with a suggestion of
squinting inward, that would be a frighteningly
large eye if opened; and by a suggestion of the
calm of childhood in the smooth lines of the
mature face – a certain puppy quality in the long
ear often helps to bring this out. If you get these,
they carry the main thought of the religion; for
one thing the face is at once blind and all-seeing.

William Empson, *The Face of the Buddha*

驚

The Awakening of Insects

蟄

The first thing I heard when I arrived in Diamond Hill was a boy's cry coming from an alleyway that smelt of piss. The cry was short and low, as if the boy was swallowing his angry breath, as if he held a grudge against being born in this shanty town infested by moths. It was before the season of thunder and cockroaches.

'Stop it, you little insect! I'll cut your ear off if you keep moving around,' a woman shouted.

Smudges of dried blood covered the belly of her pearl-white dress. Over it, her red silk dressing gown, adorned with a phoenix triumphing over nine dragons, fluttered in the breeze of an electric fan. She wore high heels and sunglasses that covered half her face. Holding a cigarette in one hand and a pair of scissors in the other, she was trying to cut the boy's hair. She looked like a faded actor who had settled on being an extra.

I glanced at the smudges on her belly.

'Don't worry, it's only chicken blood,' she said. 'This little insect will get herself killed before I lay a finger on her.'

The child wasn't a boy, though she was made to look like one. She wasn't a child either. Her hands were tied to an armchair and her mouth was stuffed with a face-flannel. She wore a big porcelain soup bowl like a hat.

The woman traced the scissors around the brim of the bowl. The girl held her breath until she couldn't.

'Keep still!' The woman put the cigarette in her mouth, rested her sunglasses above her forehead, and slowly ran the blades towards the tricky bit near the girl's temple. The girl peeked from behind her fringe and the woman blew cigarette smoke into her eyes. The girl coughed and the cigarette dropped on her knee.

I grabbed the woman's arm before she could run the blades over the girl's ear. 'Give them to me.'

'What the hell do you think you are doing?' She yanked at the girl.

'I used to be a hairdresser.'

I picked up the cigarette butt, put it between the woman's lips, and took the scissors. She tipped her sunglasses down again and stepped aside, spitting out the butt and lighting a new one. The scissors were wet and slippery. I could feel her sweat on the handles.

I crouched on the floor and untied the girl's hands. She took hold of the bowl and lifted it up an inch, so that the blades could travel over the tender bridge above her ear. Then I did the other. The girl kept staring at me all the time. It was difficult to tell her age from those strong, determined eyes. Underneath her T-shirt there were tight bandages, flattening her young breasts.

'Leave the sideburns alone. I don't want her to look pretty,' the woman said, puffing smoke at me.

The girl spat out the flannel and screamed, 'NO!'

'Another word from your insect mouth and I'll shave all your hair off!'

The girl stood up and threw the bowl on the floor. It didn't break. It was plastic.

The woman laughed. 'Pathetic!'

The girl ran away and disappeared into the alley.

'Let her go,' the woman said casually, as I was about to give chase.

The sound of her young feet was sliced thinner and thinner by the electric fan. I stood up, brushing the dark, soft hair off my T-shirt, wiped the scissors clean on my trousers and handed them back to the woman. I picked up my luggage and watched the cigarette ash landing on her pristine white leather high heels.

'They're Louis Vuitton,' she said, wiping the ash off with the sleeves of her silk gown. 'A gift from Bruce Lee. One of my exes.'

Her shoes gleamed under the fluorescent lights and I didn't say a word.

'What? Haven't you heard of LV? Country bumpkin.' She spat her words at me before admiring her own shoes.

I gathered myself and walked past.

'靚仔 (Handsome), want to come upstairs with me? Free of charge.' Her voice softened into another person's voice. 'I like the taste of a fine stranger.'

'Thank you.' I carried on walking. 'But that's not my cup of tea.'

'Go to hell.' She smirked and went back into her corrugated metal shack.

As I was walking off, a man shouted from across the street.

'柯德莉夏萍 (Audrey Hepburn)! Have you been dumped by another bald loser?'

'收撚你把坑渠口 (Shut the fuck up, you gutter-mouth).'

'你死撚開啦鬆皮雞 (Go to hell, you open-thighed whore).'

I continued down the alley and searched for the path towards the hills without a clue which direction I was heading in. The journey from Bangkok to Hong Kong was tiring, though I had travelled light, with little in my suitcase. I had been sent home by 大師 (Daishi), an old monk in Bangkok, who had disappeared some months earlier. He'd saved me from death many times. The young monks in Wat Arun said he had gone to the mountains to meditate on the Earth's sufferings. I waited and waited for him to return. He didn't, or wouldn't. Why did I wait for him? When he didn't show up after a month, I obeyed his command and ended up back here, where I began. I hated Hong Kong so much I thought I'd never set foot in this damned city again. Here I was, with nowhere else to go, seeking shelter in a nunnery. What the hell was I doing here? Why had Daishi sent me back here from Wat Arun? I missed Bangkok already.

There were no street signs. The shanty town was a maze, all its lanes and paths twisted and crisscrossed randomly. Most houses were wooden or metal shacks, one leaning precariously on another, each fitted with wafer-thin walls. Cardboard houses were built on top of tin-box houses, built on top of wooden houses. Red demolition notices were glued on all the doors. There were wires everywhere, some loose, some tangled up around lamp posts. Open gutters ran in the middle of most alleyways, funnelling a foul smell of sewage and lemon bleach. The graffiti on the rat poison notices were full of racist jokes about Vietnamese refugees and Indian immigrants. There were sexist ones too – tits and penises painted on people's doors beside foul words about women and prostitutes. The jokes about black people were the worst.

Despite its hard edges, sociability was abundant everywhere. Lives travelled through the thin walls onto the narrow streets – children shrieking after winning a game of dice, food being tossed in woks, men cursing at an unlucky horse after a race in Happy Valley, plastic flip-flops clip-clopping on hard concrete floors. Lots of people had their doors open and checked me out as I walked past. Through a low-hanging door two kids were drumming at the small table with their chopsticks, swinging their heads up and down to a private rhythm. Their mum handed them a bowl of rice. The children cheered when their dad placed a piping hot dish in front of them. Pork ribs steamed with garlic and black bean sauce. It smelt so good, my mouth watered.

I lingered around the doorway, and the little girl turned towards me, reached her hand out with her rice and said, '媽咪, 有個和尚嚟探我哋 (Look, Mum, a monk is visiting us).' As I extended my hand, her dad grabbed her bowl. '呢度剩喺有尼姑, 冇和尚! (There're only nuns here, no monks!)' I panicked and ran away, finding myself in a dead end.

Suddenly there was thunder. A 747 flew very close to where I was standing, and I could smell gas fumes everywhere. Its shiny grey undercarriage filled the sky. The metal and wooden houses shook and made disturbing noises. It felt as if the whole place was under attack. The plane dipped closer, and I could see the wheels descend for landing. It flew so close to the shanty town I swear to God I saw some of the passengers' faces. It sounded like the noise of battle. Or the terrible bombings shown in war movies.

I ducked down, and just when I thought the plane would crash on top of me it glided westward, taking its thunder away.

The noise in my brain faded but my eardrums were still hurting. There was an earth-cracking bang in the distance, as if a bulldozer had knocked down a house, or a power drill had hit bedrock.

Most people weren't bothered by the plane or the construction. They were busy having fun and gambling. Some men crouched in circles, shouting at the radio, obsessed by the machine-gun commentary from Happy Valley. Another street was taken over by table after table of men and women playing mah-jong, chattering and chain-smoking. Each table a world of its own. The clatter of tiles being shuffled reverberated through the alleys. People were jokey, overexcited, preoccupied by whoever they were playing with. Or the money they had lost or won. Everyone looked contented in their own shabby corner.

Why couldn't a paradise be built out of scraped wood, cheap metal, and cast-offs, with stray cats and dogs, and the occasional rat sneaking past?

An old man stood apart on his own, wearing nothing but a pair of white boxer shorts and flapping his arms like an angel. He caught my attention, grabbed my hand, and said, '鄧小平話馬照跑舞照跳　香港五十年不變! (Deng Xiaoping said the horses will keep racing and people will keep dancing. Hong Kong will remain unchanged for fifty years!)' I nodded and he smiled brightly as if he had won the lottery. Another 747. The old man pointed upwards with his middle finger, shouting '屌你老母啟德 (Fuck you, Kai Tak Airport).' Far overhead, three skyscraper-height cranes swung slowly, lifting steel frames into the air. He sat down on a pile of flattened cardboard boxes, mumbling words that sounded like the names of foreign places.

A group of kids ran past. At first I thought they were chasing the plane, but then I noticed a yellow dragonfly struggling over my head with a string tied to its body.

'Catch it! Catch it!' the children shouted to me.

I took hold of the string and felt the force of the dragonfly trying to escape. It was very light. It buzzed around like a toy helicopter, from left to right, right to left, scanning me with its multifaceted eyes. Everything about it was fragile – its wings, its legs, its antennae – except its strong, big eyes.

The children flocked around me suspiciously. None of them were wearing their own clothes – the trousers too long or too short, the T-shirts too tight or too loose. Two were tickling each other, some barefoot, all of them smiling.

'It's ours. Give it back,' a boy said, opening his arms.

The dragonfly flew up into the sky and I could feel the string slipping out of my hand. I pulled hard to regain my grip. The insect fell apart like a stick snapped in two.

The children shrieked and started kicking me.

'You killed it, you bastard. Pay us back!'

I fished out a small coin from my trouser pocket and tossed it into the air far away from the kids. They ran after it like a mob, except the boy who was staring at me. He stood there, without moving an inch.

'Who are you?' he asked.

His small black eyes were fixed on mine.

'I asked you who you are. Answer me!' He raised his unbroken, high-pitched voice.

I turned away and headed up another narrow alley.

One of the kids got the coin and galloped around like a firecracker. The other kids were trying to steal it from her, pulling her T-shirt and hair, but she ran away and vanished into one of the colourful boxlike houses.

I looked back to see the boy still standing there. I walked

faster. The alley seemed to go on for ever. The residents were watching me intently, instructing me to mind my own business.

In fact, I hadn't had any business to mind for quite a long time, and that was a good thing. How would the boy have described me? A bald man with a suitcase? A loser? I could now smell 白粉 (the white powder, heroin), that pure stuff glowing in the dark, a fluorescent god without a face. I could see its traces everywhere in the alley – needles, burned tinfoil, urine, blood, shit. I found a plastic bag, wrapped it round my hand like a glove, and picked up a broken needle, still spots of blood on it.

How could any place remain unchanged for fifty years?

It was two years since I had set foot in Hong Kong, and it already looked a different beast. Of course, the city still breathed money, but everyone knew what would happen in ten years' time. On 1 July 1997, the last colony of the British Empire would be handed over to China. Perhaps it was easier for me to return, knowing there was an expiry date for my home city. Before I left Hong Kong, all I knew was how to shut myself out of life. This city was a cruel place, especially to failures like me.

At the end of the alley a dog was sniffing torn rubbish bags. He looked shit-scared, like a drug addict. I wondered what I looked like in the eyes of the shit-scared dog.

Another peal of thunder, another plane. The shanty town trembled under its engines and I too felt shaken.

It took me another hour to get out of the corrugated metal labyrinth. A narrow alleyway opened to a dirt road, a green hill, and some jutting rocks. Through dense trees, the yellow-tiled roof of the nunnery was just visible. I could see as far as Lion Rock Peak. Perched on top of the mount, the bare rock did indeed look like a crouching lion eyeing its prey. I had never seen it so clearly before. I continued uphill, trying to recall the lyrics of the famous song by Roman Tam: *We are together below the Lion Rock, so throw away our divisions and find our bridges.* I'd forgotten most of them, but I hummed the melody anyway as I walked under the trees along the darkening path.

I heard the stream before I smelt it – fresh air, burning charcoal, and wet leaves. I was soon enveloped in a cloud of midges. Water trickled down the steep hill, through the moss and stones, until blocked by a pile of rubbish. I picked up a few discarded Coke cans to release the flow. Then I saw the junk downstream – diapers, plastic bags, broken glass, burned clothes, needles, toys, chairs, shattered figurines of the Buddha – detritus big and small, choking the stream.

The sun had set by the time I arrived at the nunnery. The nuns had begun their evening chants. A young nun came out and bowed to me, her palms held together by prayer beads. She didn't speak and neither did I. I followed her along a moonlit corridor and through a small meticulously tended garden leading to an annex next to a kitchen. At the far end of a mock-stone mountain and a circular gate stood a bamboo hen coop, and next to it a doorless wooden shed with a thatched roof. She took me into the shed and lit the gas lamp on the desk. I put my luggage on the single bed and sat down because there was no room for standing. She left quietly. I lay in bed with my eyes closed and my feet resting on my suitcase, listening to the distant trickling of water in a pond. There was something calming and infectious about this quiet, secluded place.

I opened my eyes and on the desk was a wooden tray with a bowl of rice, steamed tofu and bean soup on it – all stone cold. A moth was desperately trying to fly into the gas lamp. Finally, it got through the crack between the two panes of glass. It sizzled. Another come and gone. I turned the gas lamp off and started eating in the dark. Airplanes flew overhead, the noise of their engines reverberating in the surrounding hills. Between the landings and take-offs, the construction droned like a bass drum in the distance.

Later the young nun appeared again and took away the tray. She bowed and said, 'The door will arrive tomorrow.'

When I woke the sun was already at full mast. The same wooden tray with rice, tofu and bean soup was on my desk. I finished it all without complaint.

I could smell rice steaming in the kitchen and hear hens pecking and clucking. In the sunlight the wooden shed looked bigger than it had in the dark. The window by the desk had no glass or curtain. Next to the gas lamp stood a small porcelain figure of 觀音 (the Goddess of Mercy) and a burning incense stick. Though makeshift and minimal, everything inside the shed was spotlessly clean, gleaming in the sun.

I put on my only pair of sandals and the nun came to take the breakfast tray away.

'The door has arrived,' she said. 'Please install it yourself.'

I bowed and nodded without thinking twice. The door, leaning against the shed, was made of oak, beautifully sanded and showing the ring-years like orbits in a galaxy. Only when I touched it with my hands did I realise it had been custom-made for the shed. There was a note tied securely to it. It contained three words written with an ink brush: 內禁釘 (inside no nails). There was another piece of paper with technical instructions explaining how to make wooden joints and how to attach the door to the wooden hinges. With nothing else to do, I went straight to work.

It took me the whole afternoon just to make the joints. The oak was old and hard and difficult to work with. By the time the sunlight dimmed, the nun reappeared with the same tray, and the same rice. I stopped working and ate. To avoid the moths I didn't turn on the gas lamp. Soon afterwards I fell into a deep sleep.

I woke up earlier the next morning but still later than the nuns, who I could hear doing their morning chants. I got on with installing the door and time passed quickly. Kai Tak Airport had replaced my wristwatch. Every eight or ten minutes a 747 emblazoned with its airline's livery flew over the nunnery. The nuns chanted and meditated like whisperers watching an action movie.

By the end of day, I had managed to attach the hinges to the doorframe. At sunset I took a rest in the garden and realised that it was less well-tended than I'd thought. The azaleas were dead or dying and the lawn was fake. The algae in the pond were strangling the lotus.

When I returned to the shed, dinner was on my desk. Although I was aware there were people in the nunnery, I had not seen a single soul all day. I wondered if the young nun was avoiding me.

On the third day, I discovered that the door had no handle or inside lock. There was only a wooden bolt. The instructions indicated that the bolt should be installed from the outside.

Through the kitchen door across the yard, I could see two pairs of hands chopping vegetables.

'You can't come in here,' said one of the nuns, and shut the door.

'Sorry to bother you. I need to speak to somebody.'

'All the other nuns are meditating and won't be speaking to anyone.'

'For how long?'

There was no answer. I realised I hadn't heard chanting that day. So I set my heart on finishing the door.

On the fourth day, it was complete. The nuns must have still been in meditation, as the nunnery was dead quiet.

The silence lasted for another two days. They were perhaps the longest two days of my life. With nothing to do, I played with a small wooden splinter, pressing it as far into my thumb as I could without drawing blood. The hours crawled on.

In Wat Arun, I had learned that being quietly repetitive was at the heart of Buddhist training, but it was only through making a door for my own shed that my mental disquiet finally gave in, focusing on one single task. So I decided to undo the door and reinstall it to while away some more time. In the process I refined the joints, making them more at home with each other. I started to patch the windows with a roll of old Japanese paper I'd found under the bed. I stepped out of the shed, and a tray with the same dinner had been placed by the door. Once the windows were sealed off and the door installed, I could have my dinner with the gas lamp on without fear of killing a moth.

On the seventh day, this pattern was broken. That morning there was no breakfast, and at noon no lunch. I was famished and couldn't believe how much I hungered for the plain rice, tofu and bean soup. There was nobody around, not even in the kitchen. I wanted to venture further into the nunnery, but without a guide I felt I would be trespassing. I was light-headed and delirious and went to bed early.

I was woken in the middle of the night by the young nun. She gave me a bowl of warm water which tasted like liquorice. Then, she signalled me to follow her. There was a new moon and the garden was cloaked in a thin haze. She took me to the Main Temple and left me there.

On the veranda I could see the whole shanty town cascading downwards like a waterfall. The faint yellow street lamps mapped the contours of the hill. At that time of night there was still movement in some of the houses, and an occasional dog's bark echoed by another. The eastern part of the town was pitch-black; rows of houses had already been demolished. Just around the hill bend, sheltered by the pines but not far from the nunnery, there were cranes, scaffolding, dirt tracks, and silhouettes of concrete towers, lit by powerful floodlights like those in a stadium. Every five seconds one of the floodlights flickered, and after each flash, the construction site seemed to have encroached further down the shanty town and up towards the nunnery. I closed my eyes and gave myself up to my hunger. I could smell the pungent, almost sickly-sweet taste of jasmine. All I could hear were crickets and my stomach.

'What is keeping you out there?' a sharp voice echoed from inside the Main Temple.

Through the paper screen door, a flickering candle showed a figure on the right side of the temple. I took off my shoes and opened the screen. A middle-aged nun in a saffron robe sat in the lotus position, counting her prayer beads. She lifted her hand to indicate I should sit opposite her.

'It is a long-established custom that anyone wanting to join this nunnery needs to be purified by eating the same food for seven-times-seven days before they can enter the Main Temple. In the final week, they eat nothing to complete the purification. I have made an exception in your case. I understand that forty-nine days would be too long for you. After all, you have no intention of being one of us. Even if you did, you cannot.' She only looked into my eyes once she had stopped speaking.

'Thank you for starving me. I appreciate your allowing me to stay here. All the same, I don't understand the bolt on the door. It's on the outside.'

'I am the Head Nun of this nunnery. You are the only man who has stayed overnight here since it was founded. The bolt is a symbol of our distance. We have no intention of using it.'

'What's it for then?'

'A bolt is a bolt. It has no intentions.' She smiled awkwardly. 'I knew you were a drug addict, but I didn't know you were a philosopher. Heroin, wasn't it?'

My lips shook.

'Don't be alarmed. Daishi and I go back a long way.'

She stood up and turned towards the south end of the hall where a kettle was starting to boil. A small lady, I thought, but her smallness was forceful. She put a pinch of tea leaves in a tall glass and poured boiling water into it. The glass burned my fingers. I quickly put it on the floor, trying not to spill any of the tea, and the nun sat down again. In the dancing candlelight her face appeared gaunt, strong, and determined, as if she could have been a mother. It was a face that had shown and seen suffering. There was a round mole the size of a pea on her left cheek. It would have been a gift for a comedian.

'How is Daishi in Wat Arun?' she asked, adjusting her robe.

I felt palpitations in my chest. 'He disappeared without a word. The monks said he'd left Bangkok to become a hermit and is hiding in Doi Pui Mountain in Chiang Mai.'

'He hates Chiang Mai. At his age, the mountain would mean his death.'

I stopped the words I was going to say and took a sip of the hot tea instead. A moth caught the candle flame and dropped to the floor.

'Daishi is very healthy for his age. There's no reason he would leave Wat Arun because he was dying,' I said after a moment.

'He has been dying since last year, didn't you know?' she muttered, picking up the remains of the moth and rubbing it on her robe. 'Lung cancer. It's spread everywhere. No hope.'

It was difficult to detect any sorrow in her voice.

'He wrote to me a month ago, asking me to take you in. He said you needed to make peace with the past.'

She sat cross-legged on the floor, resting her hands on

her knees, palms facing the night sky, as if the gesture were shielding her from the outside world.

'I finally wrote back telling him that was a load of rubbish. No man has ever stayed in this nunnery. It was untypically sentimental of him to talk about making peace with the past. The cancer must have gone to his head. He was on the last leg of his journey when he wrote to me. I could sense it.'

The crickets were going berserk. I stood and walked towards the seated Buddha in the hall. His quiet face was barely lit, and yet even with his eyes closed I knew he was watching me. I found some change in my pocket and threw it into the offering box. I closed my eyes and prayed, though not for anything or anyone. When I opened my eyes, I could see his steady palms, facing outward.

It was a stormy night when I met Daishi for the first time. He had taken me in from the streets of Bangkok, given me tea and offered me refuge. He wasn't like the other monks who had helped me. He knew I was an addict and would need my regular shots. He went inside the private quarters of the temple and came out offering me a bag of new needles. I guessed he wanted to win my trust. He said that the Buddha's palms were reaching out, asking me to overcome my fear. I slept with the Buddha that night. Before dawn, I took the two gilded lotus candelabras and put them in my rucksack. Then I emptied all the money from the offering box, sneaked out of Wat Arun and went back onto the streets. Now, two years later, I was standing in front of another Buddha making the same gesture. I felt my face burning. Perhaps the Head Nun was right. Daishi was hiding from us because he was dying. How would sending me to the nunnery and drug-filled Diamond Hill help me make peace with my past?

The Head Nun was meditating with her prayer beads. I put on my sandals to leave and stood at the doorway looking out at the blinking shanty town.

'The developers have bought Diamond Hill from the government and the entire shanty town will soon be demolished, to give way to luxury apartment blocks.'

'And the nunnery? The cranes are almost at your doorstep.'

She laughed. 'This place is as old as the hills. It's sacred. Nobody would dare steal an inch of my nunnery. I will protect it with my last breath. Of course, the shanty town is a totally different story.'

'It isn't that bad here. People look contented with what they have got. There is poverty in every city in the world. I've seen worse in Bangkok.'

'井底之蛙 (A toad at the bottom of a well, an ignorant man).'

I didn't respond.

'I didn't mean you. Daishi told me you come from a good family. You're an educated man. You should know the shanty town is behind the times. The development is for the greater good.'

'These are people's homes. They will be uprooted and where will they go?'

'They will drift about like dandelion seeds.'

I bowed and reached out to close the screen door, but her hand indicated not to.

In my mind I pictured my suitcase underneath the bed in my shed, and inside it the only jacket I had, folded neatly, and in the inside pocket a sealed paper envelope that contained all the money I had saved in Wat Arun. A small sum, not even enough for a one-way passenger ticket on a cargo boat to Bangkok.

I reached the veranda and her voice followed. 'I want you to take all the hens to the butcher tomorrow. Keep the giblets. Quartz, my assistant, will give you a list telling you what to buy.'

I walked back to my shed. I looked at the chickens huddled in their coop. They were scrawny and sleepy. Wouldn't it be a pity to slaughter them all in one go?

The butcher didn't ask me how I came to have six hens. He only told me to return in half an hour. Quartz's list was rather short, so after shopping and picking up the hens from the butcher, I went to Café Paradiso next to the cobbler. I ordered milk tea which the waiter claimed was the best in Kowloon. They were faithful to the original recipe: they used a pair of silk stockings to filter it, making it as smooth as a woman's legs.

A television hung above the bar. Advertisements floated across the screen, mostly about cleaning products, including a new type of bleach suitable for sanitising baby bottles and killing rats. The café was busy but uncannily quiet. In one corner a group of construction workers were having an early lunch. The whole place was a crazy mismatch: the green tables, orange walls and blue overhead fans made it exotically out of date. A laminated photograph of the owner and his dog was perched on the counter, featuring rugged emerald hills and turquoise water on golden sandy beaches. There was a bright red slogan on the top of the photo: *Hawaii, the world's paradise.* Next to it was another laminated photograph bearing the gold signature of Bruce Lee diagonally superimposed over the owner, his dog, and the star himself sitting in the café.

As soon as the news at noon came on, a husky voice, presumably the boss's, shouted from the kitchen, 'Turn the damn thing off! I don't want to listen to those liars.'

The female cashier put down her cigarette lazily, blipped the remote control and the television screen went black. She had immaculately permed hair shaped like a poodle. She gave me a nonchalant look and went on puffing out cigarette smoke.

My milk tea arrived, along with a steaming plate of rice and a grilled chicken thigh with onions which I hadn't ordered. 'Courtesy of the boss,' the waiter said. His little fingernail was long and dirty and there was a faded dragon tattoo on his forearm.

I looked around for the boss in the café and the waiter pointed to a boy in oversized sunglasses sitting among a bunch of bigger teenage boys. It turned out to be the girl I knew. She gave me a cool nod and resumed her conversation with her friends. They were acting tough in an over-energetic, amateurish way, sprawling on the chairs like gangsters. Their gold chains and bracelets were way over the top. Their big mouths threw out words like 'business', 'package' and 'clean' repeatedly, just to catch people's attention. The girl was mainly quiet, minimally nodding her head. When she spoke, they listened respectfully like children being scolded by their mother.

It had been more than a week since I had eaten meat. The crispy, oily chicken skin lifted my spirits, though the milk tea was absolutely revolting. It didn't take me long to finish. The girl got up and tapped my shoulder as she swerved past, signalling her gang to leave her alone.

'Hey, Buddha boy! Nice to see you around.' She spoke in a fake, manly, enthusiastic voice that bore no resemblance to that of the helpless little girl who had been forced to have her hair cut. She pulled up the chair opposite me and sat down like a cowboy in a Marlboro advert.

'Thanks for the lunch.'

'That's a thigh from one of your chickens.' She smiled mischievously, as if she knew everything about me. 'How's sex with the nuns going? You like their 飛機場 (boobs as flat as an airport runway)? They don't often get to have sex, you know, if they've ever had it. Are they really tight? Are you loosening them up nicely? They must think you're a godsend.'

'You shouldn't talk like that. It's not funny, 細路女 (little girl).'

'Call me 波士 (Boss). That's what people call me here. I'm everybody's Boss, okay?' She took out a tiny plastic packet filled with the white powder and waved it in my face. 'It's Grade A stuff. People call it *the diamond cut*.' Her American accent came straight out of a gangster movie. She blinked and whispered, 'You don't need to look anywhere else. I run a monopoly in Diamond Hill.'

She put her finger on my lips just when I was about to speak.

I moved her hand and said, 'Don't do this again.'

She waved at the poodle-woman at the till, who climbed down from her high-stool, lit a cigarette and put it in Boss's mouth.

'How's your mother?' I asked.

She laughed and blew the smoke in my face. 'Who said she's my dear mummy?'

'Who is she to you then?'

'Whatever you like. I know you haven't fucked her yet, but I still call her an open-thighed whore.' She chuckled, and the poodle-woman laughed with her. The construction workers hastily finished their lunch and headed for the exit.

'死撚開! 唔好阻住我發達!' (Fuck your dick off! Don't stop me getting rich!) If I see your shitty asses here again, you're dead, real dead. Your wives won't recognise you.' Boss shouted. 'You're a bunch of fucking traitors!'

'Shouldn't you be in school?'

She repeated my words in a whining, childlike voice. 'Shouldn't you be in school?' She made a funny face, then a steely face.

'Fuck school!' she screamed, before raising her arms and shoving everything on the table against the wall. The plastic plates bounced on the floor and the metal cutlery made a sharp clattering noise.

I left five dollars on the table. As I walked past Boss, she put the money back in my pocket and said in a softer tone, 'My treat.' Her eyes looked as young as those of the girl who had held a soup bowl over her head, waiting for me to cut her hair.

'See you around, 佛佗 (Buddha).'

One of her teenage gang blurted out, 'Have fun with the nuns!' Then they all started whistling after me and calling me Buddha.

I handed the five-dollar bill to the cashier. She opened the till, smiling and shaking her head as if telling me I was an idiot.

While the nuns were busy cleaning the nunnery that afternoon, I was sent to the kitchen to prepare the chickens.

There was no gas fire and the whole place smelt of burning wood and charcoal. I had never been a good cook but the nuns were forbidden to handle meat. The birds were still lukewarm with their giblets thoroughly cleaned. The recipes were simple enough – chicken soup, steamed chicken with salt, and rice flavoured with chicken fat, along with some green vegetables. Judging from the quantity of rice, I was cooking for at least twelve people. The nuns wouldn't be eating meat, so they must be having guests.

Quartz stood outside the kitchen door peering in. 'I won't come in because of the meat. Please lay out the dishes in the side hall when you're done. You can take a portion for your dinner. You are to stay in your shed tonight. Forgive any noise.'

She left before I could answer.

The side hall, true to its name, was adjacent to the Main Temple. It had been decorated with bright red draperies and lanterns like a court parlour to hide the dark mahogany panels on the walls that depicted scenes from the life of the Buddha. There were new wineglasses, silverware and napkins on the table. The tablecloth was snow white, out-of-place in the hall. The wooden Buddha and Goddess of Mercy on the small altar had been turned to face the wall, prevented from witnessing the banquet.

After dinner in my shed, I went as far as the bamboo fence, the boundary to the annex. The entire nunnery was lit up with red lanterns, some with the Chinese word 貴

(Fortune or Nobility) written on them. The flames danced in the spring breeze. Against the background of early crickets, I could hear people speaking in English, Cantonese and Mandarin. There were sounds of clinking wine glasses, laughter, and faint piano music like Schubert's. Among the flow of English platitudes, I caught the insistent voice of the Head Nun speaking in Cantonese and using occasional English words. It was solemn, her sentences short and flat in tone, but what she said was translated into English, and her guests laughed politely.

My legs and arms were being bitten ferociously by mosquitoes. When two men came out of the side hall and wandered in my direction, I went back to my shed and turned off the gas lamp. I could hear somebody kick the bamboo fence. I left my door ajar and sat quietly. The new moon wasn't bright enough to show their faces. They were standing on the fake lawn and leaning against the rock mountain in the yard. There was a flash from a lighter, then another.

'Do you think the Iron Nun is serious?' one of the men asked in clipped English.

'I think she is as easily manipulated as rusty old iron,' the other man replied with a perfect English accent. They both laughed. 'Has she got any alternatives?'

'She could easily blow the whole thing.' He inhaled the cigarette fiercely. 'After all, she has the Buddha on her side.'

'But no money.'

'That's true. But nobody wants this to turn ugly or, what's the word ... filthy. I still don't trust her. Too much hinges on her. I know all the paperwork is in place and our governments are keen to see this through, but are you convinced she'll really be a part of the team? There is something weird about her. Almost too good to be true. Why is she so desperate to protect this shabby nunnery?'

'She's a Buddhist nun, what do you expect? Probably not as cuddly as a Catholic nun.' The other man blew the cigarette smoke at the mock-stone mountain. 'Trust me. We've done our homework and conducted a thorough background check on her. She is spotless. She's so clean it's sad. No relations, no strings. *Here*, this scruffy backwater is all she's got to show for herself. She would do anything to save this place. She'll throw all her principles out of the window to protect it. We've a Chinese term for her type, 鐵石心腸 (Heart and guts like iron and stone). There's no known cure for it, I'm afraid, but it suits us.'

'Well, she's called the Iron Nun for a good reason.'

'You should know better than me that everyone is dispensable.'

'How about the Triad? Are they going to play ball? Did you see the scar on that man's tattooed arm when he rolled up his shirt?'

The Chinese man laughed. 'You speak of the Triad as if they were local deities. They're flesh and blood like us.

Have you heard the theory that organised crime is a sophisticated form of chaos? The white powder has always been out of control here. It's good for the people who control the drugs and for those in distress. It was your great Empire which introduced opium to China, remember? History is a marathon relay race and now we're picking up the baton. Anyway, both our governments are turning a blind eye to these things. So why should we be bothered? You never know who can be trusted these days. The Triad could even be working for the government. I could be a Triad member for all you know.'

'*Are* you in the Triad?'

'Now you're finally showing me some respect.' He laughed louder this time. 'Do you think we're still living in the days of Kowloon Walled City? You 鬼佬 (*Gweilo*, Westerners) are always obsessed with the Walled City, the Triad, the colonial past. This is Diamond Hill, the Hollywood of the Orient where Bruce Lee made *Fist of Fury* and *Way of the Dragon*, but this shanty town has always been an eyesore. The people of Hong Kong will be happy to see it go. If I were you, I'd just leave things as they are. Let's stick to the plot and roll with the Iron Nun and the Triad. Distraction is the best cover. Remember the Trojan Horse? The more people are distracted, the less time they have for truth.'

'That's right,' the Englishman nodded. 'We're only pawns anyway. I'm just following the money.'

'My loyalty is to the crown.'

'Well, we wouldn't be giving you citizenship for nothing now, would we?'

'If I scratch your back, you'll scratch mine. Isn't that an English saying?'

'You must know that I'm not very high up in the pecking order. Those men in there have the power to change the airport's flight path tonight, so that they can listen to Schubert while drinking champagne without being disturbed. "Every man for himself" is another useful English saying.'

'I loved *Fist of Fury* by the way,' he went on. 'The scene where Bruce Lee killed the Russian man in the Japanese garden was stunning.' He made some funny Kung Fu noises and his friend played along. 'Can we swing by the studio tomorrow to see where the film was made?'

'It's long gone. Demolished,' the Chinese man replied.

I could hear their footsteps moving further away and a burst of hilarious giggles, as if they were tickling each other. Then the sound of water trickling in the pond. They must have been pissing into it.

When it was dead quiet, I came out to the pond and found the lotus disintegrated and a few petals floating on the surface beside two cigarette butts. It stank of urine.

The airplanes returned in the early morning. I pulled the pillow over my ears to try and block out the noise, before dragging myself out of bed. Quartz was already standing by the shed, waiting for me to appear. I told her I had a headache, and she said that I would get used to the planes in no time.

Quartz didn't want to touch the mess and asked me to clean the side hall from top to toe. It was a complete tip. There were uneaten chicken pieces, empty wine bottles, glasses with lipstick marks, and cigars in the ash trays. Lots of cigars. I was told to burn everything in the furnace, including the draperies and lanterns.

I removed the cloth from the mahogany panels, revealing striking scenes of the Buddha's life beautifully carved with details I'd never seen before: his mother's death after giving birth to him, him running as a boy in his father's opulent palace, his marriage when very young, his first encounter with the world outside the palace walls. The other set of panels at the far end of the hall seemed to have been carved by an even more sophisticated hand, showing the Buddha's later encounter with a diseased man and a decaying corpse with wrinkled skin clinging to its skull. I wasn't sure what had happened in between these moments of his life, apart from him preaching all over the place. The last panel was divided into two scenes: the top part showed him dying under a sal tree, while in the lower half he sat under the bodhi tree, with one of his hands stretched out to touch the ground. Daishi had told me that this gesture meant the Buddha was asking the Earth to bear witness to his pure enlightenment. I never understood why purity and enlightenment mattered so much to religion.

Distracted by the stories on the panels, I'd forgotten to bleach the surfaces and the floor. Now the pungent, lemony smell seeped into every crack and crevice.

There was lots of chewing gum on the walls in the streets outside Wat Arun. Daishi had asked me to remove them with ice, after I had recovered from my first heroin withdrawal. I remembered the ice cubes melting within seconds in the heat of Bangkok. I crouched down to unpick the sticky smudges with a paint scraper. Mistaking me for a proper monk, people treated me with a respect I wasn't used to. Some nodded as they walked past, some handed me fresh green coconut juice. One old woman even put a *phuang malai* (a flower garland) around my neck. It took me three days to remove all the chewing gum. A week later, the gum found its way back again. All my efforts were wasted. Daishi said never mind the gum, you've cleaned your mind.

I finally got the fire going mid-afternoon and started burning all the stuff left over from the banquet. It was still burning away at dusk.

'They won't come back.' Quartz appeared behind me. The glow from the fire revealed a new energy in her face. She stood next to me like a stone deity lost in a forest.

'How do you know?' I asked, tending the fire listlessly.

After a long pause, she said, 'I just know.' She handed me a piece of paper with two words on it – 樟腦 (Camphor or mothballs) – and walked away.

*

I left the nunnery in the opposite direction to the construction site and discovered a shortcut to the shanty town through a half-demolished area which looked like a film set of a warzone. Most of the wooden houses had already been torn apart, leaving flattened, empty spaces filled with rubbish, weeds and cats. Faded plastic bags clung to the cut wires like dead jellyfish. Further down, a pile of broken timber and corrugated iron roofs blocked half the road. Some children had used scrap metal and broken concrete to make a snowman with a yellow hard hat. Some of the more solidly built metal houses were boarded up, with ripped demolition notices still clinging to them. The spring sun felt much fiercer that morning. I heard a machine beeping and saw the swing of a tall crane, casting an elongated shadow over the snowman. Sweat soaked my T-shirt. A scraggy dog lay a few feet in front of me, looking dead, or sleeping in the shade.

Next to the dog was a homeless man, wide-awake, holding on to his rucksack and shielding himself from me with a piece of cardboard. As I walked past him, he made low-pitched barking noises while his dog kept its mouth shut. *Woof, woof, woof,* he went on and on.

A mulberry tree remained alone among the heaps of junk and rubble, and its young green leaves sharpened in the midday sun. Pigeons sat on its branches, nibbling on the leaves. I heard the first buzz from a cicada, and then a host of them chorusing all at once like a firework display. Through a wire fence I could see a community centre, the only concrete building left standing. All the windows were smashed. Red and black graffiti read: 走狗 (TRAITORS) and 屌你老母死英國狗 (FUCK OFF YOU DEAD BRITISH DOGS).

When I arrived at the grocery store looking for camphor mothballs, the owner seemed to know who I was and exactly what I wanted. I asked him how much I owed him, and he said it was an offering for the gods.

The streets were filled with life and a heady smell of food. Families with young children shared busy restaurant tables for hot congee and dim sum. There were hawkers selling soy milk, wonton dumplings, fermented tofu, dragon-whiskers sweets, beef tripe and tendon noodles ... I bought a skewer of curry fish balls, something I hadn't eaten for a long time. The sauce was sweet, savoury, spicy, and the deep-fried fish balls were crispy on the top and juicy in the middle, exactly as they should be.

A stream of school kids strolled past with pristine white shirts and skirts. A few looked stylishly scruffy, chattering and shrieking as if they owned the street. A handsome boy, carrying a school bag almost the size of a vacuum cleaner, threw a tantrum on the kerb, while his mother tried to cheer him up with a sweet pineapple bun. He acted up his frustration and she embarrassingly offered to help him carry the heavy backpack full of books. She forced a smile as I strolled past.

I walked on to the town's main street, which was more like a bustling market. A row of fishmongers yelled out discounts for mackerel and the fruit sellers were piling up small mounds of Californian oranges. It was an ordinary street full of market people, except that men stood aimlessly at the corners, talking to themselves, or rummaging for stuff in the bins. People rushed off to side alleys with cash in their hands and emerged again with their hands in their pockets. A mother and her children were sitting on a cardboard mat. One of the kids was resting on her lap and sucking on an empty bottle, while the other was begging.

'Please help us. My children haven't eaten for two days.'

After giving her some change, I spotted a familiar figure in an alley next to the noodle shop. Sitting on a low stool in a back-breaking position, the woman was plunging dirty bowls into a big bucket of soapy water and laying the clean ones upside-down on a tray to dry. The bowls were like the one Boss had held over her head when I cut her hair.

'I remember one of these,' I said, as I picked up a clean bowl and put it down on the tray.

She didn't look up and carried on rinsing them, bowl after bowl, without saying a word. I put my hands into the soapy water and started helping her.

She didn't acknowledge me until I fished for her hands in the large bucket. She froze. She looked like a completely different person – no makeup, no Louis Vuitton, no bravado, just a woman in a scruffy T-shirt and wellies, washing dirty dishes in an alley.

I stood up and prepared to leave. A man from the noodle shop shouted out, 'Get your ass moving, Audrey Hepburn! We're running out of bowls.'

With difficulty, she picked up the heavy tray. 'This is not me. I'm just acting in a film.'

I looked around, but there was no film crew, no camera or director.

Her face hardened and I said, 'You look great for the part.'

'*Thank you very much,*' she replied politely in a perfect British accent.

'Are you really called Audrey Hepburn? Why are you washing dishes?'

'I told you I'm acting in a film, didn't I? I'm a professional. People say you are different and smart. Haven't you heard of *method acting*? I'm the female Marlon Brando.'

I smiled and she flicked some bubbles at my face.

'By the way, I meant what I said the other day. I like the look of you, stranger.'

I could feel her wet hand inching towards mine under the tray.

'I want *you*.' She blew a kiss to me as if we really were in a film. 'But I also want you to leave my daughter alone. Don't ever speak to her again.'

'We bumped into each other accidentally in the café yesterday—'

'Nothing is accidental here,' she said, disappearing into the kitchen.

The nunnery was covered with laundry – on the veranda, the railings of stairwells, on the low-hanging beams. The nuns' white bed linen and their saffron robes were sailing in the breeze. When it blew stronger they got tangled up, and when it dropped they unravelled themselves. I was thrown by the unexpected scene of domesticity. I could hear duvets being dusted in the inner courtyard like the sound of animals being whipped with bamboo canes.

Quartz was waiting by my shed and I handed her the mothballs.

'What's happening?' I asked.

'A moth infestation. They are eating everything. Even the silk prayer scrolls.'

'Does it often happen at this time of year?'

'Yes, but not as bad as this,' she hesitated. 'This is by far the worst year. It's because of the red lanterns.'

'But the lanterns were only there last night. The moths couldn't have eaten much in such a short time, could they?'

She lowered her face and avoided me. She seemed younger and more robust. There was a flash of cloudiness in her eyes, like an ink brush dipped in water. Her round earlobes hung elegantly like those of the Goddess of Mercy. Her mouth was very small in proportion to the rest of her features, like an infant's. It was as if she hadn't been born to speak or hadn't spoken enough since she was born.

The whipping sound of the bamboo canes echoed again from the inner courtyard. 'Why did you stay so long in town?'

'I found a shortcut, but it ended up taking longer. It was a strange experience walking through the ruins in the western part of Diamond Hill, but the east is still all hustle and bustle, and full of life. Is it true that the whole town will be completely demolished?'

'I thought you knew what's happening.'

'Life goes on and not many people seem to care about the wreckage.'

'Not everyone cries when they are hurt.'

'I overheard something last night during the banquet. What's the point of saving the nunnery if Diamond Hill is gone?'

'Not gone. Redeveloped. There will be new – and better – neighbourhoods. Pain is part and parcel of any radical change.'

'Are you comfortable with what the Head Nun is doing? Don't you want to save the shanty town and people's homes?'

'It's not my place to have a view. You're a guest here.' She paused. 'Your linen and clothes need to be washed too.' She handed me a small pack of mothballs and walked out of the annex, unshrouding the mock-stone mountain and taking the half-dry linen away with her.

That night I couldn't sleep. Whenever I closed my eyes, I saw Audrey Hepburn and her bowls. I felt what she'd said was true: I had walked into a film set where she played a single mother, washing dirty dishes to make money to provide for her daughter.

I got up and walked to the pond. The two cigarette butts were still floating on its surface and I bent down to pick them up. When I turned around, the Iron Nun was standing behind me. In the moonlight, her face was silvery and emotionless.

'This is for you.'

I put the wet cigarette butts in a small dent on the rock mountains and took the packet she handed me. There were foreign stamps, my name, and the nunnery's address, all in English. The postmark was from Bangkok.

The Iron Nun continued to stand there. She clearly had no intention of leaving me alone.

'Open it.'

Inside, there was a letter and a small bamboo container the size of a salt shaker.

She clearly wanted to know the contents of the letter, but I gave a slight bow and said goodnight.

'Daishi has died. Those are his ashes in the container,' she said before I could leave.

'What do you mean?'

'He died on Doi Pui Mountain as I predicted. When he was found, his body had rotted away and been partly eaten by wild animals. The monks recovered some of his remains, but not much. It was his wish to be cremated and have his ashes distributed to those closest to him. You are to eat the ashes as instructed in the letter.'

'How do you know what's in the letter?'

'I received the same packet.'

'Have you eaten the ashes?'

'I drank them with tea. He was very controlling, in his flamboyant way. But I always respected him. Like you, he had been a heroin addict before seeing the light.'

She turned to me expectantly. 'I'm surprised you didn't know about his addiction. You stayed in Wat Arun for two years. Shouldn't you have realised?' She lifted her right leg, crossing the bamboo fence.

'Who were the people here last night?'

'They're nobody.'

'They didn't sound like nobody to me. The flight path was changed so that they could—'

'That's none of your business.'

'You're dragging other nuns into your dirty plan. Quartz has been completely brainwashed. Who the hell are you? What kind of nun would work with the Triad to harm others for your own personal gain? You should be ashamed of yourself. Whatever you're playing at, I don't want to be part of it.'

She straightened a crease in her robe. 'You've only just come back to Hong Kong and already you want to be a hero? Remember the saying 若要人不知 除非己莫為 (if you don't want anyone to know what you have done, the only way is not to have done it in the first place)? You've had a checkered past, haven't you? Born with a silver spoon in your mouth, you've ended up in a gutter in Diamond Hill. It is amazing what the power of forgiveness can do to a life. Daishi forgave you, but the question is: have you forgiven yourself? Don't stare at me. I am not your enemy.'

I walked quietly back to the shed and took my suitcase. She laughed as I brushed past.

'The sad thing about life is that it is always more predictable than we think. Go back to your ghost if you want to. Boss will feed you the white powder and give you a roof.'

'What do you want from me?'

'Daishi in his letter said you meant the world to him.' She looked at me with disdain. 'I'll let you stay on the condition that you are here only as my guest. You will follow my orders or else your past will not be safe with me. Daishi mentioned you went to a good school on Hong Kong Island and I want you to teach Quartz English. She will need it later on when the shanty town is cleared away. However, if I ever see you put your head above the parapet, you are finished.'

She disappeared through the backyard. I stood shaking.

I sat in bed for a long time, holding the bamboo container. I fell asleep and woke up, but it was still very dark, as if time had stopped. I opened the envelope and found an official letter from the clerk of Wat Arun handwritten in Thai and with an English translation in typescript telling me what I already knew, that Daishi had died on Doi Pui Mountain and it was his wish to distribute his ashes to people who were close to him, and that he wanted us to ingest his ashes as a way of remembrance. The last sentence of the letter read: *'In his will, Daishi explicitly asked us not to receive you back in Wat Arun under any circumstances. He wanted you in Hong Kong and to stay in the nunnery. We wish you well. Peace to the world.'*

The gas lamp quivered, my fist cast a strong shadow on the wall and I made animal shapes – rabbit, pigeon, deer and dog. I held the bamboo container to my chest and tried hard to remember Daishi, whose face had seemed as old as the roots of the banyan tree in Wat Arun. Did I really mean the world to him? Why did he cut me loose and forbid me to step foot in Wat Arun again? Had he liked me out of self-pity?

I felt feverish. Under the flickering gas lamp, the neat Thai handwriting looked like a train of ants levitating off the page.

A moth tried to fly into my ear. I teased it out with my finger as gently as I could, but it turned into a grey smear. My shed was filled with moths circling the gas lamp, desperate to touch the fire. The door was closed, and I wondered how they had got in.

I noticed a small hole in the lower corner of the window,

as if someone had put a finger through the paper screen. I lowered my head onto the desk. Moths squeezed themselves through the hole one after another.

Peering through the hole I recognised a blackness that was not the night. A deep, crystalline pool reflected the wingbeats against the lamp. It was Quartz's eye, unblinking in the dark and peering through. In it I could see my reflection. I thought of putting my finger through the hole to touch it.

Instead, I found my chest tightening and my left arm jerking spasmodically as if something foreign had invaded my bloodstream. It was like the panic attacks I used to have whenever I was tempted to leave Wat Arun. The idea of Wat Arun closing its door to me was as if someone had opened my ribcage and stolen my heart. I switched off the gaslight, held on to Daishi's ashes, and watched my breath move in and out, as he had taught me. I could hear him now in my jet-black shed, his fluid bass voice chanting the long familiar sutra in Sanskrit. I had never managed to memorise any of the words in the sutra except *shabdkosh*, which he said meant darkness, sleep and ignorance.

Outside my shed, I could hear Quartz chanting the same sutra about nightfall that Daishi had murmured in Bangkok. I held on to my knees and the shivers gradually subsided as her slow dispassionate chant sent me to sleep.

穀

Grain Rain

雨

The damp bed sheets clung to my legs. Audrey Hepburn started to look for a pair of clean knickers in a messy pile but couldn't find any. She got her foot tangled up in a shoe-box and fell over onto the bed, landing on my leg. I tried to get her back into bed, stroking her shoulders, the nape of her neck, her sore foot, and after a while she reluctantly returned to my arms. It had been raining relentlessly for the last three days and I had almost forgotten the feeling of being dry. The leak on the roof had worsened as the rain fell harder.

Audrey Hepburn pulled the sheets over our heads and whispered, 'Where have you gone?'

'I'm here.'

'No, you are not.'

She pulled at the small bamboo container round my neck. 'What's this ugly necklace for?'

'A memento.'

I drew circles around her navel.

'What's in your mind?'

'The shanty town, the mah-jong tiles tap-dancing on the tables, the horses in Happy Valley, the rat poison, the demolition notices, the kids playing with dragonflies, the—'

'Did you do this to your wife too?'

'Do what?'

'Blanking on her after sex.'

I ran my finger more slowly on her belly and tried not to flinch. 'Who told you I was married?'

'You're not the first married man I've slept with.' Audrey Hepburn turned sideways, nudged my cheek away with her shoulder, and tapped my forehead. 'Your mind has travelled to somewhere else. I know it.'

Beyond her shoulder blades, the rain was pelting down the windowpane.

'We all have our own ways to tame our demons.' I didn't know if she was reciting a line from a movie. She combed her hair with her hand and said, 'I used to be a well-spoken person like you. Diamond Hill has turned me into a rough diamond.'

I smiled. She got up and opened the window.

'This is not real,' she said.

'What's not real?'

'The rain.'

'It feels quite real to me.'

'This place is unreal. See?' She came back to bed, wrapped her head in the sheets and held her breath for a long time. Abruptly she opened her mouth again, drawing a deep breath. 'Try it. You won't die, I promise.'

She did it again and I copied her. With my eyes closed, my head wrapped tightly in the sheets, and my breath held,

I couldn't hear the rain on the roof, the water dripping, or the passing airplanes. I wasn't even aware of Audrey Hepburn lying next to me.

I unwrapped myself. Audrey Hepburn was still deep inside wherever she was in her own cocoon. When she finally resurfaced, she looked into my eyes and said, 'I like you. You remind me of my old self.'

We stayed in bed, letting the odd raindrop fall on us like kids playing in a tent.

'I never got on with my late father. He kept telling me that 娛樂圈係一個大染缸 (the entertainment industry is a big dyeing tank) and there's no such thing as untainted fame. He hated the idea of me sleeping with a producer or director to get a leading role in a film. He was an accountant at HSBC and never understood how much I wanted to be an actress.'

'How about your mother?'

'She was mostly kept indoors and only occasionally brought to life when my dad took her out for fancy dinners or work parties. A typical housewife of the time. I felt for her, and I swore not to follow her path. So I skipped school and milled around the film studios in Diamond Hill getting autographs from the stars.'

'Your dad must have been very proud of you.'

'Especially after I dyed my hair blond and permed it like Marilyn Monroe. He once threatened to shave my head – 我叫佢去躝屍 (I asked him to pick up his own corpse and fuck off). He eventually slapped me and disowned me. I broke my mother's heart and left home.'

'Who's Marilyn Monroe?'

'What planet are you on? Haven't you seen *Some Like It Hot*?' She widened her eyes and started blinking like Marilyn. '*Real diamonds! They must be worth their weight in gold!*'

I made a straight face and said, 'Sadly, I wasn't born then.' She realised I was lying and tickled me, finding the weak spots under my armpits. 'Dark hair suits you better.' I smelt rain in her hair. 'Anyway, you were brave to leave home. Why did you want to be an actor?'

'People sugar-coat boredom by calling it a normal life and I refused to follow in my parents' footsteps. Their narrow, repetitive existence was as repulsive as the lacklustre wallpaper all over our apartment. I got sick to my stomach seeing Mum not having a life of her own, waiting on Dad hand and foot like a mute parrot. I was sixteen and wanted to be in charge of my destiny. I moved to Diamond Hill and started working as a waitress in a local restaurant and delivering takeaway lunches to actors and film crews. The freedom was wonderful. I spent my salary on clothes and accessories, desperate to recreate the allure of Hollywood stars. On my days off, I put on lots of makeup, dressed in nice clothes, and hovered around the gates of 大觀聲片 (Grandview Studio), posing as Audrey Hepburn. I was desperate to be spotted by an agent or director.'

'Did your dad cut you off completely?'

'Pretty much. Mum came to visit me every month and gave me some money. She kept saying it was her own savings but I knew it was from Dad.'

'And you were happy to take it?'

'Of course. I needed money for beautiful things. I bought a gorgeous sunflower-yellow Givenchy jacket like the one Audrey Hepburn wore in *Charade*. I liked the idea of bugging him by spending his tight-fisted cash on the luxury he hated most.'

I laughed and rested my head on her shoulder. 'What was Diamond Hill like in those days?'

'You couldn't believe the glamour. There was so much electricity in the air! Jackie Chan was signed up by Golden Harvest Studio here in the late 1970s. Diamond Hill was a classy neighbourhood, though more modest than Hollywood. There were posh colonial-style redbrick houses built by proper British architects for the film stars. You can see the ruins now on the west side of the shanty town. Grandview Studio wasn't that grand at all. There was no security guard at the gates and the studio was cheaply built – dirt floor, high ceiling, everywhere tangled up with electric wires. The filming was chaotic, with lots of people lingering on, stargazing and looking for autographs. Sadly, the stars were always inaccessible. They arrived through a secret passage and were protected by the crew. Do you know what the magic of cinema was then?'

'The makeup artists? The editing?'

'It was the lighting. I was an extra in 《少林搭棚大師》(*Return to the 36th Chamber*), a classic Kung Fu comedy made by the Shaw Brothers Studio. With some effort, I befriended a lighting technician who agreed to cast the softest, most attractive light on my face so that I would be spotted by a director. That never happened.'

'You mean the technician or the director?'

'Both,' she laughed.

'What happened to all the film studios here?'

'There were a lot of rumours. The most famous one is that the rivalry between the Shaw brothers ended the heyday of cinema production here. The younger brother couldn't bear being controlled by his elder brother, took some money and talented people with him, and set up a new Western-style studio somewhere else. The elder one tried to keep the film business afloat but failed in the end and ventured into television. There's nothing more bitter and vengeful than when a family business goes wrong. It destroys a family—'

She massaged my neck, softening the knots in my shoulders. 'Are you alright? You look tense.'

'Nothing. That's sad about the brothers and their family business.'

'It is just a rumour. You're sexy when you get sentimental.'

'Aren't you sad that the Hollywood of the Orient is now a slum?'

'冰封三尺非一日之寒 (Being sealed off under three feet of ice does not happen after one cold day). It took years for the glamour of Diamond Hill to fade – the stars gradually moved out and the steakhouse turned into a cheap noodle joint. The sets from the film studios were used to build slum houses ... When a disaster happens in slow motion, it looks at first like a series of unfortunate events. People fool themselves all the time because thinking anything else is too painful.'

'Was that how you ended up staying here?'

She bit her lip. 'My whole body is covered with scars. I am an expert in pain management.'

I kissed the countless invisible wounds on her back and said sorry.

'No harm done. I lost any hope for this place a long time ago, but you should know that in Hong Kong no cash means no choice.'

'Don't you think we can still save Diamond Hill?'

She laughed at me in disbelief. 'You can't even save a dollar a month!' She yawned and stretched her arms out. 'The rain is making me fuzzy-headed.' She snuggled up next to me. 'This place is a shithole, but 龍床不如狗竇 (even the king's bed isn't as good as your own doghouse). Do you want to know how I met Bruce Lee?' She started before I replied. 'One day Bruce came to my restaurant for lunch. I was so embarrassed. I was late, had a hangover, and didn't notice him at first. I even started cleaning his table while he was still eating. People looked horrified and his bodyguards very uneasy. The moment I recognised him, it was as if there was an earthquake inside me. I knew it was 命中注定 (destiny) that we'd finally met each other.'

I had never seen her smile like that before. Although her complexion had been battered over the years by sun, sweat and detergent, her wrinkled face, shaped like a sunflower seed, still had a warm glow. She was beautiful, but with a kind of common, forgettable beauty that made her look shallow and almost unlikeable.

She had never asked anything about me. It was as if she didn't want to know me. Perhaps I was drawn to her for that reason. I liked that she was totally absorbed in her own world; that I was simply a prop.

'Did Bruce Lee help you with your acting career?'

She bristled and jumped out of bed, looking for her knickers again. She picked up the pair she'd worn, caught my eyes and gave me a fake smile, before disappearing into the bathroom. In the mirror, I could see the profile of her breasts and the elongated curve of her hips. She was humming an ABBA tune in the shower. I imagined I was a male actor impersonally checking out the leading actress in the spotlight.

I lay in bed, naked from the waist down, touching myself and recalling her touches. I didn't cum this time. In fact, I hadn't cum the first time either. She didn't ask, and we didn't talk about it. I had no idea if she had had an orgasm or not. We had only slept with each other twice and each time we'd gone on until she'd sat on me, then slumped on top like the lioness on the Lion Rock, holding me tightly without saying a word. Each time I had lost track of our breathing and the whole thing had ended as abruptly as it had started.

She finished her shower and quickly put on blue overalls.

'You know you are attracting quite a lot of attention in town. The first man ever to stay in the nunnery.' She wiped the steam off the mirror and put some lipstick on. 'How did you make the Iron Nun bend the rules?'

'I suppose I have my uses as a handyman. I am going to teach a nun English too.'

'Never trust a single word from the mouth of a Buddhist nun.'

'Are you jealous?'

She ignored me and grabbed an umbrella. 'This place has no future, even if they build a forest of luxury high-rise apartments here. From now on it's all just part of the shitty countdown to 1997.'

The greasy clock on the wall moved its hand to 2:32 p.m.

'Remember to get your ass out of the house before three o'clock like last time. I don't want you bumping into my daughter when she's back from school.' Her hair was still wet but there was no point in drying it, the rain was still pouring down outside.

I heard the flimsy metal door shut and the whole house shook. It was more like a rough-and-ready shack, bigger than my shed, but it felt darker and more claustrophobic. It had two floors with temporary partitions. The precarious wooden staircase was missing a few steps. It led up to Boss's room, which was guarded by a big padlock. Downstairs was a dump, or more like a crime scene after a police raid. The bed took up most of the space. There was no obvious boundary between it and the bathroom or the kitchen. A small red gas tank stood at the far end. The gas ring burner was supported by a rudimentary wooden shelf leaning against an old fridge. I could imagine a fire starting at any time. The cooking pots were the kind designed for outdoor camping and the noodle bowls were erratically stacked up on a shelf. One electric extension lead was linked to another. Cardboard and shoe boxes occupied every inch of space. I could see cockroach droppings in almost every corner. Everything smelt damp, and looked filthy and impersonal, as if it had belonged to someone else. There was a big pile of 《龍虎豹》(*Dragon Tiger Leopard*), the once popular porn magazine, dating back a decade or so. I picked one up and leafed through a dozen naked women in multiple poses. All very predictable and repetitive. The only thing that interested me was the calendar hanging next to the bed. It was a traditional Chinese calendar, with fortune-telling messages for every day of the year: 宜: 安葬, 嫁娶, 起基; 忌: 移徙, 栽種, 出行 (Good for burials, weddings, foundation laying; bad for moving house, planting, travelling). I noticed that the date on the calendar was actually yesterday's, so I tore off the wafer-thin page and stuffed it into one of the cardboard boxes.

A house gecko brushed my hand and whizzed up the wall. For a few seconds he paused in the corner as still as a stone, before darting into a spider web and stealing a green moth. The dark spots on his body looked like a constellation against the city's skyline. He gulped the moth down and slipped through a crack I hadn't noticed.

It had taken Audrey Hepburn weeks to allow me into her crumbling home. It was a big deal for her to share her mess with me. I had never once tried to tidy her house because I knew the real chaos was in her head.

I lay in bed listening to the rain tapping on the metal roof. I recalled the night when I had first arrived in Bangkok and spent hours watching the hot torrential rain flood the streets and the sewage water rise from the drains. No raindrops fell as hard as those in Thailand. They hit the ground like bullets. I had sprawled out on the streets and let the rain land on my stomach to fight the hunger for heroin. I would open my mouth and catch it. In the end it would fill me up. Even when the thick rain turned the whole city into a blur, there were people who'd hand me something to eat – a banana, a mango, some sticky rice. Since I'd lived under the roof in Wat Arun, I hadn't watched the rain for a very long time. In Diamond Hill the rain was more ruthless. It smelt and sounded like rusted metal and turned a coppery yellow as it mixed with the soil.

When I opened my eyes, Boss was lying next to me. She must have just come back from school. I pulled the sheets over to make myself decent.

'You smell like a woman,' she said, leaning closer. I could smell cigarettes on her breath.

She touched my forehead. 'Don't move. Your head is so bald and lovely. I've always wanted to kiss a bald man's head.' She moved her lips, pretending to kiss me.

I moved her hand away. 'Can you stop playing games?'

'I am serious. How often do you shave it?'

'It depends. Usually every other day.'

'Did you become bald before or after you became a hairdresser? A lot of the most famous hairdressers in the world are bald.'

'After. But not because I was a hairdresser,' I said, trying to get up and make myself decent. I put on my clothes and sandals while Boss still lay in bed, her eyes fixed on my bald head.

'How old do you think I am?'

'Fifteen? Sixteen? I'm no good with age.'

'You're so rude. I'm not that ancient.' She turned around, lying on her stomach like a flatfish. 'Do you think I look better without my breasts?'

'Why did you bandage your chest?'

'I have to, Buddha. I haven't a clue why the boys are so scared of my tits. They had obeyed my orders before they got their pubes. But when they noticed that my breasts began to show through my T-shirt, they could no longer control themselves. They stopped listening to me and started saying dirty things and making funny faces. I some- times wonder if it would have been easier if I had had all their 何B仔 (willies) cut off. A bit sadistic, I know, but it would free me from these nasty bandages.'

She sat up in bed, untying the bandages from under her white school uniform. I turned away at once.

'Don't worry, Buddha. I'm wearing my bra underneath!' She laughed.

She rolled the bandages up and aimed them at a small cardboard box. It was a clean throw and they went straight in.

'How are you finding this lovely place? Do you like the rain?'

'I don't normally mind it, but I hate the rain here.'

'Most people here loathe the rain, but I love it. When it's pissing down like this, it stops everyone in their tracks. It feels as if the sky is about to fall on the roof and this whole damned place will just melt in a landslide.'

'I'm not into catastrophe,' I said, as I tightened my belt and prepared to leave the house.

'You're unlucky then. I *am* a catastrophe.'

She placed her legs at a peculiar angle like a yogi.

'Can you cut my hair? I want to get rid of these sideburns.'

'Your mother will kill me.'

'She won't. She can't even kill a cockroach. I was going to cut it myself anyway, but I thought you'd do a better job.'

Reaching into her school bag, she took out a pair of scissors as big as her face and gave me a mischievous smile. 'Do you like them? I'm always well prepared.'

'You took them to school? Was it really necessary?'

'Of course! Not everyone knows how to show respect.' She cut a hole in the front page of a newspaper and wore it like a poncho.

I sat her down on the stool in front of the full-length mirror in the bathroom. She searched for my eyes, but when they met she avoided me. The rain softened into a mild drizzle.

'I trust you, Buddha. Do what you need to do.'

I tightened the paper poncho around her right arm and noticed a purplish bruise. 'Does it hurt?'

'Oh, that's nothing. I hit myself with a stick. I need to look tough to inspire the younglings.'

It was a bad bruise, but I wondered if she had used cosmetics to make it look worse.

'These are old newspapers. Do you know how we manage to keep newspapers in this dump?' Boss's eyes were still closed.

'No, not really. They're just old papers as you said. What's so special about them?'

'Have you seen any newspapers in town? I bet you a tenner there aren't any papers in the nunnery.'

What Boss said was true.

'My gang runs a tight ship in Diamond Hill, you know. We don't want the punters getting too curious about the outside world. The less people know, the more they think they know.' Her voice was someone else's. 'It wasn't easy for a girl like me to gain the trust of the Triad. I've had to work hard to create a shortage of the white powder, to cause a price hike. As the elders in the Triad said, we just need to sit back and let events unfold: unrest, domestic abuse, families splitting up, homeless kids begging on the streets, men and women selling their own children for sex to get drugs, and hungry people eating their own cats and dogs. It took months to train my gang, to implant an unquestioned sense of loyalty and discipline in their brains. That's the key to my success.'

'I won't call what you do a success.'

'Call it what you like. The old Hong Kong is dead and money is the future. I've learned so much management skills from the Triad. I've divided my followers according to their skills, experience and temperament. I've introduced a rec-ognition scheme called 每月最醒目專業白粉員工 (Employee of the Month) to reward and retain the most talented staff. There is even a mentoring scheme for newcomers.'

'I saw what you did, stationing your troops in the corners and alleys that were most discreet and convenient.'

'You're such an observant customer.'

'I am not your customer.'

'Your resistance is admirable.'

'Your gangland fantasy is like your mother's film-world fantasy.'

Boss got cross and raised her voice, 'Don't ever compare me to my mum. In her 柒頭 (retarded head) she is an actor but I'm completely different. I'm an artist. I make the impossible possible. Like a film director. Look, it's me that has made Diamond Hill what it is now. Why do I need actors when I've got real drug addicts sniffing the shit?'

I didn't know if she was being serious or not, but her eyes looked as determined as an arsonist's.

'You could play a big part in my movie too. Under my watch, you could be anyone you want. You wouldn't need to be a heroin addict. Pardon me, ex-heroin addict. Tell me, Buddha, who do you want to be?'

'Don't call me Buddha. I'm no Buddha.'

'Have I offended you?' She opened her eyes, searching for recognition in the mirror.

'No,' I said. 'But who told you I was addicted to the white powder?'

'I've been selling the stuff since I was a toddler and I can spot a client a mile off. It's those yellow fingers of yours. I bet they were all once blackened by burned foil. The problem is you can never wash the shitty stains away. Once you are infected by this thing, it lives in your body for ever.

It's a fucking curse. That's why I've never touched the shit myself.' She smiled cheekily. 'Of course, I have friends in Bangkok too. Thailand is a lovely country, a fertile drug-land, full of kind people and good monks.'

I looked at her smug, knowing face in the mirror and I wanted to slap it. She caught the anger in my eyes and made a funny face, playing the innocent little girl.

'Don't worry, Buddha. The Triad will protect you as long as you don't ruffle my feathers.'

'You talk big, but you can't be more than a mid-ranking soldier in the Triad. Are you 草鞋 (a Straw Sandal)?'

Boss pulled out a Swiss army knife from her pocket and flipped it open as if she'd been born with it.

'Do I look like a Straw Sandal? I've been 紅棍 (a Red Pole) for a year and soon I'll be 香主 (an Incense Master).'

'How long have you been in the Triad?'

'長個你細佬 (Longer than your penis)!'

I frowned, and she looked very pleased with herself. Her hair had a hint of waviness like her mother's. But perhaps tougher and wirier.

'Didn't Audrey Hepburn warn you that nothing good will come of it if you roll with the nuns?'

'No, she didn't. What's wrong with the nuns?'

'Ha! That's a stupid question. How could there be anything wrong with the nuns? Of course, they're all clean and pretty and pure. They're all virgins!' she said sarcastically. 'When I was young I always wanted to be a nun. But who would choose to be a nun when you can be a businessman? I am an entrepreneur just like those smart-suited men in Central. I make big money. By the way, their obsession about purity is very fucked up.'

'Selling the white powder to people doesn't sound less fucked up to me.'

'There is no clean money in this world, Buddha.'

'But some money is cleaner than yours.'

'Fuck your clean money!' She screamed at the mirror and tore off the paper poncho. Strands of black hair fell on her white school uniform and on the bathroom tiles.

Just as quickly as she had flared up, she calmed down and ordered me to continue cutting.

'Don't ever freaking lecture me again or I'll ask my boys to scoop your eyes out.'

I put my hands on her shoulders. She softened, and with difficulty, smiled.

'You're too young to waste your life like this here.'

'Do you want me to call you Dad?'

We didn't speak for some time. I didn't know if she was serious about her question. The wind rose and the rain fell harder. The scissors, touching her face, caught one of her thin sideburns. It fell on her shoulders, on her bruised arm.

'You're not that kind of girl.'

Boss shrieked with laughter.

'Oh, I can't believe you just said that. You're so sweet.' She continued smiling, until it became a demeaning laugh. 'Don't worry, Buddha, I've got it all planned. I'll be leaving this hellhole soon. I've been saving up and I'm nearly there. Next year I'll have enough money to emigrate to London. The Triad have promised after I finish helping them develop Diamond Hill, they will hook me up with the gang in Chinatown to look after their underground gambling racket there. I'm not keen on gambling myself. Too damned noisy. I prefer 清清靜靜 (a quiet profession). But once I show them what I'm capable of, they will let me handle the drugs scene. I'll escape this fucking place before the Communists come and take over. Before this whole place is flattened. Before they build those high-rises here and a few people make a shitload of money. Before the stinking rich come and buy their pathetic apartments.'

'Are you taking your mother with you?'

'She is *not* my mother. How many times do I have to tell you that?'

'Why do you live with her if she is not your mother?'

'Because I've nobody else to live with.' She paused. 'Anyway, I need a mother to get myself to London.'

'Why London?'

'Why not? I was born in this British colony. I love Great Britain. People there are so polite and sophisticated. So calm. Real gentlemen. I'll learn to speak proper English when I move to London. One day I'll be really British.'

I didn't know whether Boss meant what she said. In the

mirror I saw a little girl sitting on a stool, having her hair cut by a stranger.

'You're not a real monk, are you, Buddha? You can't hide it. There are no secrets in this place. Everybody is spying on everybody. That's what poverty means. Don't trust anyone, except *me*!'

'I never said I was a monk.'

'Then why are you in the nunnery? Those spinsters hate men and I can't believe they've let you stay in their hornet's nest.'

'I was sent here by a monk called Daishi at Wat Arun in Bangkok just before he died. He wanted to save me. He thought I needed to come back and make my peace with Hong Kong.'

'There's no future in Hong Kong, I tell you. And no peace. The moment the British leave in ten years' time, the Chinese will fuck us up big time. Even if the Chinese let us fend for ourselves, we wouldn't know how to keep the ball rolling. We have been house-trained by our foreign master for too long.'

She threw me a naughty smile in the mirror. 'I really can't believe that Daishi sent you to this crazy nunnery to save you. Damn it, he must have been desperate. Anyway, Buddha, you're here. In this living hell. Right? But you can still have a good time in hell if you play ball with me.'

I laughed slightly. 'You're done, Boss.'

'You're a pro. I like it.' She beamed. Without the

sideburns and with her new sharp fringe, she looked like a Japanese doll.

She took the scissors and put them back in her school bag. I shook the hair off the newspaper and took it and some others from the pile in the corner, putting them under my arm.

Boss saw what I was doing and said, 'I knew you were a thief. Don't show them to the nuns. They will go crazy and chop you into pieces. If you want, we have a library of 《龍虎豹》 (*Dragon Tiger Leopard*) in the corner. I am sure those nuns being locked up all night could do with some porn.'

I ignored her.

She turned on the electric fan to the highest setting and put her head close to it. Her hair lifted into the air like a shortened black cape. To the left of the metal door, I suddenly noticed a black-and-white photo of Audrey Hepburn and Bruce Lee. His arm was on her shoulders as if they were a couple.

'This place used to be full of film stars. They made films on the other side of Diamond Hill. It's true she did date Bruce Lee for like a week a million years ago. Well, that's what she says. Can you believe that before she became a total monster Mum had a twenty-three-inch waist like the real Audrey Hepburn in *Roman Holiday*?'

I wiped the dust off the photo. It was Audrey Hepburn, but it also wasn't.

'So, when will you come back and fuck her again?' Boss asked.

I opened the front door. The rain was still torrential.

'Does it turn you on, now that you know you're fucking someone Bruce Lee fucked?'

I didn't answer but plunged into the rain and shut the door.

It was impossible to keep my shed dry. The paper windows had partly dissolved, though I'd coated them with varnish. The wooden walls were softening too. The straw I'd put on the roof didn't seem to work. The only thing that withstood the incessant rain was the oak door.

The rain was so dense that I could barely see the Main Temple from my window. It blanked out all the noise and I could no longer tell if there had been thunder or planes passing by. I watched it fall into the brimming pond, battering the lilies, and through the vertical bamboos. Every two or three minutes a nun's silhouette emerged from the side temple to throw a bucketful of water down the steps.

I thought of Audrey Hepburn. The idea of a Hong Kong woman called Audrey Hepburn. What would it be like to move in with her and Boss? I had been on my own for so long. I closed my eyes and listened to the sound of the raindrops grow more and more high-pitched as they fell into a bucket at the corner of my shed.

I unfolded one of the newspapers I'd taken from Boss

dated 25 September 1982. It was a tabloid with more pictures than words. On the front page the headline read 鐵娘子跌下來 (The Iron Lady has fallen), accompanied by a full-page picture of Mrs Thatcher falling on the steps of the Great Hall of the People in Beijing, after meeting Deng Xiaoping. Two men in suits had come to her rescue but it was too late: she had ended up on all fours, as if praying in front of the Buddha.

There was a knock on my door and I quickly shoved the newspapers under the mattress. It was Quartz. She put an open package on my desk and signalled me to have a look. To my surprise, I found a set of English grammar books for young children.

'The Iron Nun asked me to give you these,' Quartz said hesitantly.

I laughed. 'Do you also call her the Iron Nun?'

She blushed. 'I don't call her by her name. I mean she's the one who does the calling. But you are right. Her name is Iron. All of us in the nunnery are named after a mineral. 鐵, 晶, 銅, 鉛, 鋅 ... (Iron, Quartz, Bronze, Copper, Zinc ...)'

'So there are five of you?'

'It's not my place to say. Some of us are not ready to meet people from the outside world yet. So you don't see them.'

'What do you all call *me*, then?'

'We don't call you anything. There is only you and me here. We know who we are. There is no need for names.'

I beamed at Quartz's strange logic and she smiled back.

The rain dripped onto Quartz's head and her saffron robes. She wiped it away with her sleeves and moved the heavy bucket to catch the drips. With her head lowered reticently, she came closer to the desk and put her hand on the books. 'She said you would teach me English. She said you went to a good school on Hong Kong Island when you were young. Which school was it?'

I was speechless. I could feel blood rushing to my head and my earlobes burning with rage and embarrassment. Quartz stood there like a withering fern threatened by a sudden change of season.

'It was St Paul's.'

'St Paul's is a famous school in the Mid-Levels. It's only for the elite. 你係富貴人家 (You must have come from a prosperous family). Unlike the rest of us here.'

I laughed in disbelief. 'Me having been to a good school doesn't make me part of the elite. Look at me now.'

Quartz tried to hide her unease. 'I've nothing against the elite. I don't care whether you are one of them or not, but you are certainly not one of us. That's fine. We don't need to be like two peas in a pod.'

'What else did the Iron Nun tell you?'

'She said people in Bangkok were impressed by your English. Particularly Daishi. You call yourself a hairdresser, but I know you aren't just a hairdresser.'

Quartz wasn't just Quartz either, I thought. She must have had a life before Quartz.

'I apologise. I spoke out of order.' She bowed.

'There is no need to apologise. You're not the person I am angry with.' I emptied the bucket and moved it to the other side of the shed because the wind had changed direction. 'How can you stand her being so controlling?'

Quartz paused and took her hand off the books. 'At some level we always just do what we are told.'

'What gives her the right to boss you about?'

'It takes two lifetimes to be a boss. For me, one lifetime is trouble enough.'

'And why does she want you to learn English?'

'She said that at some stage I would need it to teach children because they want us to open a small school for the displaced local girls.'

The rain now seemed to have subsided and there was even a glimpse of faint blue in the sky.

She put her hands on one of the grammar books. 'I've heard about the poor girls in the shanty town. Some of them are immigrants from Vietnam, India and Mainland China. Some of them are homeless. They might have lost their parents on their way here, or their parents have abandoned them. I also heard that some parents just put their children on the train or the ferry with the traffickers, hoping that they would have a better life in Hong Kong. Even though some of them may have parents, they won't be the kind of parents we think of as real parents. But I do want to help, if I can.'

'You can help save the shanty town.'

'It's beyond salvation. I feel sorry that people have to live in such a desperately poor and ... filthy place.' Her pause was telling. 'No child should be brought up among drugs and prostitutes.'

'When was the last time you visited the town?'

'I have never been. I've found out from the other nuns.'

'Perhaps you should see it with your own eyes.'

'I'm not allowed to see the outside world.'

'Does the Iron Nun forbid you to leave the nunnery?'

'No. It's myself. I don't want to see the world or people.'

'Those people you refuse to meet have a normal life in the shanty town. I've seen children going to schools, families enjoying dinners, people doing daily groceries. How will you feel if the property developers come and start demolishing the nunnery?'

She turned aside, about to leave.

'Do you want to be an English teacher?'

'I do what I am told.'

'Is that what being a nun means?'

'You don't understand. I want to be subservient. I want to lose a bit of myself every day, so that when I depart from this world, I am nothing but a chrysalis.'

I was lost for words.

'Didn't your time at Wat Arun teach you to lose part of yourself?'

'I never thought about it that way. It was only for two years.'

'Intentionally or not, that's what we do, shed more and more of our skin until we become a shell.'

'Learning a new language doesn't sound like letting everything go.'

She ignored me.

'Do you have any English? Have you taught English before?'

'I know what English is,' she replied. 'It's a language as Chinese is a language. But I don't *have* English just as I don't really *have* Chinese. I don't own anything.'

'That's far too philosophical for me, Quartz.'

She smiled. 'I suppose we will find out, one way or another.'

She bowed and left the shed. On her way out, the sun broke through and landed on the back of her shaved head, which gleamed like a mirror.

The next day after breakfast, she returned with a notebook, pencil, ruler and eraser. I pulled the desk closer to the bed, so that I could sit on it and she could have the chair. The sky looked fickle; it was bound to rain any minute.

She started reciting the alphabet to me, all twenty-six letters in a perfect queue. She pronounced the last one as *zee*, the American way, which wasn't how I would have pronounced it.

'You'll need more than the alphabet to teach these children English.'

'We should always start with the foundations. You don't need to dampen my spirits. The day is already wet enough.'

The first chapter of the grammar book was on parts of speech, and we started on pronouns. After fifteen minutes explaining the possessive pronouns, I realised that knowing grammar and teaching grammar were completely different beasts. I'd forgotten how I learned English myself. Quartz was patiently copying out the pronouns in the notebook. Her handwriting was strong and neat, perhaps too strong, and she repeatedly broke the pencil nib. Sharpening the pencil wasn't the only cause of frustration. She struggled with the possessive pronouns to the point of giving up. Why shouldn't she? After all, as she said, she did not own anything.

'Why can't I say *this is me watch*? Why must I say *this is my watch*? What's the difference between *this is my watch* and *this is Quartz's watch*? How can there be an *its*? How can it, something inanimate, possess anything?'

When it finally came, the rain was much heavier than I'd expected. I pulled the bucket from under the bed and moved the desk to stop it ruining the books. Quartz's questions had been as ceaseless as the rain. I looked at her delicate, small mouth and wondered why she'd ended up becoming a nun at so young an age. There were lots of questions I wanted to ask about her life but somehow her urgent curiosity about English grammar made everything else seem insignificant. Towards the end of our first lesson, she had mastered an understanding of *not mine*, and from then on, I knew that English pronouns would gradually take root in her mind like a sapling invigorated by the spring rain.

All night the torrential rain fell like lead on the thatched roof, and at dawn I jumped out of bed convinced that the roof was collapsing on me. Instead the rain poured through the reeds, soaking my pillow and blanket. The paint had started peeling off the walls. It would have been safer to be out in the storm than in my shed. I found shelter under the solid roof of the veranda.

The sky was a heavy mackerel. The curve of the roof and gable, the construction cranes and the shanty town were all blurred in the wash. The vertical rain soon turned into a flood, the nunnery steps into a waterfall. I watched as everything around me dissolved.

Quartz emerged panting from the side temple. She was barefoot and her saffron robes had turned a damp copper red.

'There has been an emergency. The police have just rung the Iron Nun. They said there was a landslide down in the shanty town and the fire brigade is calling for help.'

'How bad is it?'

Quartz kneeled down to hide her bare feet. 'It sounds serious. Everyone's worried. You've seen the tin shacks and wooden houses. God knows many families may be affected.'

She handed me a flimsy umbrella. 'The Iron Nun wants

you to help the fire brigade. We will stay here and pray for the rain to stop.'

She frowned deeply but didn't say another word before leaving.

I took the sheltered path through the woods to the shanty town. Despite the thick green foliage, the downpour had broken many branches and a few bird's eggs had been dislodged from their nests. My umbrella took the brunt of the storm, but the moment I came out of the woods the weight of the deluge broke the frame and I was pelted.

There were no floodlights at the construction site, but the cranes were trembling precariously.

A black cloud rose from the heart of the shanty town and I could hear banging and shouting in the distance. I chucked the umbrella away and started running.

The town's main gate had been fenced off and barricaded with petrol barrels. Black smoke welled up from rubber tyres thrown on a bonfire. A group of men were holding cricket bats and metal bin lids as shields to defend themselves against an attack. They chanted '保護我家 反對當局 視死如歸 (Protect our home, oppose the authorities, death is nothing).' Some of the older villagers were sitting under big parasols, looking after young children. A gang of teenagers were waving machetes and cleavers. I couldn't see any guns but there was a smell of gunfire in the air.

The three policemen present were heavily outnumbered.

They were keeping themselves safe and dry in a van and had no intention of calling for backup.

The chief fire officer spoke over the loudspeaker, repeating again and again that they were here to rescue the survivors buried beneath the landslide. The crowd wasn't convinced and shuffled anxiously. I saw the firemen had no rescue equipment, not even hoes and spades. There was no ambulance on site either.

A young man shouted, '屌你老母冚家鏟 佢哋呃我哋 佢哋嚟攞我哋塊地 (Fuck your mother, all your family is dead, they trick us, they come to take our land).' He began to bang the shield with his cricket bat and the others followed suit, drumming and chanting. A plane flew past as if the world were still in order. Some teenagers started bashing their machetes and cleavers on the metal fence.

The racket continued until a gun went off. Everyone heard it. Everyone was silent. The rain droned on.

Then a man with tattoos all over his chest howled like a wolf and the shouting and knife-banging resumed with greater intensity. Some children went crazy and rolled an old armchair into the bonfire. A bunch of teenagers poured petrol on the fire and it shot up a storey high. It was hard to breathe and see things clearly. Some people stood as if trapped in time. By now the police had quietly driven off. The fire brigade jumped back into their truck and rolled up the windows. I thought they would stay but the officer started the engine and did a U-turn. The crowd cheered.

I saw Audrey Hepburn jostling her way through the crowd, holding a handgun with a white marble handle. There was blood on her face and T-shirt. She came straight up to the barricaded gate, trembling like a moth on fire.

'Did you fire the gun?' I shouted through the barricade.

'I can't find her. I don't know where she is. I can't find her.' She was sobbing and screaming simultaneously.

'You mean Boss?'

'I can't find her. She is not in the house. I thought she had come home late last night, but the door was padlocked.'

'Your hand is bleeding very badly. What happened? Where did you get the gun?' I wrapped my fingers around hers through the metal mesh.

'I couldn't break the padlock. I got the gun from the Triad and shot at it and it blew up in my face and shrapnel went all over the place. But she wasn't there. She wasn't in her room.'

The wind changed direction and brought the choking smoke to the crowd. The gun dropped from Audrey Hepburn's shaking hands and landed in a puddle. A teenage boy with a leopard tattoo picked it up and hid it in the back of his trousers.

I jumped onto the gate and started climbing. People quickly began throwing things at me. I must have struck them as a traitor, having appeared with the police. Soft drink cans, broken umbrellas, the legs of an old chair. I managed to climb over. As I was putting my foot on one of the petrol barrels, a boy threw a brick at me. I dodged, lost balance, and found myself falling before my brain could register any pain.

When I woke up, Audrey Hepburn had already bandaged my head. She handed me some painkillers and said, 'We need to find my daughter.'

At the site of the mudslide, five or six houses had been totally destroyed. Furniture, toilet bowls and odd metal structures jutted out of the yellow sludge. I found a pair of children's socks at my feet. There were two bodies on the ground covered with a tarpaulin. Audrey Hepburn rushed to check them, and a man pulled me aside and asked me to help lift a metal frame, under which an old woman's leg was trapped. I got a strong grip on the rusted metal bar, but the structure was too heavy for four men to lift. Someone went to get a chainsaw.

'It's not her. Thank god it's not her,' she said when she put down the tarpaulin. 'These men say they haven't seen Boss, but there might still be people trapped under the mud.'

'Why don't we call the fire brigade for help? The situation is out of control.'

The man who had asked me to help tut-tutted. '收埋你 把口 你知乜撚野 (Shut your mouth. What the fuck do you know)? We can't trust the authorities. They are behind all this. Didn't you realise? They want us to leave. They want us to die.'

He left me alone and found another tarpaulin for the

old woman whose leg was trapped. He wanted to shield her from the rain. Her leg looked dead to me. Her face was wooden.

'She is a fighter. She survived the Cultural Revolution. She'll pull through,' the man said, putting his hand gently on her forehead. She barely had strength enough to raise her eyelids.

Audrey Hepburn was running around aimlessly, asking people if they knew where Boss was, talking to herself, picking up odd pieces of junk from the mud. She was as helpless as any mother looking for a lost daughter. The brown sludge was warm and thick. I plunged my hands into it and imagined catching a child's arm or hair.

A stainless-steel blade shone in the mud and I pulled it out.

'What is it?' Audrey Hepburn asked.

I could barely open my mouth, 'I think they belong to Boss.'

'What do you mean?'

'I cut her hair with these scissors a few days ago. She took them out of her school bag.'

Her eyes widened, and I could feel something black and inflamed inside them. She screamed at the rain and collapsed. I tried to pull her up, but she took the scissors from my hand. Rough with anger, she pushed me away and threatened me with them.

I struggled to keep my feet steady. It was getting dark

and some men with torches came to check whether we were victims or rescuers. Audrey Hepburn threw the scissors away and plunged her wounded hands into the mud, burrowing like a frantic mole. The men ignored her, and the torchlight left us.

Holding her tight against my chest, I felt we were sinking into the ground. I finally found a solid foothold and pulled her up. With nowhere else to go we headed towards the sodium lights, finding our way home on autopilot.

Audrey Hepburn's house had been broken into. Nothing downstairs had been disturbed or stolen.

I marched into Boss's room. It was the first time I'd seen it. The tiny over-perfumed room was beautifully decorated in an English style I remembered seeing in magazines, complete with floral wallpaper, a cast-iron bed and mahogany wardrobe. On the dressing table I found an antique hairbrush, an expensive-looking fountain pen, a pink diary with the words 'My Diary' on it, and at least a dozen fragrances of all shapes, colours and sizes from the big French and Italian brands. I opened the diary; it was completely blank. Everything in the room was pastel-coloured. The blue checked curtains matched the pink floral bedding. A teddy bear was tucked into the bed. There was a bookmarked *Pride and Prejudice* on the bedside table, and above it, a nondescript print of what looked like Westminster Abbey or the Houses of Parliament. Beside it hung another of a British naval ship, somewhere exotic with palm trees, perhaps India or Malaysia. On a small bookshelf by the window there were complete leather-bound sets of Jane Austen, the Brontë sisters and George Eliot. They turned out not to be books at all, but wooden props perhaps from some movie. It was as if I had walked into someone's dream, a history museum, or the film set of a period drama. Why did Boss have such a meticulously decorated English room in Diamond Hill, on the second floor of Audrey Hepburn's dirty shack?

'Someone's been here.'

I thought she would be shocked by the break-in, but instead she rushed downstairs, scanning every corner. She started rummaging through her castle of boxes. I didn't know what she was looking for. With hundreds of boxes to go through, my heart sank as she set about digging her nose into every single one.

When she took down the Chinese calendar and flipped through the pages something fell out. The photograph of her and Bruce Lee had been taken out of the frame and hidden in the calendar.

At the back of the photograph, four small words in pencil read, '百無一失 (None Lost in a Hundred).'

'She is alive! Look, it's her handwriting!' She was jumping up and down.

'What?'

'It's a coded message between us in case of emergency. She is in trouble. But thank god she is alive.'

'What trouble?'

'The Triad.'

'She works for them. Why—'

She collapsed in bed, looking utterly exhausted. I hugged her, sending her into a deep sleep. I suspected under the tricky circumstances with the Triad, she didn't want me to stay, so I decided to leave. When I got outside, the rain had already turned into a thin cottony drizzle.

On the dark uphill path to the nunnery, I met the beggar, without his dog, lying on the ground by the metal fence. He was curled up like a kitten, trying to fit his body on a small piece of dry cardboard. He had taken off all his wet clothes except a pair of white boxer shorts. I checked if he was breathing. Just when I was about to shake him, he opened his left eye and stared straight at me. I jumped and ran away without drawing breath. The darkness in front of me was as empty as the eye of the beggar.

The gaslight in my shed cast an incomplete shadow of a nun on the paper windows. It must be Quartz, I thought.

'I have been waiting for you,' the Iron Nun said without acknowledging me.

I took off my wet T-shirt. Her face, half-hidden in the shadow, did not move. But her eyes did. She looked at my face, and then my bare chest.

Sitting at my desk, she examined me from top to toe. I acted as casually as a cat, taking off my sandals, loosening the top button of my trousers. I wanted to embarrass and unsettle her: that was the least I could do. But the inquisitor's eyes were unflinching.

'Take them off if it's more comfortable,' she said.

I lowered my trousers. The gaslight seemed mellow in the cotton-like rain. I lay down on my bed and tried to ignore her.

'Do you know that today's the auspicious day of 穀雨 (Grain Rain)? The rain is supposed to fatten the grain at this time of year.'

I didn't respond as it wasn't a question. She sat with her back to me. Her shadow wavered on the wall like some ancient cave painting.

'You may have heard a service will be held for the dead families in seven days,' she said.

The two bodies under the tarpaulin flashed in my mind.

'People are still being rescued. Isn't it a bit early to be talking about the funeral service?'

'The dead are dead. I can only chant for their safe journey to the afterlife. People also need closure.'

'Wasn't it the Buddha's mission to save lives?'

'How could these lives be saved when they wouldn't even let the fire brigade in? It doesn't surprise me that the police left them to their own mess. But I don't blame them for not trusting the police either.'

'How do you know what happened? You weren't even there.'

'I didn't need to be there to smell the burning trash.'

'You sure are quick to judge.'

'How old were you during the 1967 Riots?'

I couldn't answer as I had no memory of the riots.

'I guess you weren't even a teenager. I didn't support the Leftist protesters—'

'Leftist ... Meaning?'

'The pro-Communist movement. Don't laugh, young man. The working conditions back in the Sixties were terrible and not a single minister in the colonial government raised an eyebrow. Nobody had faith in the Police Force as they were so corrupted and brutal. There was lots of violence on both sides. The government imposed emergency regulations – curfews, widespread searches – and worst of all the police were granted special powers to arrest and convict thousands of protesters. Those were the darkest moments in Hong Kong. If you had seen what the British did to their own subjects here, you would never trust them again.'

'Protesters? Didn't you say it was a riot?'

'Good question. It's funny that often only one version of the story ends up in the history books – if the story is allowed at all.'

The rain poured down more fiercely for a moment, then subsided.

I imagined the police in armour, with batons, shields and guns, lining up against protesters throwing bricks, metal objects and petrol bombs. The Iron Nun was right, I was too young to remember anything, and the events weren't taught in schools or in the history books. There was no mention, nothing to be erased. But it was hard to forget it now, once I'd heard the story.

'Did you find that girl?' she asked out of the blue.

I heard a rumble of dry thunder in the hills. The wind rose sharply in response and the gaslight lost its flame. Lying in the dark, I felt overcome by a sense of mutability. It was as if I had been caught red-handed like a protester and the Iron Nun was the policewoman who had handcuffed me and left me on the ground.

When I refused to respond she said, 'I know you know who and what I am talking about. Your silence tells me everything I need to know.'

'I haven't a clue what you're talking about.'

'One doesn't need to be naked to look naked. You have been here long enough to know that. Because there are no secrets in Diamond Hill, everything is secretive. We are in a state of transition here. In fact, everyone in Hong Kong is obsessed with one single date: 1 July 1997. The whole city is in a state of violent change, moving from one regime we are used to loathing, to another one we are loath to get used to. People think there is only one life, but they are wrong. The only thing I'm certain of is that there is no such thing as honesty in this life, but at least tonight darkness is cloaking our nakedness, and we can speak without shame.

Your suspicions about me are justified. I'm working with the Triad and helping the developers. A conglomerate, they call themselves. Sometimes one has no choice. Soon, the skyscrapers will sprout up all over the place like bamboos, but this nunnery will stay where it is. This religion is older than capitalism or communism.'

She paused, though not for long.

'I know more about you than you would like to admit, and I think you know more about me than you like to accept. So we are the same kind of creature. You have nowhere to go and neither do I. In her tiny head, Quartz thinks that 我前世欠你 (the two of us are indebted to each other in our previous lives). Indebted, as if we had been husband and wife.'

'In our previous lives,' I smiled. 'Do you think so?'

'I think we don't need to have been husband and wife to be indebted to each other. And it is definitely you who are indebted to me.'

I coughed with laughter. In the almost pitch-dark shed, sounds seemed to penetrate more deeply. 'Why are you so certain I am in your debt?'

'Because I am a nun and you aren't. If I owed anybody anything in my previous life, it would have been to the Buddha himself.'

'You do know Boss and her gang call me Buddha, don't you?'

The Iron Nun didn't reply and sat there quietly.

'That night you hosted the banquet, I heard two guys say that you were desperation personified. You would do anything to save the nunnery. Why are you getting in bed with these people?'

'Money brings out the worst and best in humanity. Even religion is not immune to cash. Everybody knows I have no option. That doesn't make me weak.'

'What do you mean by saying you're working with the Triad and helping the developers? Is that the British or the Chinese?'

'I trust nobody except the Buddha. British, Chinese – they are all the same to me. Exploitation has no nationality and what people call international business is just the latest incarnation of greed. You haven't forgotten we are still living in a colony?'

I hesitated. 'Why are you so interested in Boss?'

'You're a clever man. Why do you ask me if you already know the answer? She *is* dangerous. Anybody calling themselves Boss is dangerous.'

'You're the boss here.'

'There is no boss in this house, not even the Buddha. You can't call 虛無 (Nothingness) anything but itself.'

She paused for my response, but I found myself at a loss for words. She straightened her sleeves. 'Boss's heart isn't in this place. Just like her pathetic mother eaten up by Hollywood rubbish, the girl wants to be someone some-where else but knows she will never be able to escape and transform herself. That's why she is so dangerous. She will always be a caged tigress. Those who have once been caged can never be free.'

'That's a load of nonsense.'

'Freedom and imprisonment are both nonsensical. They stopped making sense to me years ago. I have made peace with nonsense. I've been watching Boss the way you'd watch any dangerous caged animal. We only cage animals if they are hard to tame, or close to extinction. You should know that preservation and control are spectator sports. Look what's happening to Hong Kong. The whole world is watching us – the Americans, the British, the Chinese, the Russians. Don't we love being watched, being at the centre of attention?'

She stopped in her tracks for a second or two. 'And you? You have secured a special place between the legs of the woman who calls herself Audrey Hepburn. But aren't you fond of Quartz's eyes too?'

'What the fuck are you talking about?' I grabbed what I thought was her wrist, but it turned out to be her knee. I held on nonetheless.

'You know exactly what I am talking about.' She swatted my hand away like a fly.

'Don't drag Quartz into it. Don't disrespect her.'

'There can be no disrespect when there is genuine attraction. She brightened up like a sunflower facing the sun the moment I granted her permission to be taught English by you.'

'You're just using Quartz to manipulate me.'

'I do want her to teach English to the poor homeless girls in the near future. With respect, I know you are reasonably educated, but what qualifications have you actually got, apart from having been to St Stephen's, that posh secondary school in Stanley?'

Stanley was a lovely word and a beautiful place. I hadn't heard that word for over twenty years. But she was wrong. I didn't go to St Stephen's in Stanley. It was St Paul's.

'This whole business of having a man around is totally new to Quartz. I know you are not the monogamous type. God knows how many women you tricked to sustain your addiction in Bangkok. She is like Eve and you are the nearest Adam.'

The night was dead quiet, except for a startled bird's cry on the roof. 'I know what you're doing. Ever since I arrived you've done nothing but provoke me. If you dislike me so much you could have kicked me out and made me homeless. Like Quartz I am one of your caged animals. Soon you'll be bored of me and ask someone to take me to the butcher, just like you did with the hens. I know you're letting me stay because for the moment I am still useful while this crap you call transition is taking place. Yes, I had a checkered past, but you know nothing about me, not even an atom of mine will ever be familiar to you. Don't fool me and don't fool yourself. We don't owe each other anything, in this life, in any previous life or afterlife. If your religion matters so much to you why on earth did you serve meat in the nunnery to your powerful cronies? Also, don't make jokes about Adam and Eve. You demean your own religion when you demean that of others.'

'I remember that feeling,' she said. 'The blood rushing to the genitals before the brain. I've played with a few cocks in my time. Despite the common preconception, I didn't become a nun because I hated men. Don't be mistaken, I love cocks and I loved them inside me. If you were to show me your erect cock now, I would still be physically tickled and my vagina would still be wet at the sight of it. But would I now want it inside me? No. Not because you are an unattractive man. Not because it would be inappropriate. It is because my heart does not want it anymore. As I've said, I've played with a few cocks in my time but I have never played with someone's mind. Not intentionally. You know very well why you are allowed here. It's not because of me, or whether I like or dislike you. It is because of Daishi and my respect for him. You are old enough to know one does not devote oneself seriously to any religion without being damaged.'

The wind blew more strongly and flicked the shed door open. A slice of moonlight slipped inside between the passing of two clouds.

'Who's there? Show yourself,' the Iron Nun barked.

The door screeched on its hinges and a dark figure slipped in. Bald, I noticed.

'Quartz? Is that you?' I asked.

The first thing we saw was a small pistol pointing into the dark, shaking at us. The moon gleamed on a bald head. It was Boss but freshly shaved. She was damp, muddy and misshapen like a new chick fallen from a nest and yet so determined to fly that she'd forgotten how badly she was hurt.

芒

Grain in Ear

種

Since Boss's abrupt arrival, she had been kept in the Main Temple. Her fever and chills wouldn't subside. I wasn't allowed to enter. Quartz nursed Boss day and night; she said that she had never seen so much sweat. It was as if a volcano was erupting inside the girl. The whole nunnery was infused with the bitter, acidic smell of medicine boiling in a clay pot. Quartz gave me a long list of ingredients for a broth, which I had to fetch from the shanty town: 蓮子 百合 蒼耳子 枸杞 雷神藤 馬兜鈴屬 甜艾草 柳樹皮 (lotus seed, lily bulb, cocklebur fruit, goji berry, thunder god vine, birthwort, sweet wormwood, willow bark). It would have been a better recipe, she claimed, if 乾海馬 蟬衣 (dried seahorse and cicada chrysalis) were allowed in the strictly vegetarian nunnery. Quartz tended the fire all day, adding just enough coal to keep the flame gently burning. The smell reminded me of the medicine that Daishi had used to help me quit heroin. It had seeped into my clothes and bedding. I tried burning more incense and washing my clothes frequently, but the smell lingered throughout the nunnery.

The messages Quartz left me were short, often only one word: 水 (Water), 炭 (Coal), 冰 (Ice), 布 (Cloth). I would immediately get them for her, place them by the temple door, and knock on the wooden floor three times. Quartz would appear, take the items, and give me a brief, tired look to reassure me. Every time I saw her I found her stronger, more present, as if caring for the girl had released a hidden energy in her. To my relief the Iron Nun instructed me to tend the vegetable patch by the side temple. I had no experience with soil, but I set my mind dutifully on the tomatoes, cucumbers, potatoes and lettuces, and thought about nothing except vegetables and Boss.

In the middle of the third night, Quartz came to my shed and told me that the volcano had stopped erupting and that Boss had finally gone to sleep.

'What's happened?' I asked.

Her mouth opened slightly but made no sound. She bowed and just when she was about to turn away, I reached out with my hand, hoping to make her stay. She retreated swiftly like a bird seeing a cat.

'Tell me what's wrong.'

'Nothing is wrong.' She paused. 'The girl needs to be looked after.'

'I don't imagine she can be better looked after. Don't exhaust yourself. Please get some sleep.'

Quartz didn't respond. I hit a mosquito on my arm, or I thought I did.

'There is no point killing one when there are so many,' Quartz said.

I smiled and hit another one on my face.

'The girl called for her mother over and over again. I wonder where she is.'

'She's in the shanty town.'

'Do you know her?'

'Yes, I do. She calls herself Audrey Hepburn, like the Hollywood star.'

Quartz could tell instantly that I'd slept with her. I tried to be as wooden as a door, but she simply opened it and walked in. The mosquitoes reigned rapturously around us and I could feel sweat dripping from my armpits. It smelt like the horrible Chinese medicine.

'Why are you still in the nunnery? Go and see your Audrey Hepburn.'

'We're just friends,' I panicked. 'I am worried about Boss as much as you are.'

She turned away, as if I were a stranger, and walked quietly to the bamboo gate. 'Your priority should be the cucumbers. Most of them have stem blight.'

'Tell me what to do about it,' I asked, though my mind was elsewhere.

'There's nothing you can do now. Just burn them all, including the soil. We won't grow cucumbers in that plot next year.'

Quartz opened the bamboo gate. Under the full moon, her shadow climbed to the roof of my shed.

'By the way, the Iron Nun wants you to go to the shanty town tomorrow. Remember to take your barber's scissors.

You have been asked to cut the hair of the dead before their cremation. It turns out all the hairdressers have left.'

At daybreak I sneaked into the Main Temple hoping to see Boss, but the door was bolted. I fetched a bucket of water and went back to my shed to shave my head. I had stayed bald since Daishi's death. I wondered if the Iron Nun would have allowed me to stay if my head weren't shaven. To pay respect to the landslide victims, I wanted to look clean. Without a mirror, I had to glide the razor blade slowly over my head, and the further my hand went towards the back of my skull, the trickier it got. I often cut myself. A thin trickle of blood ran down the nape of my neck and I wiped it with my finger. I rubbed the blood lightly on my lips to give them a nice colour. I then sharpened the scissors, found my only pair of socks, and put on a fresh white T-shirt and black trousers. Another deafening plane was landing at Kai Tak. The construction site resumed drilling and the wind blew drifts of yellow dust all over Diamond Hill.

The mudslide had cracked open the tarmac of some of the side roads in the shanty town. A burst waterpipe had been ignored by the authorities and people used it like a public fountain to wash their clothes and clean the streets. Children jumped up and down over a gush of water, shrieking with excitement and flapping their arms like hungry ducklings. More houses had been emptied. A family was piling their belongings into a trailer ready to head out to the city.

The blockade to the shanty town still stood but the brown sludge on the main thoroughfares had been cleaned up, leaving almost no trace of the disaster except the mile-long white funeral draperies running along the main street.

I could see that on the whole life had returned to the area – the noise of shuffling mah-jong tiles, the radio broadcasting the horse races, and people jumping the queue outside the last pawn shop in town, hoping to get a better price for their precious belongings. The height of the lychee season sweetened the stink of mud.

In an alley, four boys crouched down in a circle and were forcing a praying mantis to fight an armoured beetle. A sudden roar came from another alley and a shirtless man shouted at the top of his lungs, '我中咗三重彩 (I've won a tierce in Happy Valley)!' People around him started whistling and clapping, as the man dashed up and down the street, showing people the lucky betting slip.

The only thing missing was the white powder. Boss's gang was nowhere to be seen. A few nervous men hovered hopefully at the street corners, their desperate faces and jittery movements all too familiar.

I was on the point of asking for directions to the Taoist shrine, when an old man stopped me in my tracks and kindly took me there. A crowd of thirty-odd people followed us, including family members of the deceased carrying a vast array of 紙紮 (joss paper offerings) which would be burned for their loved ones to take with them to the afterlife. I could see a miniature two-storied house with a front garden, sofa, food, clothes, handbags, TV, car, chauffeur, dog, and a servant boy and girl. A man was playing a funeral tune on a transverse flute and another was striking handbells and cymbals. Some women were scattering handfuls of 陰司紙 (hell money) into the sky, hoping that whatever obstacles the dead might face in their passage to the underworld would be removed by it. The colourful papers pirouetted in the wind, landing on the ground, in the gutter, on people's heads and faces. I caught one and it was printed in sterling, with so many zeros that I lost count. Was it £10 million or £10 trillion? There was the face of the god of the underworld, 冥帝 (Hades), with a fine crown and lush beard, and next to him a logo and the words *Bank of Hades, Heaven and Hell Common Currency*, all printed in elaborate cursive. The banknote was authorised by the Secretary of the Treasury whose signature in English I couldn't read except for the surname Wong, a rather fitting surname, as it had the same sound as 'King'. I let go of the banknote; it was bad luck to keep it.

From the corner of my eye, I saw the beggar. He followed the crowd on its journey, as if he were one of the mourning relatives. He was carrying a pile of cardboard under one arm and pushing a supermarket trolley full of his belongings wrapped in red-white-blue plastic bags. His dog trailed faithfully behind. The crowd stared at him, tutting and shaking their heads. He imitated the crowd, tutting and shaking his head too. Someone shouted '死乞 兒 死屎開 (dead beggar, fuck off)' and others followed suit, calling him a torrent of profanities. The beggar mumbled their foul language back at them. He started picking up the paper money and putting it in his pockets. People got furious. A few men grabbed him by the neck and shoved him out of the procession. But the beggar charged on with his loaded trolley, screaming whatever came into his head: '我想上北京賣鹽鴨蛋 (I want to sell salted duck eggs and die in Beijing)', '英女王好靚 (The Queen is beautiful)', and '我 媽冇奶畀我 (My mum has no milk left for me)'. A teenage boy rushed towards his dog and kicked her in the belly. She yelped and curled up by the kerb. The homeless man dropped everything – his cardboard, trolley, plastic bags – and ran to save his dog. The crowd laughed and left the two of them behind.

It was almost midday when the procession arrived at the Taoist shrine, a hut with a corrugated-iron roof, wooden floorboards and bamboo beams and pillars. There were still pools of rainwater dotted all over the place and rat poison littered the corners. The sun came through the roof, bringing the wind with it, but 文昌王 (the God of Literature) and 關二哥 (the God of War) stood unflinching in the middle of the shrine, taking no notice of the living or the dead.

In front of the two small wooden deities lay three

bodies – a girl about three or four years old, a young man of thirty at most, and an old woman. There was no family resemblance between them. Dressed in clean refrigerated clothes and wrapped loosely in rough hemp, they lay flat, each on a bed of straw mixed with dry ice. Their frozen bodies had been powdered with white chalk. From a distance, I imagined that with their pale, muted appearance they looked like the wild exposed limestone of Doi Pui Mountain where Daishi had gone to die.

An old man handed me three sticks of burning incense. I bowed to the three bodies, and then to the gods. Then he took the incense sticks from me and put one on a tray at the foot of each corpse. Many women in the crowd started sobbing and a child started screaming.

'You have until the end of the incense stick. I guess it's about half an hour if the wind drops. Please stay here until they have come and collected the bodies. They will give you cash. Thank you for coming.' The old man turned away before I could ask a question. When he left, I couldn't remember anything he'd said.

I had cut a dead boy's hair before, but never a girl's. She was as young as a pea. Once in Bangkok a young monk about twelve years old had lost consciousness for seven days after being hit by a tuk-tuk. Daishi brought him back to Wat Arun, laid him down on a silk robe by the Buddha's feet and asked me to shave the boy's hair. The monks thought the boy was still alive as his hair and fingernails had grown noticeably though he'd been dead for a day. I told them that they only appeared longer because the skin around them had dried up and retracted. The monks didn't believe me and kept screaming, 'No! No!' as the boy's body descended into the incinerator.

My hands were a broken compass, trembling as the scissors touched the girl's delicate fringe. I cut her fringe to eyebrow level and tidied her hair at the back. Once I'd finished she looked like a sleeping acorn.

I took a deep breath. The artificial sweetness of the incense burned my throat. I had just two-thirds of the allotted time left.

I realised the young man had a very fine face when my scissors touched his temples. There was a mole hidden in the tail end of his right eyebrow, not quite a birthmark but distinctive enough. His small, gentle mouth laid bare a touch of femininity probably invisible when he was alive. He was almost stubble-free, and I guessed he must have shaved just before the mud came down on him. I thinned his hair, reduced the weight at the back, cut the sideburns and applied a thin hair-gel to keep his parting in place.

The crowd's impatience outside was palpable. Thankfully, the thumping and hammering sounds from the construction site drowned out the noise of the crying children. A glint of sunlight filtered through a tiny gap in the rusted metal roof, revealing the hidden lives of dust motes and landing on the old woman's face.

When I had seen her six days earlier the old woman's leg had been trapped in debris. A survivor of the Cultural Revolution who came to Hong Kong to find another life. Now, lit up by the sun, her chalk-white features seemed detached from the rest of her body, like a face uncovered after an avalanche. Her wrinkles had been smoothed over by the chalk and her thin curled-up lips appeared to be smiling. The mortician must have stuffed cotton buds in her mouth to give a semblance of vitality to her cheek-bones. Her hair was so thin that no cutting could give an illusion of lushness. I touched her forehead as the man had done. She was colder than white marble. I combed her thin hair to little effect.

The incense stick still had about three minutes left. I sat idly at the foot of the door, feeling the heat of the crowd outside and the stagnant air in the shrine. The incense rose like some spirit unleashed by fire. I thought of Daishi on Doi Pui Mountain, hiding from us so that he could die alone without being seen or pitied. Was he in a cave or under a tree? Did he pass away lying down or sitting in the lotus position? Tigers would have found him later, if there were still any tigers left. I pictured his unburied corpse providing sustenance for birds, festering with maggots and fungus, before having been found and burned to ashes. In his amateurish Cantonese, he used to say '色即是空空即是色 (Reality is a phantom and all phantoms a reality).' I used to repeat it over and over in my mind when I was withdrawing from heroin, convulsing in my own shit and urine. I still haven't a clue what he meant by phantoms or reality. But when I thought of Daishi's body rotting away in the remote mountains, I had no idea if his hiding from us was an act of bravery, cowardice or apathy. I was angry with him for leaving me behind and sending me back to Hong Kong, but I didn't have the energy to think about it. He had found a way to forgive me, even though I couldn't myself. If seeking silence and letting his body rot in the open were what he really wanted, I would have to find a way to understand him.

I jumped when someone knocked on the door. Six strong men came in without greeting me and carried the three bodies away on bamboo stretchers. I watched as the crowd and the loud funeral music disappeared. A woman handed me money in a white envelope and said, '多謝 (Thank you).' I found myself alone in the empty shrine.

It was only when I had finished picking up the hair that I noticed Audrey Hepburn standing by the door.

'How long have you been there?'

'Longer than you think.' She picked up a few strands of hair from the ground and handed them to me. She closed the door and a patch of light landed on her face.

'I kissed Bruce Lee in this shrine. It was the summer he was filming *Fist of Fury* up in the hills. I was blossoming, 花樣年華 (in the prime of my life) as they say. It was just a silly kiss. Many things start with a kiss.'

'What was he like?'

'You mean his lips? They were as soft as ripe plums, like yours. He was bewildering, but vulnerable and foreign. He caught my eye one day in a break from filming, and the following day he found me in the alley. We were like an item, complete with our glamorous hats and sunglasses. It happened so suddenly. It was as if I had been hit by a bus. Did I say how sweet and vulnerable he was? And such a gentleman.'

'Is Bruce Lee Boss's father?'

She laughed ironically, not taking my question seriously.

'Are you serious? Don't you know what Bruce Lee looked like?'

'Vaguely. I have seen photographs of him, but never any of his films.'

'How could you not have seen Bruce Lee? That's a tragedy I'll help you fix. You can't say you're from Hong Kong if you haven't seen a Bruce Lee film.'

'How long were you together?'

'I don't remember. It was a secret, anyway. All good secrets are timeless.'

'Who is Boss's father then?'

'I'm not in the mood to be investigated. It's so damn hot in here.'

'Being a single mum is no picnic. Did the father offer any support?'

'收撚你把口啦 (Shut the fuck up)! I'm sick and tired of your questions.'

Her face changed and her mind drifted somewhere else. 'How's Boss doing?'

'She came out of her fever last night.'

She stared at a dark spot on the roof; a swallowtail butterfly that had flown in and perched there.

'Is she feeling better?'

'I can't tell. I'm not allowed into the Main Temple. A young nun has been looking after her day and night and giving her medicine.'

'Quartz is the last of the good ones.'

I picked up the remaining strands of hair and put them in a plastic bag. She kneeled and started praying to the gods.

'Hang on. Do you know Quartz? How did you know Boss had come to the nunnery?'

'Where else would she go?' she said, her eyes firmly closed.

'Quartz said Boss called out for her mother during her fever.'

'The girl looks tough, but she is as soft as a teddy bear inside. We've never been separated from each other. Not even for a single night. Even though she and her gang sometimes work through the night, I always keep my eyes open and check until she's home safely.'

I hesitated. 'Are you her real mother?'

Bowing down with her palm closed, Audrey Hepburn was as quiet as a corpse.

She stood up and said bluntly, 'Just because I've slept with you once or twice doesn't mean you own me.'

'This has nothing to do with us.'

'Then what's between me and my daughter has nothing to do with you either.'

'I know you care about her.'

'What do you know about love between a mother and daughter?'

'I was born from a mother's womb too.'

'Oh, really? Look where you are now. And where is your mother? I'd bet my life on it that 你老母死咗你都唔知 (you don't even know if your mother is still alive or not). If she was alive, she'd be ashamed of you.'

'You don't know a thing. Why don't you keep your mouth shut?'

'That's what you want, isn't it? You want to shut everything up, don't you? Look at yourself. "Buddha". Do you really think you are a Buddha? I don't need to question you to get the dirt on you. You can't fool me with your shaved head and tatty clothes. 我同你一樣咁折墮 我知你喺度玩緊乜野 (Like you I didn't start as a lowlife, so I know the game you're playing). You think living in the nunnery makes you a saint? However high and mighty you sound, and with all your fancy education, everybody knows you're a loser, an ex-addict with nowhere to go. Why don't you get the fuck out of Diamond Hill and get a proper job on Hong Kong Island? Oh, I forgot. Nobody is going to hire a fake monk like you. Can't you see how low you've sunk, cutting dead people's hair? Yes, I'm stuck in this hellhole like everybody else, but at least I'm not a parasite. And yes, they all think I'm mentally ill and living in my bubble. I like being called 柯德莉夏萍 (Audrey Hepburn) and I want to *be* Audrey Hepburn. Why not?'

Her eyes were fiery. She tilted her head up and down, mumbling English-sounding words that didn't mean anything, before dropping her chin to her chest like a puppet.

'Do I look like a mad woman to you?' She laughed, pulling at her hair dramatically and sucking her thumb. She spat at me, 'Don't ever call me a retard or say I'm not right in the head. Just because you're not from this dump doesn't mean you're immune from our madness. You're 垃圾 (trash) like me. You're worse because you don't even know you're trash. Keep staring, I am all yours. You don't scare me. Come on, pick up your scissors. Stab me if you want. You know what? I only fucked you because I pitied you.'

She laughed and turned towards the wall. I gathered my belongings and headed for the door.

'Why are you using her to hurt me?' she muttered.

'What are you talking about? Nobody wants to hurt anybody.'

'You've come between me and my daughter to drive us apart. Is that what the Iron Nun wants? I know you're one of her puppets and that monster always manages to get what she wants. Are you happy now that Boss is in the nunnery with you? Are you planning to adopt her? Don't you know you are nothing but a total stranger? 屌撚開 (Get your cock out of my way)!'

'What the hell? Why do think Boss seeking refuge in the nunnery has anything to do with the Iron Nun? They hate each other. I'm surprised Boss came, and that the Iron Nun let her stay. Boss loves you and she said she's emigrating to London with you one day.'

'Yes, London,' she smiled. 'She was always obsessed with Britain, even as a little girl. It was probably my fault teaching her all those silly songs in *My Fair Lady*.'

She licked her fingers and stiffened her eyelashes, before singing the famous song about the rain, Spain, and the plain. The sun occasionally dappled on her face as she danced, lifting her invisible dress and showing me her delicate footwork.

'Shit, I can never quite remember this bit. Is it *In Heartfort, Hearford, and Humpshire, the hurrycake hardly happens*?'

I burst out laughing. She sat sulking by the wall, hands on both cheeks, pouting her lips like Eliza Doolittle fed up with the speech exercises.

I huddled up next to her.

Audrey Hepburn turned to me. 'By the way, did Boss say she also wants you to come to London with us?'

'Yes. I thought it was just one of her jokes.'

'Not at all. We've been planning it for years. The moment we caught wind of the Triad getting involved with land sale in Diamond Hill, Boss persuaded me that her working with the Triad would be our way out of this hellhole. I've been the casualty of misfortune for far too long. This is our only chance to make a new start. Now Boss is in trouble and I'm worried the Triad will sell us down the river.'

She looked lost in her thoughts.

'Why am I part of your plan for London?'

'I know you don't belong here. You – *we* – deserve better than rotting in this dump. Anyway, Boss has always wanted a dad. We can be one big happy family.'

She came closer to me and kissed me in a wet violent way, scratching my lips with her teeth. I gave myself up, our tongues twisting in each other's mouths like two electric eels. I grabbed her breasts and she stroked my groin. It was quick, messy and unsatisfactory, leaving me wanting more. But she'd lost interest. We sat on the floor and saw the butterfly reappear and land on the head of the God of War.

'That's a good omen,' she said, pointing at the swallow-tail with yellow specks. 'It means we'll be at war with each other for the rest of our lives. I knew I'd have a difficult life like Audrey Hepburn's – divorces and miscarriages. Now the god has spoken.'

'Why don't you come with me and see Boss?' I asked.

'I will *never* step an inch into that nunnery. Not in my lifetime. She'll be safe there.'

I held her hands, which were hot and alive. The shrine darkened. The sun must have been setting.

'She is my sister.'

'Who is your sister?'

'The Iron Nun,' she paused. 'But you mustn't tell anyone.'

The morning sun was so fierce that I was drenched in sweat and sick from the choking heat. I could hear Quartz laughing but couldn't believe my eyes when I saw Boss in the courtyard – upright, energetic, sunflower-like – dressed as a proper nun in full Buddhist robes. She was helping Quartz in the vegetable plot. She put a cherry tomato in Quartz's mouth, making the juices spatter all over her robes. They laughed at each other like silly lovers.

I gave them a fright when I appeared behind them.

'你個衰樣好似同你老母送終咁 (You look as if you've just been to your mother's funeral). What's wrong?' Boss asked.

'I haven't shaved.'

'You'd need more than a clean shave to look like a Buddha,' Boss said, exchanging playful glances with Quartz.

'It's good to see you fully recovered,' I said.

Boss ignored me.

'I was going to clear the rotten cucumber plants,' I said to Quartz.

'We've got it all under control,' Boss replied.

'Do you want to continue with English grammar later, Quartz?' I asked.

'We've got that under control too. I'm going to teach her the tenses today,' Boss said matter-of-factly.

I'd become the subject of a conspiracy between a teenage gang-leader and a nun. I moved a few tangled leaves and Quartz walked off, picking some young green beans.

'You're not giving them a chance to grow bigger?'

'You really haven't a clue. The plant is overwhelmed. It needs to channel more energy into fewer pods.'

'You don't want me to teach you English anymore?'

I could see blood rushing to her cheeks.

'She'll have the chance to learn from a better teacher,' Boss interrupted, and Quartz went over to the far side of the plot and started weeding.

'When did *you* learn to teach English?'

'*Chill out, man.*' Boss spoke in a well-practised accent. 'Of course, I can teach English. I learned it in school and from the company I work for. Posh foreigners need my good stuff to relax. Quartz saved my life and I'm just helping her out.'

'It looks like you're doing more than helping her out.'

'You're damn right. I like her a lot – she is much sweeter, gentler and more caring than my mum. I was a wreck and she brought me back to life. We must get on. I haven't got time to entertain you, Buddha.' Boss showed me a pile of rotten cucumbers. 'See, we've got our hands full.'

I stood under the burning sun, watching the pair of them weeding side by side. Their bald heads gleamed like two fishes. Boss looked so different without her hair. It was as if she had always been a nun. As the heat rose, they went in and out of focus, more like a mirage than real people. Through the boiling haze, I saw Boss lean towards Quartz and wipe her face with her hand. Boss smiled at me deviously as if she had stolen something precious from somebody.

When I got back to the shed, I noticed that Boss had already removed some of the grammar books. I picked up one of those she'd left behind. Flipping through it, I found a series of type 3 conditional exercises: 'If this thing had happened, that thing would have happened (but neither of these things really happened).' I suddenly had a moment of déjà vu. I remembered sitting in this same shed, confronted by the same English grammatical puzzle about the conditional. I didn't even know if my mother was still alive. I felt as if my mind was running in circles inside an impenetrable vault with thick concrete walls. The example given in the exercise book was: 'If it had rained, you would have got wet.' Underneath was a blank space where I'd written: 'If I had died in Bangkok, I would have been cremated there and never come to Diamond Hill.'

At the crack of dawn, Quartz knocked on my door with two beautiful hens under her arms. She instructed me to carry a new stove and two cylinders of gas from the entrance gate to the kitchen. I asked her where she got the hens from and whose idea it was to get rid of the old charcoal stove. It was all thanks to Boss. There were four hens already in the coop. She added the two under her

arms and tore some dry bread into small pieces for them.
The hens nosed around the coop, ruffling up the straws
and rubbing their beaks on the bamboo, before pecking
at the bread.

'Why do you keep hens in the nunnery? You don't
eat eggs.'

'Before the hens were slaughtered for the banquet, I
used to collect the chicks and give them to the children in
the shanty town. I also collected the unhatched eggs, and
every few weeks, walked up into the hills and put them in
a cave for the bats.'

'I thought bats only ate insects.'

'I have been mothering the bats in a secret cave for
years and spoiling them with eggs. They've gained quite
an appetite.'

She looked pleased feeding the healthy hens.

'I love bats,' she said. 'I want to be reincarnated as a bat
in my next life.'

'Why a bat?'

'Early Buddhism started thousands of years ago in the
caves of northern India. I think bats were the only thing
living in those caves, so they must have been the creatures
closest to the early Buddhist masters.'

I was moved by Quartz's strange and stubborn imagination. I didn't know what I wanted to be in my next life. I
didn't even know if I believed in reincarnation.

'Can you show me the cave next time you feed your bats?'

'If you help me carry the gas stove, I will consider it.'

She squatted by the coop and talked to the hens in the language everyone talks to hens.

By mid-morning, I had finished shifting the last cylinder, a heavy one. I had twisted a muscle in my back, but it wasn't too bad. Boss was busy in the kitchen connecting the gas cylinder to the stove. I left the spare one outside, hidden behind a bush by the pond.

After turning and airing the big pile of compost, I found a shady spot by the side temple to sit and have a drink of water.

'Don't be cross with me, Buddha,' Boss said, grabbing my bottle and emptying it.

'I'm not angry. I'm worried.'

'You're always anxious about something. That's why you can never be a proper drug addict.'

'Now you're making me cross.'

'Whatever.' She squeezed herself into the last bit of shade, sat down next to me and wiped my sweaty forehead with a towel.

'So, the gas stove?'

'Yes, today is the dawn of a new civilisation.'

She turned on the hosepipe near the vegetable plot, wetted the towel and put it over her head. The water dripped down the sleeves of her new Buddhist robes.

'You look rather good bald.'

'死開 (Piss off).'

'I'm telling the truth.'

She squeezed herself back into the fast-disappearing shade.

'真係熱到我老母都唔認得呀 (It's so hot I wouldn't recognise my mum). I hate summer.' She pointed at the sun. 'Look at that cocky motherfucker up there. I'd just die for a cool breeze. I'm melting. God, I'd give anything to throw myself into an ice pool.'

A crow called in the hills. It could have been a cicada, but I thought it was too late for cicadas.

'It will be cooler in London in summer. I can't wait to live there. My savings are growing as we speak. I'm nearly there, Buddha.' She paused and then in English, said, '*All in the fullness of time.*'

It was the first time I heard Boss using such an English idiom. It was beautiful, and it reminded me that Daishi liked its Chinese equivalent, uttered in a half-Thai, half-Cantonese accent.

'What are you thinking?' Boss asked. The sun beat down and cancelled out all other sound in the nunnery.

'I'm wondering about why you are here.'

'Buddha, the truth is I didn't quite do what I was told. I'm in trouble and needed a place to hide, to let the storm calm down.'

'Are you OK now?'

'No, not really. It's a real mess out there. I am really scared.'

She leaned on my shoulder and her sweat dripped onto my knees. I stroked the back of her head and she started to cry.

'I was recruited by the Triad at the age of seven. Mum had been very sick after seeing one of her clients, and after three days I'd finished off all the food in the cupboard and was famished. Neighbours didn't help because I was the daughter of an unhinged prostitute. One day, a Triad leader was sniffing about Diamond Hill and he spotted me picking a half-rotten mango out of the bin. He handed me a Swiss army knife and said if I dared to stab the fat man crossing the street, he would give me a corner to look after. I remember the compact knife, with its dark plastic casing the colour of dried blood. I remember the white-cross logo. I didn't think twice.'

'You really stabbed a man just like that?'

'Yeah. It was easy. You don't think when you stab someone. The knife slid in like a dream and came out quick as a flash. I did it just the once to prove a point, but since then, I've had lots of others who'll do it for me. Violence isn't my style, and anyway, you don't need it if you've got the white powder.'

I had nothing to say as her arm moved matter-of-factly, flashing an invisible army knife in the air.

After a few goes, she got bored and said, 'They asked me to do a crazy thing.'

'What crazy thing?'

Her voice was racked. 'One of the 香主 (Incense Masters)

in the Triad from 油尖旺 (Yau Tsim Mong District) asked me to threaten some random families and order them not to leave their houses. Those precarious houses by the hillside.'

'Threaten the families? How?'

'Weapons – knives, scissors, or anything sharp. I told them I'd slash their throats if they dared set foot outside. It was an order from on high, so I obeyed. I've always been a good soldier. No fuss, no questions asked. I instructed my boys to keep a night-watch on the families to make sure nobody sneaked out—'

'So those poor people would be smothered by the mud?'

'I had no idea there would be a landslide. Anyway, the problem was I was getting too soft. Some of my boys were worried about the deluge. They said the soil above the houses had got very loose and debris had started to fall. Once I heard that we stopped harassing the families.'

'Three people died.'

'I didn't have a choice. It could have been much worse.'

'What's going to happen to you?'

'I'm hoping things will calm down. I've been told things always cool down after a while. I don't think I would be walking around if there hadn't been some fatalities. I just need to lie low for now. Nobody apart from my most trusted boys can know I'm hiding here. My boys told people in the slums that I'm in Cambodia visiting the poppy fields.'

'Audrey Hepburn knows you're here.'

'Mum is a smart woman. She won't say a word.'

'I gather she is not your mum.'

'Did she tell you?' Boss paused. 'Wow, she really trusts you. Did you fuck her again?'

I didn't respond.

'Anyway, it's probably good she told you. Yeah, she is not my biological mother, but I really do see her as my mother. I know it sounds weird but being here makes me miss her. We've never been apart. She brought me up when nobody else gave a fuck. She is the only family I've got.'

'And what about this grand plan of moving to London?'

'It's a real plan, Buddha. The Triad is a multi-billion-dollar international business. Like company executives, Triad leaders relocate all the time, moving from Hong Kong to America, Europe, Australia, even as far away as New Zealand. Have you heard that *the milk snatcher Margaret Thatcher* was re-elected as Prime Minister yesterday for the third time? The bigwigs are over the moon, though there will be more hard times to come.'

'Wow, you've got your finger on the pulse of British news.'

'We serve quite a lot of expat clients. London has become a new hub of underground gambling in the Chinese community. What do the exploited, depressed chefs and waiters in Chinatown spend their money on? Mahjong, poker, roulette, horses. I was told one of the gang leaders in London's Chinatown has gone rogue, tripling interest payment randomly and losing a lot of customers. They want someone new with no strings attached to restructure the business there. I'm young and able, and have shown I've got potential to be a future leader. Well, that was before I fucked everything up.'

She picked up a discarded broad-bean shell and tore it into pieces.

'If I somehow manage to weather the storm, I can take you to London too if you want. Then the three of us can be one big happy family.'

'Funnily, your mum said exactly that.'

'You would be a good dad.'

The sun climbed right above my head. I lost track of time, and Boss's wild plan. If Boss was right that Hong Kong would be dead in ten years' time, her escape to Britain would be a smart move. But what did she and Audrey Hepburn want from me? What would I bring to the table that they didn't already have?

The midday heat was so oppressive I could feel Boss melting in my hand or my hand melting on her head. We sat there, her head still on my shoulder, while in front of us the stifled green hills looked smothered in the haze. Now and then, there was a sea breeze and a patch of trees swayed backwards and forwards as if seasick. Sadly, the wind never came as far as the nunnery. Apart from Boss's drowsy breathing, I could only hear the nuns' midday chanting, their soft slurred voices repeating a sutra and folding the world around them in one big cocoon.

'Who is your biological mother?'

'Some woman, I guess, who couldn't be bothered to bring me up. Maybe I'm a casualty of the one-child policy in Mainland China. Who knows? I don't blame her, whoever she was, even if she's still alive out there somewhere. I wouldn't want to have a baby around my neck either.' She sounded like she really meant what she said.

'Have you ever asked Audrey Hepburn who your mother is?'

'She hasn't a clue. I wouldn't trust her anyway. She isn't always on it, I mean, sometimes her head is a bit 藕線 (cross-wired).'

'Well, she calls herself Audrey Hepburn for a reason.'

'Exactly. She's lived in her own head all her life. She said she found me in a basket by the gate of the nunnery one evening when she was looking for Bruce Lee. Mind you, she was always looking for Bruce Lee, and if it wasn't him, it would have been other stars like 陽帆 (Yang Fan) or 王羽 (Jimmy Wang Yu), Humphrey Bogart or Clark Gable. She'd longed for a son to appear miraculously without her ever being pregnant. And there I was. A godsend. At first she treated me like a boy and cut my hair short. I often had this dream where I woke up and thought I was a character in some movie. She would be playing an independent woman single-handedly bringing up a little orphan, while I was the screwed-up daughter who should really have been the son saving his poor foster-mother from poverty.'

'Is that why your room is like a crazy Victorian film set?'

Boss blushed and straightened her back. 'I adore Britain. I'm going to live there soon. I need to get used to it, to prepare myself. My Mum isn't exactly Mary Poppins.'

I laughed, and her tone changed. 'If I find you've touched anything in my room, I'll pull your fingernails out one by one. I'm not joking. It's one of the most painful methods recorded in ancient torture books. I haven't had a chance to try it on anybody yet, but I've got the instruments all ready.'

'I like the idea of you consulting ancient Chinese torture books. Are you also going to do 五馬分屍 (five horses attached to the body to pull the head and limbs apart)? You're just like your mum, but living in a different movie.'

Boss laughed with me. She stood up and said, 'I will not become a failure like my mum. But it's true that I'd love to live in a movie! Didn't I tell you I was born to be a film director? Once I'm settled in London and earn enough money as the head of Drug Trafficking for the Triad, I will 金盆洗手 (wash my hands in a golden bowl), leave the Triad, and study to be a film director. I want to be the best Hong Kong female film director in Britain – in fact, in the world. People all over the globe will see my films, and I'll be remembered in America, India and Brazil. I'll win the Oscars, the Palm thing in Cannes, and the Golden Horse!'

I was moved by the passion in Boss's eyes, the energy in her hand gestures.

'So, what'll be your first film?'

'Obviously, I want to make my first film about myself.

How do you call it? 自傳 (autobiography)? Rich people are obsessed with stories about lowlifes, aren't they? People are happy to pay good money just to see some loser put a dirty needle in his vein, and a prostitute bend down to suck some cocks. Seeing the suffering of others makes us all feel lucky and strong. Isn't that what you call sympathy?'

Boss wiped the sweat off her forehead. 'I'll give the world what it wants. I'll sell my lucrative life story to make millions. My first film will be set here, in this stinky, fucked-up shanty town. I want people to see the world through my eyes. The camera will follow me through the narrow alleys like that.' Her hands moved like those of a professional cameraman. 'I'll zoom in to the gutters full of broken needles. See? I'll yell *Cut!* and sit in a director's chair with my name on it. I want the world to get excited about this exotic place. I want people to realise how crazy and talented I am.'

'Sounds amazing. What'll you call your first film? How about *Diamond Hill*?'

'Not bad, Buddha, not bad at all. But who the hell knows what Diamond Hill means? I'll call it *The Boss from Hell*. Or how about *Hell Boss*?'

'They both sound good to me. What's the twist in the tale of your *Hell Boss*?'

Boss straightened up and laughed smugly. 'You, Buddha. A total stranger arriving in Diamond Hill. Lost and clueless with no idea who you want to be.'

I remembered how Daishi, when meditating, used to make a gesture where his thumb and index finger joined to form a circle, like the sign for OK, except that the other three fingers were tucked into his hand. He said the circle, like the passing of time, has no beginning and no end.

A cicada called from a tree behind. This time it was definitely a cicada, not a crow. A late cicada, the last survivor.

'Buddha, you know what: if I die, I need you to look after my mum.' Boss looked into the green hills. 'You don't need to marry her. I know she is a nutcase, but I want you to keep an eye on her. The Triad have helped me get my will sorted. I've left everything to her.'

'Do you really think they'll try to kill you?'

'Like me, these people are capable of anything. I'm prepared for it, Buddha. A good show can't run for ever.'

She reached for my hand and our fingers interlocked. 'Don't worry, Dad. I'm definitely safe here. No man would dare harm me in the presence of the Buddha. The Triad are particularly superstitious about these things. That's why I've shaved my head. As long as I look like a nun, they won't touch me. Anyway, my boys are keeping watch in the shanty town. The moment they hear that 風吹草動 (the wind blows and the grass moves), they'll alert me.'

It was strange her calling me 'Dad', but I had no idea how serious she was.

'Do you like living here?' she asked.

'It isn't that bad. I've got a roof and a shed. I'm getting used to it.'

'Was it easier living with monks in Bangkok than being surrounded by these uptight virgins?'

I knew when her mood changed, and I ignored her.

'Anyway, take it easy with Quartz. She's fragile.'

'What do you mean?'

'You know she suffers from memory loss, don't you?'

'Memory loss?'

'I don't know the details. All I've heard from the other nuns is that she has no recollection of her childhood. Not a single sliver of memory of her life before she arrived in the nunnery. It's a bit odd and sad. I can't imagine living like that, as if one of my limbs had been cut off.'

'How's that possible? She looks fine.'

'I didn't ask her. 你話係唔係真係慘過死老母 (Don't you think that's more tragic than having a dead mother)?' There wasn't a hint of self-pity in her voice.

'I told her I'm an orphan just to see if she would open up to me. But she said nothing and took no notice. Clearly, she is hiding 好撚大個傷痕 (a fucking great scar). I didn't want to mess with that can of worms. Don't worry, Buddha. Quartz is fine. Buddhism suits her and she's thriving here. Just don't push it too far with her. It's obvious the Iron Nun is using her to seduce you. But I can sense that Quartz likes you. That's a no-no. She is a nun and more of a nutcase than my mum.'

I changed the subject, 'Where did you get the gas stove and the cylinders? And the hens?'

'My boys sorted it. Just a small token of thanks for the nuns. No big deal.'

She used the wet towel to cover her forehead and groaned. 'I'd die for a cigarette, Buddha. Nothing better than smoking like a chimney in the heat.'

'Have you still got the pistol?'

'Nope. My boys took care of it. A mind like yours shouldn't think too much about lethal weapons.'

Over the next few days, Boss embedded herself into the fabric of the nunnery. She showed the nuns how to adjust the fire and temperature of the gas stove. She helped chop vegetables. She gave Quartz a three-hour English lesson each day, or so she said. She weeded the entire vegetable plot. She cleaned and refilled the pond. She hand-washed the bed linen. She wiped the floors of the Main Temple. She attended the prayers before daybreak, at noon, sundown and midnight. She showered with the nuns. She ate and slept in the same room as they did.

The nunnery was transformed by Boss's presence. All the doors and windows of the Main Temple and side temple were kept open from dusk till dawn. The fresh summer breeze seemed to refresh everyone's mind. The nuns' chanting became clearer and louder, invigorated by Boss's hyperactive enterprise. They started speaking more frequently with each other, giggled and laughed more freely in public. Even the tofu was seasoned with a more generous helping of soy sauce.

The weather coincided with a new sense of openness – dry, high heat, with a regular breeze that swept away the usual humidity.

Boss gradually gained the nuns' trust while I withdrew from the day-to-day life of the nunnery. Most days I hid in my shed, mulling over the past.

The night Daishi took me into Wat Arun, he had found me passed out on the street. On the second night, the torrential rain fell like bricks on the roof and the monks were busy with mops and buckets, keeping the gold-plated Buddha dry. I was overwhelmed by a craving for heroin and every vein in my body was furious, itchy. I scratched my arms until I drew blood, but seeing my blood only made me crave heroin more. The dried blood smelt like a rare steak. I kept licking the wounds for comfort. The withdrawal process was agonising, and it felt as if someone were grabbing my throat and trying to strangle me. Sometimes I would scream at the top of my lungs when I looked at the hungry veins in my arms. I wanted to pull them out one by one with my teeth.

To stop me self-harming, Daishi and the monks once rolled me up in a bamboo mat and tied it with strings. Sweat leaked from my pores. I vomited until there was no liquid left in my stomach. In the darkest hours, Daishi held a wooden spoon to press my tongue down, keeping it intact during my tremors. He forced salty water down my throat to keep me hydrated. Every inch of my body tingled like an open wound. It was as if I'd been split in two – one half yearned for needles to shoot up my arteries, the other wanted to petrify into stone, so that the needle would snap when it touched my flesh.

Over the following days, I passed out again and again, twisting and wrestling with myself. One night I saw a tall figure standing next to me. It wasn't a he or she. It had no gender, no physical details, no face – a human outline dripping with water. It reappeared night after night. It was as if I'd invited it into my life for all the wrong reasons, and now it wouldn't leave. I could feel it looking down on me. Sometimes I could feel its hands creep under the bamboo mat and touch me all over.

Then one day I woke up and felt I'd come through. The ceaseless rain had run out and I was still tied up. The wooden spoon, fallen from my mouth, was shaped like a battered limb dented with my teeth-marks. I called for help but nothing came out of my mouth – I had lost my voice. Lying there, bound up like a captured animal, I couldn't stop weeping, though I had no tears. My throat burned. My lips were chipped. I bit my tongue, which felt like sandpaper, and all my teeth were loose. I rolled back and forth like a spring roll deep-frying in oil until I started banging my head on the door, trying to catch someone's attention.

Eventually, a monk heard me and called Daishi, who untied me. As the bamboo mat slid off my body, I discovered I was stark naked. I was too weak even to cover my groin. I asked Daishi what day of the week it was, and he said it had taken me seven days and six nights to survive the withdrawal. My skin was imprinted all over with the pattern of the bamboo mat, which now looked like my shell. At first it felt unnatural to live in a body without heroin, but gradually I realised it was natural to feel that it was unnatural to live in one's own skin.

I lay in bed with my door and window open, letting the summer air drift into my shed and thinking about the figure in Wat Arun. I had not seen it since.

Boss and Quartz knocked at my door and giggled mischievously. They were holding hands.

'Come on, Buddha. We've got something to show you,' Quartz said.

I followed them out into the courtyard, and we all rushed past the mock-stone mountain, lily pond, hen coop and bamboo gate. It was already dark on the veranda of the Main Temple. I was reminded of standing at the exact same spot for the first time, seven days after I came to the nunnery. The yellow sodium streetlights had almost disappeared from the shanty town, leaving patches of unlit wasteland like black holes. There was no movement down below – no stray dogs barking, no dinnertime charcoal smoke. Three tall cranes overshadowed the eastern hillside, hanging over the high wire fences and surveillance cameras. A few concrete towers had sprouted up, at different levels and still under construction. I had no idea how high they would rise. Unfurled above the cranes was a banner proclaiming the new residential area 東方荷里活 (Hollywood East).

We took off our shoes before entering the Main Temple. The wooden floor creaked under my bare feet. I stared at the imposing figure of the golden Buddha sitting in the middle of the room. Boss and Quartz rushed ahead like two bats flying to their nest. I waited a few seconds until my eyes adjusted to the dark. I could hear voices whispering at the far end of the temple.

As I walked round towards the back of the Buddha, I saw a blue light wavering on the walls as if the Main Hall had turned into an aquarium. I couldn't believe it. There it was – a small Sony combo TV with a video-cassette player, turned on and showing a blank blue screen with the word *Play* in the left-hand corner. The faces of all the nuns were lit up by it. Boss and Quartz sat down on the floor in the front row, while three other nuns sat behind them. One of them covered her face with a headscarf as soon as she saw me.

Boss jumped up and pressed *Play* on the machine and the screen changed to a grey, rainy sky with a black mountain range on the horizon. A deafening thunderstorm filled the temple as torrential rain pelted down on the screen. Then there was a jump to the next scene in which a man stopped his rickshaw outside a gate. It dawned on me this must be the legendary Bruce Lee. He was dressed in a white suit, with white shoes, and was carrying a white suitcase. He clambered out of the rickshaw and ran through the gate of a big house to find shelter from the rain.

'Come and join us. It's 《精武門》 (*Fist of Fury*). Bruce Lee's just arrived. The opening sequence is classic.' Boss whispered so loudly that it sounded as if she was shouting.

'What the hell – sorry ... what's happening?'

'The Iron Nun's away tonight. When I found out there was a combo TV here, I asked my boys to get some films. Like you, the nuns have never seen a Bruce Lee film, so you're not the only 處女 (virgin) here!'

The nuns giggled. I stood in front of the flickering screen, not knowing whether I should stay or ask them to stop watching it.

They were glued to the screen. There was a brass band playing some solemn music in the rain while a coffin was lowered into the open grave. The film looked dated and artificial, but somehow the studio with its fake rain and wind made the drama more realistic. The crowd was drenched by the storm. A group of men in mourning clothes lifted their spades and covered the coffin with soil, which soon turned to mud. It was an electrifying scene, and the camera quickly zoomed in on Bruce Lee dropping his umbrella as he ran into the crowd. His face was grief-stricken as he screamed '師傅! (Teacher!) 師傅! (Teacher!).' He tried to throw himself into the grave but was stopped by two big men. He tried again, swinging his arms up in the air like a madman. Although the two strong men tried to restrain him, they couldn't, and Bruce Lee crouched on top of the grave shouting, 'Teacher! Teacher!' He was frantically removing the earth from the coffin lid with his bare hands.

'師傅而家咩嘢都聽唔到 (The teacher can't hear you now),' the eldest apprentice said.

Bruce Lee was frenzied, banging on the coffin harder and harder. The rain howled relentlessly.

The nuns were totally absorbed, frozen and covering their mouths in terror. Quartz was crying quietly. Her tears drew two long lines down her face.

On the screen, some other bystanders rushed forward to stop Bruce Lee, but they were all forced back by his fists of fury. In desperation, the eldest apprentice bashed Bruce Lee's head with a spade. The second he was knocked unconscious, there was a clap of thunder. The nuns screamed. Boss was transfixed.

The funeral scene came to an end. The theme song launched, and with an abrupt flash, the TV screen went black.

'做乜撚嘢 (What the fuck)?' Boss shouted.

'I think the electricity has gone,' Quartz said. 'It happens quite often.'

In the dark, I sensed the nuns brush past me as they

rushed out of the Main Temple. I groped to find my way out, but my hands accidentally touched a nun's face. She screamed and I fell over.

Crawling on the floor and unable to find my bearings, I was startled to hear a rustling. I thought it was a nun's robes brushing my feet, but it had nothing to do with the nuns. I kicked the empty air. Something was nosing around my neck and ear. When I tried to grab it, it became air again. I told myself it was a rat and I wasn't scared of rats, but the way it moved around me in the dark suggested that whatever it was, it wasn't scared of me either. I shouted out to Quartz and Boss for help, but there was no answer. Then, as I looked up at the ceiling, I saw it emerging from the dark: the same dripping figure I'd seen in Wat Arun during my withdrawal. It was now standing right above my head, looking down, like a man hanging from one of the ceiling beams. My panic attack started as if the figure had wrapped a plastic bag around my head.

Someone tapped on my shoulder and tried to comfort me. I panted as they stroked my back in a calming rhythm. Gradually, my breathing slowed down. When I dared to open my eyes, the TV screen showed a black-and-white random dance of dots. The Main Temple was filled with electronic white noise.

'Turn it off!' I screamed, covering my ears.

'What do you mean?' Quartz asked.

'The white noise. It's so loud it's hurting my ears.'

'I can't hear anything. The power cut has broken the TV,' Boss chipped in, massaging my shoulders.

The howling in my ears faded away. Their worried faces were covered with the dots. My head was spinning.

Boss teased me. '男人老狗你怕黑 (How can an old dog be scared of the dark)? I heard you screaming all kinds of nonsense.'

Quartz tried to help me sit upright without touching me. Boss propped me up and said, 'It looks as if he could do with some water.'

Once Quartz had gone to get some, Boss whispered in my ear, 'You were shit-scared, Buddha. Do you often have panic attacks? What did you actually see?'

'Nothing.'

'You're lying. You must have seen something, otherwise you wouldn't have been crying like a baby. Tell me. Did you see the ghosts of the three people who died in the landslide?'

She looked scared and kept talking to herself. 'I'm the one who was responsible. Why did they appear to you? I heard that you cut their hair. That was an act of kindness. Then why did they come and haunt you? That doesn't make sense. They must be coming for me. Do you think it was a warning? Did you take anything from them when you cut their hair? Maybe you still have some of their hair on your clothes? Maybe they came back to take their hair.'

Her train of thought was so fast that I couldn't catch up.

'Boss, stop! I told you I didn't see anything. I tripped up in the dark and must have passed out for a moment or two. That was it.'

'You're lying, and this can't be the first time you've had a panic attack. I've seen lots of people have them. They don't go away unless you do something about it.'

When Quartz returned with a glass of water, Boss sat in front of the TV without saying anything else. The screen wavered unpredictably. The longer I looked at it, the more my mind strove for some kind of pattern in all the randomness. The tiny screen filled the entire Main Temple, projecting a veil of white and black dots on the walls and ceiling, on the back of the golden Buddha.

The three of us sat on the floor, glued to the screen.

'It looks like it's snowing inside.' Boss said, reaching out as if to catch the flakes.

I returned to my shed with the damaged videotape. Boss had tried to pull it out as gently as she could, but it was tangled up inside the machine and we had no choice but to yank it out by force.

It must have been three in the morning when I woke up with a snowstorm in my head. I lay in bed with the videotape on my chest, replaying the opening scenes. I had to admit Bruce Lee really was handsome – great body, full of charisma. Had Audrey Hepburn really dated him?

I couldn't sleep and wandered back to the veranda

outside the Main Temple. Diamond Hill was asleep. There were only seven street lamps left in the shanty town now and one dim fluorescent light was visible in a tin shack. Perhaps an old man was making a night snack for himself, probably instant noodles. My stomach rumbled. I could hear the hens moving around in the coop. It was a windless summer night with no moon.

In the distance, somewhere between the jagged outline of the construction site and the edge of the demolished area of the shanty town, I spotted a posh car. It pulled aside and parked in the middle of nowhere, its headlights blazing. It was dark inside the limo, but I could just make out three people sitting in the back and a uniformed chauffeur in the driving seat. Someone rolled down a window. Then, the flash of a lighter. A tall man stepped out. He looked too big to be Chinese. A small figure also emerged, then a third. In the headlights, I saw the Iron Nun in her elaborate robes. The third figure, a shorter man, waved his hands up and down to explain something, but the Iron Nun seemed uninterested. The tall man finished his cigar and tossed it to the ground. Sparks bounced on the street, then went out. He turned towards the car and the chauffeur switched off the headlights.

I waited for a few minutes, expecting the limo to pull away.

I heard a creaking sound and the gate of the nunnery swung open. I rushed to find somewhere to hide in the shrubs below the veranda. From where I crouched, I could see the Iron Nun making her way up the steps of the Main Temple. She was on her own. I was tempted to follow but didn't dare.

Just when I was about to get out of the shrubs and return to my shed, I caught sight of a torchlight on the uphill path heading towards the nunnery. The powerful white light illuminated a large circular area, revealing the dark green leaves overhanging the path, odd insects, the rusted metal gate, the concrete steps, the veranda, and finally the man himself, holding his torch in front of the Main Temple. I realised I'd seen this Chinese man in the nunnery.

I held my breath, frightened of being discovered among the shrubs. He looked preoccupied. He might have come to pray.

He switched the torch off, put it down on the veranda, and took off his shoes, before carefully opening the sliding door. The creaking sound of the floor became fainter once he'd stepped inside. Coins rattled into the offering box.

He must have stayed in the Main Temple for quite a while. I looked up at the sky, which was divided into two. One half was brown and yellowy, polluted by the lights from the airport. The other half was pitch dark, sheltered by the dense woods in the foothills and the cliff face of Lion Rock.

The man finally came out of the Main Temple, put on his shoes, and picked up his torch. I decided to follow him. To make sure I was unnoticed, I waited until there was a good minute's distance between us. Though he'd just walked up it, he struggled to find the right path back to the limo and took a wrong turn. I tried hard to stay calm, carefully keeping my distance. There were moments he stopped in his tracks because of the strange insects or animals lurking in the trees, or when his arm got caught by a branch, or his legs tangled up in ivy in the undergrowth.

When he finally reached the outskirts of the shanty town, he took an odd turn east, on a new path towards the construction site I hadn't taken before. It started as a dirt track, but round the corner it abruptly turned into an evenly laid concrete road, well lit with new street lamps. With nowhere to hide, I let him walk ahead towards a dead end. We were sandwiched between two sets of tall metal fences like border security. The land beyond the fences had been systematically cleared, leaving no trace of the slums of Diamond Hill. There weren't even any weeds.

A blackbird flew at one of the street lamps. In fact, it was a bat, circling frantically around the light. The man tried to ignore it, but the agitated bat flew down and shaved the ground, swishing up and down the path as if taunting him. As he backtracked, the bat charged him head-on. He ducked down, hoping it would fly away. After a moment it soared upwards. He seized the opportunity to hide under some trees. Like a black dart, it attacked the man's face. He screamed, missed his step, and tripped, before landing on his head.

He was badly hurt. One of his ears was bleeding. I approached him, tore up my T-shirt and pressed it firmly on the wound.

Under the yellow sodium light, the blood on the path turned into a dark brown pool, where a few flies had begun to feast.

I asked him if he was OK, but he didn't respond. After about two or three minutes, he moved – first his head, then his arms and legs, and finally his whole body came back to life in a contorted way like a puppet that had got all its strings tangled up. He coughed up some phlegm and retched. When he opened his eyes, he screamed. I had never heard anyone scream like that before – raw and guttural – the voice of a terrified man. His eyes swirled around giddily. I held him until his breathing slowed down and his vision steadied. He needed water, but there wasn't any around.

'You must have landed on this side of your head. You'll be all right. Five minutes ago, you were bleeding badly but it's looking a lot better now.'

I helped him move aside to sit against the metal fence, and noticed his immaculately ironed white shirt, expensive linen suit, and matching light grey tie as silky as fresh sardines. The shirt was soiled with blood, the top two buttons ripped off, the elbow torn. His posh leather shoes were muddy and scratched.

'Bloody hell, I deserve this,' he said in English. 'That

fucking bat was onto me like a vampire. Were you following me?'

I hesitated. 'Yes, I was.'

'Good job you did. Otherwise I'd still be lying here. You work for the Iron Nun?'

'No. Should I take you to the hospital?'

'I don't suppose it's life-threatening. I've a friend who is a top surgeon at St Teresa's Hospital. I'm sure he'll sort me out.'

He tried to feel his wound without touching it. 'Ironically I'll end up getting one of those cauliflower ears rugby players get. I hated rugby in school.'

He paused.

'Why aren't you speaking in Cantonese?' I asked.

'It isn't my mother tongue. My parents were anglophiles and they always wanted me to become British, whatever that means. You've surprisingly good English for someone like you. I'm sorry. That sounded terrible.'

'It's fine. I'm not from Diamond Hill.'

He had all the features of a refined Chinese businessman in his forties who'd got a bit pudgy: shiny hair with a fine parting, bushy eyebrows, a high nose and well-proportioned mouth. The only imperfection was his rather small, mean-looking eyes. I had no idea what cauliflower ears looked like.

'Do you know you have quite a posh English accent?' he asked.

'I went to St Paul's.'

'The one on Bonham Road?'

I nodded.

'It's delightful to meet a St Paul's alumnus here. I went there too, so do my two daughters. We always say it's the Eton of Hong Kong.'

I forced myself to smile. I found it hard to imagine he was a family man.

'What on earth are you doing in Diamond Hill? You do know this place will be completely flattened in a few months' time, don't you? Are you working for a charity?'

'Yes, I am working for a homeless charity to help displaced residents. It's my night shift.' It seemed better to lie.

He gave me a pat on the back. 'Noble work you're doing. It's always a bit of a shock to come across the poor in Hong Kong. Have you seen people living in those "coffin houses"? Aren't they called 棺材屋? They are literally the size of a coffin, worse than being in a cage. We're in the wealthiest capital in Asia. Every time I visit Diamond Hill I see more of these poor people coming out of the woodwork. It's shameful, isn't it?'

'Are you one of the developers?'

He beamed. 'I wish. Diamond Hill is a piece of prime real estate because of its proximity to the city centre and of course the faded glamour of the Hollywood of the Orient. The sale is going to break world records. I'm just a lawyer, a middleman.'

'Oh, a fellow from the infamous profession.'

'Ha, I take it as a compliment.'

'That was my intention.'

'I can't complain really. It's not a bad trade, especially after the signing of the Joint Declaration. Land sale has grown exponentially and become extraordinarily complex, often involving negotiations between the three governments. Analysts forecast that the frenzy will carry on for at least five years. It's a brilliant time to be a property lawyer.'

'Three governments?'

'Never forget the People's Republic of China. The waking dragon on our doorstep.'

'I thought you meant the Triad.'

He didn't hesitate. 'The Triad is just another international corporation. It's hard to know if the Triad is the host or the parasite in strange times like ours. Isn't it a Cantonese saying that 有錢使得鬼推磨 (the wealthy can get the dead to do their dirty work)?'

'I suppose the Triad can be classified among the wealthy. They recruit the most vulnerable and treat them like dirt.'

'You are spot on. I'm actually feeling a lot better. By the way, how did you get into the charity sector?'

'Oh it's a long story.'

'Fair enough. I should get on.' He looked at my arms and hands. Could he tell my fingers were stained yellow from addiction?

'What brought *you* up here to the nunnery in the middle of the night?' I asked, playing dumb.

'I was praying for my family. What else does one do in a nunnery?'

I was about to open my mouth, when he interrupted, 'I have to maintain client confidentiality. It's a messy situation, as you might have seen.'

'You mean the landslide and fatality? Or the drug gang?'

'Have you heard that curiosity killed the cat?'

I nodded.

'Well, I'll say no more. I don't normally feel indebted to anyone, but I do owe you for helping me.' He rummaged for something in his pocket. It dawned on me that he wanted to give me some money.

'No, no. Please, I don't want anything.'

The man laughed. 'Don't fool yourself, my friend. We all want something.'

There was nothing on the empty piece of land in front of me. Nothing except concrete, concrete, and more concrete. Through the metal fence, I strained to see a flash of red from the traffic lights on the main road. For a moment, I thought I could see the dripping figure. But there was not a soul to be seen, only an ear of barley that had seeded itself in the cement.

The man struggled to his feet. I put his arm around my shoulder and slowly set off. The path led us to a thin stretch of land overgrown with thick shrubs and tall trees.

'This is a hellhole.' He took out his torch and I was shocked to see that the ground was covered with used needles and condoms. 'If it wasn't for the crazy rain last month, this wasteland would have been cleared by now and we would be walking on a decent path.'

Further into the woods, I could hear a faint rustling as if there were invisible people nearby. I listened again.

'Don't worry. It's just a couple of pansies killing each other.'

I didn't know what he meant. After a minute or so, I could see the headlights of the limo through the dark screen of foliage.

'You can leave me here. That's fine. Thank you.' But as soon as I took his arm off my shoulder, he lost his balance.

'OK. I obviously do need some help. But whatever happens, don't say a word.'

We stepped out of the woods. It was a vintage Bentley. The last time I'd seen a Bentley was during the King of Thailand's visit to Wat Arun. I had looked through the keyhole as the King stepped out of his immaculate car like a deity.

The Bentley was parked about two hundred yards away from the construction site. Massive cranes towered up like ladders to the heavens. The site was clean and tidy, except for the many foul words sprayed on the wooden boards protesting against the demolition.

The engine fired up the moment we appeared.

The driver's door opened and a young blond chauffeur came towards us.

'What took you so long?' he asked in an English accent.

'I was attacked by a bloody bat and fell over. This chap helped me.'

'Who is he?'

'An alumnus from St Paul's. He is working for a charity.'

'Are you still bleeding?'

'I don't think so.'

'He doesn't want blood in the car.'

'Of course.'

'What are you waiting for? Get on with it. Chop-chop.'

He quickly returned to the car and sat in the driving seat, resting his pristinely white gloves on the steering wheel. A foreigner in the back stayed motionless.

'The chauffeur is quite bossy. Who's the foreigner in the car? I have never seen a Bentley as shiny as this one.'

The lawyer loosened his arm from my shoulder. He looked more anxious than ever – the frown on his forehead deepened, his eyes blinked, and he was tongue-tied.

He hobbled to the car, opened the front door, and struggled in. The engine revved aggressively. It pulled away before he'd managed to close the door, heading straight at me like an angry bull. I closed my eyes helplessly, raised my arms over my head, and waited for the impact.

But nothing happened. There was a sharp braking noise and the Bentley ground to a halt a few inches away. The front wheels screeched on the coarse cement as it changed direction. Then it floated past serenely.

The back window of the car rolled down just enough for a hand to drop something out. The two red tail-lights zoomed out of focus and disappeared round a sharp bend.

When the dust settled, I found a crisp banknote at my feet. It was a ten-pound Bank of England note, not unlike the paper money from the Bank of Hades, except this was real sterling. On the front, the young Queen smiled calmly, her jewelled crown sitting firmly on her soft, wavy hair.

I held the banknote up to the streetlight, looking for any signs or marks. There was no coded message.

I walked back through the woods. Leaves and branches brushed against my skin. The sky had turned paler and bluer. A thin trail of mist hovered over the ground. Through the bushes I could see two naked men touching each other. The hairy-chested older man was overweight and had a complicated dragon tattoo on his right arm. The smooth, skinny boy had no pubic hair. He was barely a teenager. I didn't move an inch and stared back at their naked bodies. After a while, the tattooed man put his hand on the boy's shoulder, they picked up their clothes and walked away.

The sun had not risen yet but the shanty town had woken up. I could hear the sound of water trickling in the open sewers and smell the morning congee and fresh-baked bread.

Boss stood at the far end of the concrete path. No longer in Buddhist robes, she'd changed back into her jeans and T-shirt, and the familiar heavy gold chains around her neck and wrists. She wore a red, oversized American baseball cap, though it was obvious that her head was still as bald as a newborn's.

'Good morning, Buddha!' She dashed towards me with arms outspread, wiggling her hips breakdance-style.

She kissed me on both cheeks and did the breakdance again with her eyes closed. Her gold chain and gold hoop earrings jangled in the morning sun. She looked like a character from a Hollywood B-movie.

Leaning against the fence, she half-hummed, half-sang a tune with some rude English words in it and handed me a cigarette. I waved to say no and she put it in her mouth and lit it, inhaling deeply, holding the smoke in her chest, before puffing into my face.

She bent down and plucked the ear of barley without thinking.

'野草燒不盡 春風吹又生 (No fire can clear the wild grasses. A soft breeze blows and soon it rises).' Boss recited some lines from a popular classical Chinese poem and raised her eyebrows. 'I can play the scholar too.'

'It's an ear of barley, not grass.' I spoke in English.

'Whatever.' She tossed the barley on the concrete and started whistling.

She must have followed me from the nunnery, and I felt strangely betrayed.

'Is barley the same as Bally, the Swiss fashion brand?'

I ignored her silly question. 'Why did you follow me?'

'Why did you follow the lawyer?'

My face reddened. 'I asked you first.'

'I didn't know we were playing a game of who asked who first.' She rolled her eyes, tossed the cigarette away, and put some bubblegum in her mouth. She blew a big pink bubble until it covered half her face. When she tried to make it bigger, it popped and stuck to her and she laughed at herself. I wasn't in the mood to laugh along.

'你個樣成嚹豬仔包 (Your face looks as angry as a hot pork bao).'

She peeled the gum off her face and stuck it on the fence. 'I followed you because I wanted to make sure you didn't kill him. He went to St Paul's, your old school, and has two lovely daughters. He is a top-notch lawyer who looks great in a pinstripe suit. You must be jealous of his success. We don't want another family tragedy. You've no idea how hard it is to be an orphan.'

She pretended to look sad. 'OK! OK! I'll tell you the truth. He and I are on the same wavelength when it comes to love of money. He came with some great news for me. They said I'd done a *sterling job* and agreed to double my manpower and my share of future profits! I'd been so scared they'd cut me loose, but it turns out I've hit the jackpot. They'll also sort out my transfer to London. I'm over the moon.'

'Isn't he a property lawyer?'

'Don't be fooled by his looks. Haven't you heard the

English saying that *you can't judge the cover by the book*? What're you laughing at?'

'You mean *you can't judge a book by its cover*?'

She shrugged and popped some more chewing gum into her mouth.

'Did they say anything about the three dead people?' I asked.

'You mean the unintended consequences? The families will get a massive payout and have been promised a nice apartment in one of the new high-rises, once they're built. They won't need to work for the rest of their lives. They are *overjoyed*.' She said 'overjoyed' in English with a proper accent, as if she had stolen the word from the Chinese man.

'I don't think you can say they're *overjoyed* after what happened.'

'Don't disrespect the power of money, Buddha.' Boss shook her head.

I was getting tired of her games and set off towards the shanty town. She ran after me and grabbed my arm. 'Have you ever thought of being a father?'

I held her arm loosely, not quite committed to it.

'What did you see out there, Buddha? Did you see the British man? Did you see his amazing car?' She fired these questions at me, as if to divert our attention from the idea of me being a father. 'Please, Buddha. What did he look like? Nobody has ever seen the Top Dog. People say he looks like Roger Moore in *Live and Let Die*. Even the Triad respects him because he's so loaded.'

'He has a vintage Bentley,' I said.

'What's a vintage Bentley?'

I turned uphill to the nunnery. Boss halted and let go of my arm.

'Where're you going?' I asked her.

'I'm going home. Where else would I go? It's September and business as usual.'

She blew me a kiss. 'So long, Buddha. It's been nice knowing you.'

The first plane of the day flew over and the drilling had started at the construction site. It was hard to tell which was louder. A dog woke and started nosing around. A train of schoolchildren in blue and green uniforms ran past Boss, who pulled a funny face and made all the kids laugh. Some villagers waved and said hello to Boss as she walked past, others turned away and avoided her gaze. She paused at the crossroad and turned back to look at me. Through the steam from the congee shop, I caught her smile. I wanted to wave but she had already disappeared into an alley. A gust of wind hit me with a cloud of yellow dust from the construction site. The dog barked furiously at the sky and the people in the street went on with their lives.

白

White Dew

露

The day Quartz found out Boss had left the nunnery and returned to her drug gang, the weather turned autumnal. She was wide awake and sitting barefoot on the veranda of the Main Temple. She had surrounded herself with white porcelain saucers. It was a beautiful morning. A thin line of blue mist, part vapour and part incense, clung to the sky-high cranes in the construction site, which was expanding fast. Trucks and bulldozers arrived early each morning carrying a constant stream of steel and sand, while the concrete mixer churned ceaselessly, sometimes past midnight. The shanty town shrank in all directions. The noise was worst when the drill hit bedrock. It sounded as if they were using explosives to blast it open. When that happened, the whole area shook and even the noise of the planes was drowned out.

I hugged myself to get warm. Her eyes were closed and she sat in the lotus position, as stationary as a pole of white birch.

I joined her and felt time widen between us. Occasionally a bird – a crow or an owl – called out in protest. I mixed my breath with the misty morning air, until I could hear nothing but the ringing in my ears.

This was a familiar sequence of events: whenever I wanted to leave Wat Arun, I suffered a bad attack of tinnitus, and in a few seconds I could no longer breathe. Daishi had told me that if I persevered, one day I'd be able to send the tinnitus back to where it came from, deep in my imagination, and I would be able to breathe like any normal person without the fear of an invisible hand grabbing my throat. I asked Daishi what would happen if I got rid of my panic attacks. He told me the world would be a better place because there would then be one less bugbear.

I often thought what Daishi said was a load of pious bullshit. Would he have thought that the shanty town was just a blip in the course of history, and we should embrace mutability?

Trying to meditate with Quartz on the veranda, I kept wondering how long it would take for a panic attack to kick in, now that the tinnitus was rioting in my ears.

Daishi had known from the start I had no feeling for Buddhism. I'd always thought it was an ostentatious religion, full of gilded statues, sitting and chanting. All the different schools of Buddhism sounded the same to me. At Wat Arun, when I was ordered to clean the floor or polish the bronze offering bowl, I let Daishi know how sceptical I was. He told me that self-scepticism was the road to enlightenment. Sitting there with Quartz outside the Main Temple while Diamond Hill was being torn down, I rediscovered my distrust. I hated to think the sacred refuge offered by the nunnery had something to do with the gilded Buddha smiling in the lotus position behind closed doors, as if sitting and smiling were the answer to the world's problems.

With no warning, the sun appeared from the hills and an army of tree shadows emerged from the mist across the dirt tracks left by the trucks. The sun swallowed up the cobwebs on the wooden banisters, the sodium street lamps in the shanty town, the mutilated frames of demolished houses, and the towering yellow cranes among the piles of concrete blocks. A veil of dew masked everything.

Quartz picked up the white porcelain saucers one by one and tipped the dew from them into her mouth. Touched by the trickle of condensation, her lips turned redder. Was this another Buddhist purification ritual?

She did it again the following day – twenty-three saucers of white dew and nothing else – and the following days. In the time ahead, I lost count of the days of the week and the weeks of the month. The nuns didn't intervene, as they'd retreated into some form of self-punishment after Boss's departure. Each day, they obsessively brushed the courtyard to get rid of fallen leaves and served thinner and thinner congee in the morning. Finally, I was served a bowl of hot rice water with no grains. Confined to the temple halls, day and night the nuns subjected themselves to hours of endless chanting. When exhausted they would start frantically cleaning and gardening, before returning to their chanting all night long.

Quartz lost weight rapidly, looking progressively more skeletal. One afternoon, when the Iron Nun was praying alone in the Main Temple, I asked her through the screen door what we could do about it. She replied only, '重蹈覆轍 (Let mistakes be repeated).'

I watched Quartz getting thinner and thinner day by day, starving herself to death. The first thing to disappear was the colour in her cheeks, hollowed out as in a total eclipse. Later, her collarbones came to form two triangular reservoirs full of nothing but air. Her pupils floated on two dark pools, her knuckles swelled up like boiled chicken claws. Her flesh contracted around her bones. She wore her robes as tightly as she could, as if trying to become invisible.

Despite her rapid metamorphosis, Quartz continued to play her part with the other nuns: tending pumpkins, cleaning the floors of the Main Temple, dusting the Buddha and Goddess of Mercy, hanging the endless laundry, without missing a single prayer or chanting session. In the courtyard I overheard some nuns say Quartz was purifying herself of any traces of Boss and the pleasures they'd found in each other's company. In fact, I could see no traces of Boss in the nunnery, except the gas stove in the kitchen and the spare canister gathering dust and cobwebs behind the wall.

In the more and more insular, tongue-tied nunnery, I spent my time watching Quartz becoming her own tyrant, consuming her bodily reserves and chafing her brain. I supposed what she was doing to her body was similar to what I'd done to mine in Bangkok. While I'd entwined my life with heroin, she was investing hers in weightlessness. She wanted to depart the world as nothing but a chrysalis. She looked pretty much like a chrysalis now, and I wasn't convinced anything substantial could emerge after any metamorphosis.

In the hours when Quartz was out of my sight (which were many), I watched the wind doing its violent work. One morning it snapped branches on a fruit-laden plum tree, one afternoon it drilled through the rain-stained paper windows of my shed, and one night it shaved off parts of my thatched roof, slipped through the cracks, and toyed with my earholes, mouth and nostrils. I was aware the wind came from China, the unstoppable East Asian winter monsoon that marches across the vast continent from the north, passing through Mongolia, 華山 (Huashan) in Xi An, 武當 山 (Wudang Shan) in Hubei and 武功山 (Wugong Shan) in Jiangxi, finally arriving at the southern coast of Guangdong. The Siberian wind had to travel across so many mountains, only to be destroyed by the equatorial heat.

In those stifling September nights in Bangkok, I'd longed for these dry cooling winds from Mongolia. Night after night I would sit on the wet cardboard in my underpants, picking up cigarette butts and scraps of food tossed away by pedestrians.

I heard a faint ringing in my ears and felt my chest tighten whenever I thought about Bangkok. But when the autumn wind rose in Diamond Hill, memories of Bangkok rose too. I could only stop the flashbacks by watching Quartz grow thinner, but whenever the wind dropped, I found myself back in the steaming heart of Bangkok.

One unbearably sticky night in the Thai capital everyone was waiting for the coming storm. I had pickpocketed a woman's leather purse and thought I'd won the lottery for the night, but it had nothing valuable in it – a cheap lipstick, a tampon, photographs of her two young daughters, and a handwritten blessing from some monk in a local temple. I chucked all her stuff into the river and handed the purse to a drug dealer, who said the leather was fake, and the bag was worthless. I hit him in the face and took everything he had on him. Rushing back to the riverbank, I went to sit behind the big willow tree where I'd hidden my emergency stash of syringes. Unfortunately, some other addicts must have found them and almost cleared me out. I found one after a panic rush, rinsed it in the river, and shot the stuff I'd stolen from the dealer into my left arm. I was unable to find any fresh arteries, so I switched to my right arm, which I saved for emergency shots. I was instantly high and felt good for a few hours.

My left arm was now completely healed. I moved the gas lamp over it and saw the faded scars of so many needles. The teeth marks of vampire bats. I opened one of the few grammar books left on my desk and found a long table of unusual irregular verbs, similar to those I recited as a child:

Abide, Abode, Abode
Arise, Arose, Arisen
Behold, Beheld, Beheld
Dwell, Dwelt, Dwelt
Fall, Fell, Fallen
Forbid, Forbade, Forbidden
Forsake, Forsook, Forsaken

I continued to '*Withstood*', the last word on the list, and repeated the whole table again, as if chanting a sutra. Past participles don't exist in Chinese, and my tongue often tripped over the last hurdles, just like in primary school. The book called this problematic tense 'the past perfect'. I'd always struggled with the concept of the past being 'perfect', but now I could see the past was the God of Chance disguised as a clock face.

I thought of all the displaced people in Diamond Hill, and how useless I was not helping to save them. My hand reached out for one of the old newspapers hidden under the mattress. I wanted to look again at the photograph of Margaret Thatcher fallen on the steps of the Great Hall of the People in Beijing. The image somehow both saddened and reassured me at the same time. The journalist claimed this was an ominous sign for the future of Hong Kong. The next page had a cartoon of her falling over, accompanied by a rhymed couplet in classical form: 睡醒飛駕中國龍 臥伏膽怯英國獅 (The Chinese dragon is rising from his sleep; the

British lion is crouching and too scared to creep). A few pages on, there was a big slogan printed on the top of the page: 香港死亡 (THE DEATH OF HONG KONG).

I chanted the irregular verbs with my eyes open. My breath formed white steam in the cold air, the wind from China. It was as if the wind, not me, had been reciting the past perfect tenses and pulling them apart blow by blow.

'Please can you stop?' I heard Quartz whispering outside. I moved to open the door, but she said, 'No. I won't come in.'

Her index finger pierced a hole in the paper window of my shed. The bony finger stayed there like an orphan in a puppet show. Her fingernail had been clipped too short, exposing the pinkish nail bed. I touched the tip but she didn't react. I reached down to the first knuckle, but all I found was a thin layer of skin on the bone. I gently squeezed her finger and grabbed it, caressing it to warm it. I held on to it for a while, not knowing what else I could do. Should I lick it?

Its stillness made me think of my own death.

Or the many deaths I had come across in the streets of Bangkok.

I stretched my tongue out. As I stared at the tip of my tongue and the tip of Quartz's finger, I stopped. I blew at her finger. It quickly retreated, leaving an empty hole. I fixed my eyes on it. Gradually, Quartz's profile came into view – her robes, hands, hollowed cheeks, lifeless eyes, all blanched white in the moonlight.

'Please can you stop reciting those words?'

'Why?'

'I can't sleep.'

I wanted to ask if she was hungry but didn't.

'Why can't you sleep?'

'I am bothered by those English words.'

The wind whistled through the hole and lashed my eye. I blinked.

'Why? Is it because of Boss?'

There was a long pause.

'Boss said there is no such a thing as the past perfect and I don't need to learn it. It's useless.'

I sat back in my chair and Quartz slipped from view. 'Well, Boss is wrong. You wouldn't be able to have a proper conversation in English without the past perfect tense.'

She remained very quiet and I wondered if she had left the courtyard.

'Quartz, are you angry?'

'Why didn't you make her stay?'

'You know I have no control over Boss's coming and going. She is a wild wind.'

'She is young and nothing is set in stone. She needs someone to guide her towards the right path and forget the scars of her early life.'

'She trusts and respects you. There is a real bond between you and—'

'My past is anything but perfect,' Quartz interrupted.

She came closer to the hole in the paper window.

'I have no memory of my childhood. People think memories are stories we conjure up to survive the trauma of being alive. Actually, memories are the food that feeds the mouths of trauma. Imagine if Diamond Hill was to have no memory of its demolition and Hong Kong no memory of British rule. In that case, nobody would suffer from a sense of disillusion.'

'What was your first memory?'

'I remember arriving in the nunnery on my own. It was 1975, at the beginning of autumn when the maples started changing colour. The other nuns say I was a teenage girl, but they didn't know my age.'

She paused.

'I refused to speak and eat when I first arrived. The nuns say it was as if my mouth had been stitched up with invisible threads. For days, I only drank water through a straw. The nuns tried to force-feed me, but I refused to open my mouth. In the end, as punishment, the Iron Nun ordered me to meditate on the veranda in front of the Main Temple at daybreak and surrounded me with twenty-three white porcelain saucers. She forced me to drink 白露 (the white dew), which she said would purify my heart from the infection of my past. I drank the white dew for over a month, forty-nine days to be exact. At first I was overwhelmed by hunger. I never knew emptiness could lie so heavily in my stomach. I hated how the saucer touched my lips and the dew slipped down my throat. I felt violated and abused. Gradually my mind grew clean. I thought I was addicted to the ritual, and some of the younger nuns said my starvation was just a show. Later, I realised I was addicted to autumn and the white dew. If it wasn't for my mouth, the dew would have been stolen by the sun.'

'What made you change your mind on the fiftieth day?'

'My desire to live was stronger than my desire to die.'

Through the hole I could see Quartz's small pursed mouth. The tiny hairs on her upper lip shimmered with phosphorescence.

'Everyone in the nunnery said my starving myself was an act of defiance. Afterwards I had no more defiance. I came to this nunnery with nothing – no father, no mother, no siblings – and I will leave this nunnery and the world with nothing. That's the best I can do to repay my debt.'

'Your debt? You spoke devoutly about nothing this and nothing that. Why are you so bothered by the past being broken if it doesn't matter to you?'

I heard her moving away from the window and sitting down by the oak door. When I tried to open the door, I found that she'd bolted it from the outside.

There was a sudden lull in noise from the construction site. A cock crowed in the hills, or down in the shanty town. A dog barked three times. The cock crowed again. Was it our conversation or the sun that had woken the birds in the hills? First there was a single high-pitched call, and then the starlings and blackbirds started up. Within a minute a chorus of birds was announcing another daybreak. I moved to the floor of my shed, and pressed my ear to the oak door that I'd assembled two seasons earlier. Quartz was quiet as a mouse, though I could sense her emaciated body, her tiny doll-like mouth.

Just before the sun rose, there was a hushed suspense like the moment before the curtains open and a play begins. A razor-sharp beam of sunlight came through the hole in my window, marking a full stop on the wall.

'Would you like to go to the caves with me to feed the bats?' Quartz asked.

'I would, but you haven't eaten anything for weeks. You don't have the energy to trek through the woods.'

She unbolted my door. When I opened it, she was gone, leaving her rucksack by my shed. Inside I found five boxes of eggs, dried rice cakes, and a woollen jumper.

Quartz and I left the nunnery before anyone was awake. She wrapped a thick shawl over her robes and put a big bottle of water in my rucksack. We set off when the sun was half-risen on the horizon. Instead of walking downhill towards the shanty town, she led me on a dirt path along a stream. An autumn lethargy had spread across the entire hillside. There was nobody else on the narrow footpath. Trees – I hadn't a clue what their names were – grew thinner as we climbed upwards. Quartz took an unexpected turn leftwards, leaving the stream behind and descending into a thick wood. After about ten minutes of nondescript woodland, we sat on a rock and took a sip of water. She handed me a piece of dry rice cake, and munched away while stroking a dense patch of moss with her hand.

I had never felt so remote and far away from civilisation. Now, sitting in the middle of nowhere, I could hear things I hadn't heard for a long time – particular calls of unidentifiable birds I remembered from long ago, a hubbub of excited insects, and leaves shuffling in the wind. She said she could hear the stream, but I couldn't. We must have left Kai Tak's flight path, as the noise of landing planes had disappeared.

Quartz looked ill, but still disturbingly attractive. Her hand combed the moss on the rock, and I drew closer until the hairs on our arms brushed against each other. She lowered her chin but the second my fingers touched her hand, she recoiled and turned away.

Quartz started walking again. She didn't say much. We had been walking for at least half an hour bearing west, with Diamond Hill and Hong Kong Island behind us. Gradually the woods opened into a clearing and we climbed a well-worn track. And now I smelt the stream.

Unlike the murky river downstream, the water up here was crystal clear. Quartz took a handful and drank while I washed my face.

We walked on, and after ten minutes or so we reached a steep hill. Quartz nimbly got herself up the slope. My hands and feet looked for stable footing stone by stone.

The higher I climbed, the louder the river became. The final push brought me to a small waterfall. I couldn't quite believe how rapid the water was, gushing through tight rocks and falling forcefully into a small pool.

I saw shadows darting in and out. At first they looked like birds, but they converged and turned into a human shape emerging from under the waterfall. I shivered and there were goosebumps all over my arms. Had the apparition been following me? A dog appeared from the water and sat at Quartz's feet. They seemed to know each other. Then a man waded through the waterfall and stood stark naked in the pool. As he walked towards us, I recognised the poor beggar from Diamond Hill. Unburdened by his belongings and filthy clothes, he looked refreshed, like a water deity taking human form. I was shocked by his nakedness and raised my arms to protect Quartz.

'It's all right, I know him and the dog. They'll do us no harm.' She squatted down to the dog's level and started petting her on the base of her neck and under her chin.

The man examined us from head to toe, before turning away and heading back through the waterfall. He whistled, and the dog followed.

'Don't be fooled. Sometimes 地藏菩薩 (Dìzàng Buddha, one of the four principal bodhisattvas) disguises himself as a beggar. I've seen this man ever since I arrived in Diamond Hill. Years have gone by, but neither he nor his dog have aged. I can't even see a strand of white in his hair or a wrinkle on his brow. Other nuns have seen him too. We don't think he's human. He's the protector of Diamond Hill.'

I wanted to laugh but she looked deadly serious. Then she closed her palms and her eyes and bowed to the waterfall.

Quartz led me uphill along the unmarked stony path. If the beggar was really sacred how could he be wandering in the shanty town like a madman? If he was the protector of Diamond Hill, how come everything had been demolished?

The narrow path broadened, and after a few paces it opened to another clearing with a gigantic rock face on the left and dense trees on the right. Quartz pointed at an arrow-shaped crack, which looked impassable. 'Here's the entrance.' Before I could express my disbelief, she had already slipped through the gap and into the rock.

The rocky entrance was very tight. A dry cool breeze blew from the cave. I ducked my head to brace myself for the darkness ahead, groping like a blind man, feeling the rock with my palms. The passageway got narrower and lower, twisting this way and that before opening out. I called Quartz's name but only my echo answered. I'd never been frightened of the dark, but the claustrophobic cave was bone-chilling. It was as if I'd trespassed on the hidden tomb of the First Emperor, without knowing if I was surrounded by rivers of poisonous mercury. I couldn't breathe and my heart pounded in my chest like an angry mob. I shouted Quartz's name again and again, and my echo mocked me. I ran out of oxygen as my chest got tighter and tighter.

I felt something crawling near my feet. I tried to kick it, but it wasn't there. I felt it again. Something brushed past my leg and neck. Without warning, Quartz blew into my left ear. I screamed, missed a step, and when I was just about to fall, she took me by the arm.

'I hope that will teach you a lesson. Last night you blew on my finger. Now you know how it feels to be blown at,' Quartz said jokingly. 'Can you hand me the eggs?'

I barely had time to catch my breath, but reached into the rucksack and gave her the egg boxes. I was amazed by how much I could 'see' when I forgot my panic about not being able to see.

'Are you ready, Buddha?'

She struck a match and the whole cave came alive, showing hundreds of bats hanging on the ceiling. They vibrated in a soft, orderly rhythm. Some flew in and out of the cave and some circled overhead. The match went out and Quartz struck another.

She blew a loud whistle and the bats whirred down to the eggs. They poked the shells with their jaws and claws. I'd never seen anything like it. When the second match blew out, Quartz said, 'Let's leave them to it.'

I stood there trembling with fear and excitement. She grabbed my arm and took me over to the edge of the cave.

'Don't sit down, Buddha! We're walking on an ocean of bat shit.'

So we leaned against the walls and listened to the

bats enjoying their feast and making animated, high-pitched calls.

'Don't worry. The bats won't bother us, they've known me for years. They treat me like a mother.'

It didn't take long for the bats to finish the eggs. Within minutes, they flew back to the ceiling and the cave returned to its silence.

I rummaged in the rucksack for water. 'Look, I found another egg.'

'You better hide it. I don't want to get the bats excited again. They've had enough,' she said, reaching for the water bottle.

I cracked it gently on the wall to create a small hole. 'I love raw eggs.'

'Does it taste good?' Quartz sounded curious.

'The egg white and yolk are 天作之合 (a marriage made in heaven).'

'Can I taste it?'

'I thought you don't eat meat.'

'Eggs are not meat.'

'They're alive, like a living organism.'

She laughed. 'Just like a cucumber then. I want to be a bat in my next life. If my bats are fond of eggs, I want to try one.'

She took the egg and finished it.

'So, what do you think?'

'A marriage made in heaven.'

I laughed as she handed me the empty eggshell. Despite the chill that filtered through the cave, a faint warmth radiated from the bats overhead.

'Can you feel their warmth too?' Quartz asked. 'Soon they'll be hibernating here, but I still come throughout the winter to check if they're alright. I warm myself up here too. In the days when the winter monsoon brings the north wind, the cave is a lot warmer than any of the rooms in the nunnery.'

'It's strange to have my eyes open but not be able to see anything. It's as if I'm meditating.'

'What do you see when you meditate?'

'What do you mean?'

'We all see things when we meditate.'

I hesitated. 'I can't meditate. I get bad tinnitus whenever I try, and this is followed by panic attacks.'

'You had a panic attack the night we watched *Fist of Fury*. You weren't meditating then.'

'That was different.'

'You were white as a ghost.'

'I saw something I used to see in Wat Arun during my heroin withdrawal. I hadn't seen it for years.'

'What did you see?'

'A person, wet, with fuzzy outlines, as if they're made of fluid. It looks like a person but it's also inhuman. It used to stand in the corner of my room whenever I shivered and ran out of breath.'

'Was it looking at you?'

'Yes, though I couldn't find its eyes. Sometimes its colours change spasmodically, turning from red to blue to brown, green to black to white. It is as if I'm gazing into a luminous void. Often I feel I am suffocating, as if it is swallowing me.'

'It sounds like an octopus to me.' Quartz took a deep breath. 'I see a jellyfish when I meditate. Other nuns see a shrimp, a grouper, a sea urchin, even a sea cucumber. The mind is an ocean.'

My laugh echoed through the cave. 'I'm not sure an octopus could stand in the corner of my room in Wat Arun.'

'The panic attacks, tinnitus, and this strange figure – they are all in your imagination. Why can't an octopus be in your imagination? It's possibly one of the most imaginative creatures on our planet. It has three hearts, and nine brains – one in each leg and one in the head.'

'Well, one heart and one brain are more than enough for me.'

Quartz laughed.

'Daishi said I needed to send the tinnitus back where it came from and the panic attacks would stop.'

'One can't breathe without imagination.' She paused and reached out, touching the bamboo container on my chest. 'I know Daishi meant a lot to you, otherwise you wouldn't be wearing him around your neck. But I don't think Daishi is right. What you need is to become the octopus, not fight it.'

She explained in great detail that it had taken years for her to become that single jellyfish in her mind. When she was younger, there had been innumerable species of jellyfish in her head – transparent crystal ones with short tentacles, petite round ones with fat tentacles, poisonous blue ones with long trailing tentacles. Month after month, she'd learned to recognise the different physiologies of these mysterious sea creatures. Gradually, the number of species had dwindled and there was only one jellyfish left: a gigantic, red coral one with thousands of tentacles as thick as a lion's mane.

She cleared her throat. 'One day I described this jellyfish to the Iron Nun. She said it was my fault, not the jellyfish's. The poor creature was in my head for a reason. Instead of focusing on my own perspective, I should look at my mental world from the perspective of the jellyfish. It was all the inhospitable fluid in my brain that proved so disturbing for the creature.'

'It sounds like bat shit to me,' I said.

'I thought so too, until one day I practised what the Iron Nun had taught me. I abandoned my prejudices and imagined how the jellyfish in my brain would see me. It sounded mad at first, but it did work.'

'So you stopped seeing the jellyfish?'

'No. I started seeing myself through the eyes of the jelly-fish. It was like turning a camera on myself. Except that I'd become the camera. Ninety-nine per cent of the time, most people, including me, are unable to see beyond the surface of things. And even in those one-per-cent moments, we're actually too scared to look at what's there.'

'Are you talking about the poor people in Diamond Hill?'

'No, I'm thinking about everyone in Hong Kong. The nuns have been talking about the Handover happening in ten years' time. I have no idea if China is the jellyfish or not, but even if it is, it isn't inconceivable that we can enter the mind of the jellyfish and learn something about ourselves.'

'People are scared about the future.'

'Are you?'

'Not until recently.'

'It's ironic that it's the rich and the powerful who are fleeing the city to go to America, Canada, Australia, and of course, Britain.'

'A lot of rich and powerful people are planning to stay on to make more money too. That's why the demolition is taking place to make room for more skyscrapers.'

'I am very torn, Buddha. I don't know if the new sky-scrapers are a good or bad thing. Do you want to save the shanty town? The Iron Nun said you are totally deluded.'

'Everything seems to be disappearing and what can I do but watch?'

'At least you are here watching what's actually happen-ing. Better than those who cling on to the past.'

'For those who want to leave Hong Kong, I guess from their perspective, Britain is their future, their jellyfish.'

'How about you? Is Britain your jellyfish?'

'No, but Hong Kong is my octopus.'

Quartz laughed.

'Have you given up hope of remembering your life before the nunnery?'

'Can you swear that you've given up the white powder for life?' she asked. 'What made you leave Hong Kong for Thailand in the first place?'

'What would you do if the nunnery was demolished?'

'Have you ever killed somebody for drugs?'

'Do you want to go to London with Boss?'

Like two interrogators locked in an interview room trying to identify a criminal, Quartz and I directed our questions to the pitch-dark cave without answering any of them. They echoed and pricked my skin.

'Did you know your name means time?' I asked.

Now she answered. 'I don't understand how quartz crystals are used to keep time.'

'Something to do with electricity passing through the crystals . . . I've forgotten what I learned about it in school. Why did the Iron Nun name you Quartz?'

'She wanted me to embody the forward movement of time and forget about the past. My quartz watch is always ticking forwards into the future, never backwards.'

A bat flew in, another flew out of the cave.

'Anyway, it's time to go. Follow me,' she said.

*

Quartz took me back to the dirt path. We carried on walking uphill through a tunnel of trees. The bumpy track was as unpredictable as the morning weather – a sharp right turn overgrown with ivy, a left turn clear of any. The rising mist had evaporated, and the colder high-altitude air cleared my head. I put on the jumper Quartz had given me. Monkeys called in the hills and jumped from tree to tree. The dense woods gave way to grasses as tall as me, and I could see a signpost to 獅子山頂 (Lion Rock Peak) and the paved stone steps leading there.

There was less and less vegetation, and the climb became more demanding and precipitous. I imitated Quartz's movements, holding on to tree roots and finding secure footholds in the gaps between stones. The hard granite was sharp, but she climbed nimbly like a deer. Everywhere I looked I was surrounded by evocative rock formations – grey, speckled, wind-weathered stones jutting out – here a horsehead, there a raven's beak. After about ten minutes of this dizzying climb, Quartz pointed out some stone ruins.

'This is my favourite ruin – 頂天立地傻人塔 (the Idiot Pagoda). Five idiots came up here with stones and cement in the Sixties and built a pagoda, which was destroyed in the Seventies. Some people said that it was the typhoon, but others said it had something to do with protests against the Republic of Taiwan. Look, there's a poem on it.'

'雙山抱海浮游鯉 一塔擎天起睡獅 (A carp swims in the open sea between two hills. A sleeping lion is awakened by a sky pagoda). It doesn't sound idiotic at all. It's rather grand.'

Quartz laughed. 'I think it's idiotic. A lion is more likely to be awakened by a carp than by a pagoda.'

We continued the steep ascent until we reached the first mountain crest where the head of Lion Rock was clearly visible. Walking gingerly along the lion's back, we were surrounded by the folding green hills on one side and a sea of skyscrapers on the other. Quartz ignored the sign that said 懸崖危險 請勿前進 (Danger – Steep cliffs. No access beyond this point) and took me to a vantage area. She walked fearlessly on the cliff edge and found a precarious rock to sit on, waving for me to join her. My feet felt like jelly and I could feel my bladder tighten.

She placed both her hands on the rock, hauled herself over the cliff, and disappeared.

'No! Quartz!' I shouted as I ran towards the edge.

She stood below me on a big rock, which might well have been one of the ears of the rocky lion.

'Sorry, you gave me no choice. I had to fight fear with fear.' Quartz smiled, inviting me down with her hand. 'I don't want you to miss this view.'

Hundreds of skyscrapers of different height, shape, and colour were stacked up like gigantic Lego blocks. They housed millions on an impossibly confined and mountainous island. Some buildings were perched on sharp hills, responding harmoniously to the contours of the land, whereas others had had to invent their locations at the price of flattening the hills. Where the sea met reclaimed land, the coastline was as straight as a ruler. High up on Lion Rock and with the Hong Kong skyline below, I realised I'd lived too long in Bangkok. Diamond Hill and the nunnery were just other forms of confinement.

Quartz's eyes were fixed on the panoramic view. 'Diamond Hill is the only place I know. Everywhere else is just place names – 啟德機場 九龍城 旺角 中環 赤柱 (Kai Tak Airport, Kowloon City, Mong Kok, Central, Stanley). Other nuns talk of them with fondness, revulsion or apathy. They've lived, worked, visited, and embodied these places before becoming nuns. They've come from somewhere and belong somewhere, while I'm just a prisoner of Diamond Hill.'

The morning sea was buzzing with cargo tankers, yachts, fishing boats and the Star Ferry carrying passengers across Victoria Harbour. The sea looked calm and the sun thinned the clouds. The whole city was alive, as if I'd never left it behind. I told her stories about the neighbourhoods she mentioned. How only the most experienced pilots were able to guide their planes over the buildings in Kowloon City to land at one of the world's busiest airports. Landing was so dangerous that pilots were awarded a bonus for every successful touchdown. The chaotic, overcrowded and crime-fuelled district of Mong Kok, where locals and tourists combed the congested streets for bargain souvenirs, T-shirts, and the latest high-spec cameras from Japan. The city's commercial hub of Central, the emblem of global capitalism, stood like a financial god made of awesome glass and steel, where dreams were made and crushed by fluctuations in the Hang Seng Index. And of course, the extraordinary pace in Central where everyone walked at least three times faster than normal, just to get ahead of the competition. And the beauty of Stanley, which I had only visited twice in my lifetime, and could still break my heart. Once a small fishing village, it had retained its charm even though wealthy expats had built expensive houses all along the waterfront. I spoke like a local as if I hadn't ever fled to Bangkok and become a heroin addict.

'Thank you, Buddha. That's beautiful.' Quartz said, wiping her face with her sleeves. 'How about the places that matter to you? Where were you born?'

'I was born in Tsan Yuk Hospital in Sai Ying Pun on Hong Kong Island, in the Western District. It's a lovely red-brick building which once belonged to the London Missionary Society. It was one of the first maternity hospitals in Hong Kong.'

'Did your family live in Sai Ying Pun?'

'They lived near Sheung Wan Market when I was a boy. It's next to Sai Ying Pun. My father was a self-made businessman who owned a few metal shops.'

'Tell me more about Sheung Wan.'

'I remember the pungent smell along Des Voeux Road West where much of the street was occupied by store after store selling all sorts of dried seafood – dried shark fins, sea cucumbers, seahorses, abalones, fish lips, fish stomachs. On sunny days the owners used to put out their bamboo baskets full of exotic sea creatures to dry. The whole street fell under the spell of a strange fishy aroma. Some people said it smelt like armpits, but I thought it smelt of the sea.'

'Did they have dried jellyfish and octopus?' Quartz said, smiling.

'They did. In fact, it looked as if every imaginable edible sea creature was on display.'

'Other nuns said there is a famous street filled with all sorts of Chinese medicinal ingredients.'

'Yes, you would like Ko Shing Street. It is also called Medicine Street, which was the hub of the wholesale Chinese medicine trade. I remember being obsessed by the big glass jars on the walls filled with ginseng from countries like North Korea, Canada and America. The intricate root plants looked like human limbs. The street reeked of revolting medicine like you brewed for Boss. I hated that smell when I was young.'

'I'd like to visit Medicine Street one day.' Quartz took a sip of water. 'Did you enjoy your time in St Paul's?'

'My father was obsessed with sending me to a posh Christian school. Many of my classmates came from families of bankers, judges, politicians, artists and millionaires, so I was a misfit from the word go. I wondered how I got in. One day, out of the blue, a boy started calling me 口水燕 (swallow's spit), and that became my nickname. After one particular parents' evening, a boy teased me by mimicking a swallow's flight, darting around in the corridor and chirping 'spit, spit'. Dad dashed off without saying a word and I walked home with Mum. We stopped for an ice-cream which started melting before my tongue could lick it. She handed me a handkerchief. I looked up and all her make-up was dissolved by her tears.'

'Are you sure it wasn't sweat?'

'I wish. She told me to be strong and said I mustn't repeat the words – swallow's spit – to my dad because that was how I was admitted to St Paul's. Dad's best friend owned the Chinese medicinal store which sold the best bird's nests for the famous soup.'

'You mean it was bribery?'

I was tongue-tied.

'Forgive my intrusion.' She looked back out over the city.

'That explained how I never belonged.'

'Was that why you went off to Bangkok?'

'我冇做生意材料 (I don't have an instinct for business), so I ruined my father's company. I should have made a living with words, like a journalist or teacher, but I was the only child. Money and I were never on good terms.'

'What happened to your father's business?'

'To be honest, I still don't exactly know what happened. I worked my socks off for years to build up the company, but the market was changing and if I hadn't done something drastic, the business would have gone under. Maybe it was all down to my misguided ambition. I took out a big loan to expand the business, but the gamble didn't come off. I had to borrow more money from other sources to keep the company afloat. In one season, our debts snowballed to seven figures. I had to choose – kill myself or leave Hong Kong.'

'So it was money that made you leave Hong Kong.'

'No, it was shame, which is worse than money. The same thing that melted my mother's makeup.'

'There are many things worse than shame.'

'Such as?'

'Cruelty. Our ability as a species to … harm ourselves and each other.' There was an awkward pause before she said 'harm'.

'You could still be a journalist or a teacher, or both,' she said. 'It's never too late.'

'How about you? Can you imagine not being a nun?'

'I would have died if I hadn't become a nun.'

A gust of wind rushed towards us and knocked me off balance.

'Where's the city's border with China?' Quartz asked, looking north.

'We can't see it from here.'

'One day, I want to see the border, and cross it.'

She climbed back over the rock and offered me her hand.

'Thanks for being my tour guide. I hope you'll show me all these places, before everything disappears.'

We retraced our way downhill without saying a word.

The silence broke as we walked past the entrance of the cave.

'The Iron Nun will be away for three days. Can you go to the shanty town, find Boss, and bring her back to the nunnery?'

'Why—'

'I want Boss to have a second chance, to leave the drug gang.'

A bat flew past us and slipped into the tight gap. A raindrop fell into my eye. Without waiting for my answer, Quartz rushed on into the shady woodland leading to the waterfall, the pool, and the many trees I couldn't name. I finally found my own way. The path took me down to the nondescript nunnery gate, the place Quartz had arrived as a teenager with no memory of her childhood and where Audrey Hepburn had found the baby Boss in a basket.

The dry gale nagged me endlessly that night and I worried about the precarious thatched roof. I woke up with the wind still in my head and found Quartz's rucksack by my door. She had packed me a change of clothes for a few days and a huge bag of rice crackers. There was a handwritten note: 三日為期 無音勿回 (I'll give you three days for the return of Boss's voice). I put my toothbrush and towel in the bag and headed out.

The noise of the construction site at the bottom of the hill shook the trees. There was no birdsong, no insects' calls.

The row of colourful tin shacks on the town's fringes, which once housed a dozen families, were now empty. A father and three young children were rummaging through them, looking for trophies – a plastic bucket with a broken handle, a wooden stool with legs chewed by a dog, a yellow helmet discarded by a construction worker, an old metal saucepan scored with burn marks, an outdoor parasol large enough to shelter four people playing mah-jong from the sun, and a scruffy canary with yolk-yellow feathers fidgeting in a cage. The father helped his three little scavengers stack up their precious finds onto a metal trolley. The youngest, a girl about five years old, looked alarmed, nervously guarding the birdcage as I walked past. I smiled at her, but her face said: don't touch me.

The main street wasn't as busy and bustling as it had been during the summer. Or rather, it was a different kind of buzz – edgier, less authentic. The main street had become a film set choreographed by an invisible director. Many of the market stalls had closed down and the few remaining grocery stores were inundated by long chaotic queues. Some people jumped them and made scenes, but order was quickly restored by the store owners' foul-mouthed tirades. As I joined the queue, many people whose faces I recognised from the funeral procession gave me cold impatient stares.

A group of teenage boys wearing New York baseball caps, oversized T-shirts and gold chains policed the main street. They looked like sentinels from a highly disciplined organisation, controlling the crowds with efficiency by whistling and using coded hand signals. Their faces were young and unfamiliar. None of them had any stubble. Boss was nowhere to be seen.

The moment I turned into a side street, I realised I'd been deceived by the orderly façade maintained by the teenage gang. The alley, once a popular and charming hot-spot for housewives' mah-jong marathons full of laughter, food and improvised profanity, had become an outdoor drug den. A dozen heavy-eyed, middle-aged men crouched down against the wall – some holding empty needles, some smoking a cocktail of who knows what substances. A few old men lay on the ground like a pile of inflatable plastic dummies. A bald man in his seventies was touching himself and singing an obscene Cantonese pop song.

There were three women in the alley, all looking older than their age. One of them must have been in her seven-ties, sitting with her legs wide apart. Another woman in her mid-twenties was begging for a free joint and showing off her cleavage to two teenage gangsters. Finally, there was a girl on the cusp of puberty. She walked up and down the alley, picking up used needles, examining them closely like a doctor, and separating them into different plastic bags according to her personal standard of cleanliness.

Some men extended their hands, begging for money. The two teenage Triad boys stared at me. The younger one pulled out a machete from under his red leather jacket. I closed my palms and pretended to pray like a monk. They shoved the woman with the exposed cleavage against the wall and stopped me in my tracks. I closed my eyes and chanted a sutra. The boys conducted a full body search like two experienced police officers. They touched my groin, stroked my cock, and jiggled my balls.

The boy in the red leather jacket laughed at me, holding his little finger up in the air.

'你條柒頭細個條蝦毫 (Your cock is smaller than a baby shrimp).'

I kept chanting and hoped he would let me pass. Instead, he got more annoyed and put the machete between my legs. I wanted to twist his hand, grab his knife and kick some sense into his head, but I saw his dilated pupils. He was elsewhere, sky-high.

'What the fuck are you chanting?'

The sutra went on circling in my head and an old man shouted out, '佛祖乜野都睇到 (the Buddha sees everything). He is going to save us all.'

The boys rolled their eyes and let go of me.

I was desperate to leave the alley but felt a pull on my sleeve. It was the little girl.

'Do you want one? Ten cents for one. Buy two get one free.'

Many of her syringes were still filthy, though she had obviously tried her best to clean them.

'Take it or leave it. 唔好阻住個地球轉啦 (Don't get in my

way and don't stop the Earth spinning)!' She put the needle back in her plastic bag and walked away.

The beggar's dog rubbed his nose against my trousers. At the end of the alley, the beggar waved at me discreetly. I followed him into another backstreet full of debris and stray cats. He walked on faster with his dog rushing ahead. He seemed to know the dark maze of hidden passages like the back of his hand. Finally, the dog stopped in front of a battered banyan tree. Many of its aerial roots had been hacked off to make space for a barbed-wire fence, which had been hammered into one side of its trunk. Standing on the root-torn pavement, the beggar came to a rest and leant against the tree. The dog sat quietly beside him.

The banyan tree had become the boundary landmark between the shanty town and acres of fresh concrete. From where I was standing, it wasn't clear whether it was Diamond Hill or the outside world that had been turned into a cage.

Three boys had somehow found their way inside the fence and were using the space as a football pitch. They passed the ball with cool accuracy.

Rummaging in his jacket pockets, the beggar found something and cleaned it with his tongue. He handed me a plastic mah-jong tile on which 發 (prosperity or wealth) was engraved and painted in auspicious red. I'd no idea what he was up to. He shook his head like a child refusing to eat his vegetables, then took my hands in his. They were surprisingly soft and warm. He put the mah-jong tile in my pocket, and said, '救救石英 (Save, save quartz).'

'You mean Quartz, the nun?'

'救我 救我 (Save me, save me)!' he yelled and turned his head away.

Then he started mumbling the familiar nonsense I'd heard him chanting during the funeral procession – '我想上北京賣鹽鴨蛋 (I want to sell salted duck eggs and die in Beijing)', '英女王好靚 (The Queen is beautiful)', and '我媽冇奶畀我 (My mum has no milk left for me)'. The beggar kept repeating the three phrases in a hypnotic rhythm and moving his head in a circular motion. Was he possessed? The dog started barking at his feet. The quick wind shook the old banyan tree and its leaves ran riot.

I put my hand on his burning forehead and found myself humming the last line from the heart sutra, the first Buddhist scripture I'd learned: '揭諦 揭諦 波羅揭諦 波羅僧揭諦 菩提 薩婆訶 (*Ga-te, Ga-te, Para-ga-te, Para-sam-ga-te, Bod-hi Sva-ha*).' Daishi had recited this line to me whenever I wanted to leave Wat Arun. He would then touch my forehead to calm the turbulence inside. When the dog stopped barking, the beggar quietened down.

He touched the mutilated tree trunk and trailed his hands along the fence. The three football kids laughed and kicked the ball hard in his direction.

'死乞兒 死和尚 兩條廢柴 (Dead beggar and dead monk – two pieces of useless charcoal)!' They mocked us until they lost interest and kicked the ball away, running after it like a pride of lion cubs.

The beggar signalled the dog to chase the boys, but she couldn't get through the fence. The dog laid her head on his lap. Putting his hand on her head, he started repeating the heart sutra: '*Ga-te*, *Ga-te*, *Para-ga-te*, *Para-sam-ga-te*, *Bod-hi Sva-ha*'.

There wasn't a whiff of Boss and her gang anywhere. A crowd had gathered in front of the noodle restaurant. I could hear Audrey Hepburn quarrelling with the owner. They were at each other's throats. I jostled my way forward. There was a plastic bucket on the ground, along with noodle bowls, chopsticks, and a huge splash of soapy water.

'你隻死臭雞 有屎用 (Dead smelly hen-whore, you're no fucking use to me)! I gave you a chance to clean up your pathetic life, and now you turn against me?' The owner's face was as red as an overripe autumn plum.

'你條死粉腸 你以為自己有條硬撳屎 (You dead floppy dough, do you think you still have a rock-hard cock)? There's no way on earth I'd move to 天水圍 (Tin Shui Wai) with you. It's a godforsaken new town in the middle of fucking nowhere. I'm not your slave.'

'You owe me. All these years I've let you work here, come and go as you wish, and paid you an honest salary. What's wrong with Tin Shui Wai? It has everything we don't have here in this dump. I've treated you as one of my own family.

You're a venomous snake, just like your daughter, poisoning the town. We would have prospered here if it weren't for this plague of the white powder.'

Some of the crowd was cheering him on. They shouted how much they liked the new town, the clean streets, the electrified railway system, and most of all, the brand-new apartments with kitchens, bedrooms, and flushing toilets. Some sided with Audrey Hepburn, calling the new town a sham, a conspiracy cooked up by the government to steal their precious land. Some of the children said they'd love to play in a proper playground without syringes, while a few elderly people said they'd prefer to die in Diamond Hill than become vagrants in a soulless place with no history. People started baring dirty secrets about their enemies, revealing each other's weakness and bringing up forgotten scars and scandals.

'I've no time for you and your ignorant types Don't rubbish the new town if you haven't even seen it Your whole bloody family is a fossil Can't you see what the Communists are doing to us No wonder your son is a retard The city hasn't even been handed over yet and they're already stealing our land I don't want my daughter growing up among drug addicts and the Triad I've already lost my husband to the white powder and the new town will be a fresh start The white powder will follow him wherever he goes You're lucky to be allocated anywhere at all Half my profits go to pay protection money to the Triad I'm just a homeless piece of shit How much compensation money did you get from the government My parents gave me this land and even at gunpoint I'm not moving an inch You people are all traitors We must stay here and take back control Look at the state of this fucking place I can't wait to leave It's no longer the village it was First there was the landslide then the demolition and all the new construction works They said we'd be given first choice of the new apartments How much pocket money did you give the official Some apartments even have a sea view and we'll be able to see the fireworks in the harbour Fuck the fireworks The British betrayed us No the Chinese are betraying us We *are* Chinese Dumb-ass can't you see you're betraying yourself and your offspring I don't trust the Hong Kong government anymore they have sold us down the drain I just want to die here where I've lived all my life Sure you do bitch the rats would kill you first if not your husband and the white powder Those high fences give me nightmares Fuck the fence I don't even have enough rice to feed the kids'

The raw voices of residents rang out in the streets like bursts of machine-gun fire.

The noodle-restaurant owner towered over Audrey Hepburn and spat in her face. She wiped herself like a wounded cat. The crowd booed and cheered. She leapt up in the air and hit her employer square on the nose. He fell over, blood dripping down his chin.

'I'll kill you! I'll gouge your eyes out and feed them to the rats. You wombless bitch.'

A little girl started screaming.

Audrey Hepburn picked up a piece of sharp broken plastic. The owner threw a pile of plates at her, which she dodged quickly. The plates hit various people in the crowd. She tutted and mocked him. He jumped up like a clumsy Kung Fu amateur, but somehow managed to kick the plastic weapon out of her hand. He grabbed hold of her hair, pushed her to the ground, and started undressing her in front of everybody. Despite her kicking and screaming, he managed to rip her top off, exposing her battered yellowing bra. She tried to hide her sagging breasts, but he had won and threw his arms in the air to claim victory.

I bustled through the boisterous crowd, desperate to take Audrey Hepburn away. She had curled up in a pool of soapy water and would not be touched. I draped my jacket over her naked shoulders. She pulled it up to hide her face.

'Let's get out of here. You'll be fine,' I said, provoking a stream of foul language from the victorious noodle-shop owner.

'你條冚家鏟喺邊撚度爬出嚟 (Where the fuck did you and your bulldozed family crawl from)? Look, everyone, the fake monk is trying to steal her from me.'

'Just leave her alone. You've done enough,' I said.

'Don't talk to me like you own her.'

'Nobody owns her.' My hands were on Audrey Hepburn's shoulders, trying to reassure her as best I could.

'你個契弟正白癡 (You son of a bitch, you're a retard)! I

certainly own her, and many other men here own her too. She moves around like a conveyor belt. She used to be bouncy, tight and tasty, but look at her now. When I fucked her a few months ago, I could barely feel anything. Now if someone paid me a thousand dollars, I wouldn't let her dishwashing mouth come anywhere near me.'

Some men in the crowd cheered and whistled. Others shuffled uneasily.

I couldn't stand it anymore and lunged at him. He dodged easily. Someone threw him something shiny which he caught with one hand. He raised it melodramatically, steadied his feet, and stabbed my upper left arm with a syringe. I could see the silvery point of the needle enter my flesh. It happened fast, but it played out in my mind in slow motion.

I went blank as I fell down on all fours. The restaurant owner addressed the crowd, 'That'll teach this loser a lesson. Next time he messes around on my home turf, I'll pump air in his veins and let's see what happens.'

'You scum! What have you done?' Audrey Hepburn looked at him in disbelief.

'Come on, it's for old times' sake. Everyone knows he was a drug addict. Isn't this what he really wants?'

I could see the unforgettable number 2 mark on the barrel. My marker. Many times I had wanted to up the quantity just to tempt fate. On those desperate days, getting the yellowy liquid over the number 2 mark wasn't as easy as I'd hoped. I never got it right: shaky hands, blurred eyes, not enough powder, not enough cash, or worse, cowardice. Strangely I used only to think about overdosing, never about injecting air into my bloodstream. That would have been a lot cheaper.

I pulled the needle out of my arm and wiped the trickle of blood off with my hand. The colour had drained from Audrey Hepburn's face. She touched my cheek and kissed the small needle mark on my arm.

The owner erupted once again and started kicking me.

A few men in the crowd shouted, '踢死佢 (Kick him dead)!'

'Who's bothering my mother?' A voice pierced the crowd like a fire alarm. It was Boss. 'Out of my way!'

Four big teenage boys cleared the spectators and grabbed the restaurant owner, locking him in a torture position.

'Where's your tongue? Answer me, noodle man. Why are you messing with my mother?' Boss rolled up her sleeves and one of the boys gave her a machete.

'I didn't touch a single strand of your mother's hair. This loser started it. I'm totally innocent. Everybody knows the government has asked me to open a noodle restaurant in the new town and I just want your mother to help me set it up. That's part of her job.'

Boss sneered, 'Who said my mother is leaving Diamond Hill?'

'It's an open invitation. Of course, it's absolutely fine if she wants to stay. I know many people have decided to stay. There's nothing wrong with me choosing a different path, is there?'

Boss handed the machete back to the boy, who started using the restaurant owner's chin as a sharpening stone. The blade made a nervy metallic sound on his stubble as he kept his face still. Some well-built middle-aged men, supporters of his in the crowd, made grumbling noises in protest.

I lifted Audrey Hepburn to her feet and we retreated.

Boss shouted to someone in the crowd, 'You, woman with the ugly mole. Tell me, is this human trash lying to my face?'

Nobody said a word and she went on. 'OK, you dumb mole.' She picked on another unsuspecting victim in the crowd. 'How about you, you with the pig's belly, did this bastard hurt my mother?' The man lowered his head and turned away. Six strong teenage boys jostled their way into the crowd, showing off their knives, hammers and machetes. People started to disperse. Within seconds the entire crowd had disappeared, leaving only Boss, her boys and their prey.

'Old man, you know what? My mum always said you're just a spineless pile of human ash. Boys, take his clothes off. I can't see any spine on your back, Mr High and Mighty Noodle Man. Let's cut his back open to check.'

Two boys flattened the man like a roast chicken on a chopping board. They chose the sharpest knife and pointed it at the middle of his spine. The noodle man winced in anticipation of the blow. When they were about to stab him, Boss raised her hand.

'You two stupid flies, it's your job to know when I'm joking. Piss off.'

Boss came face-to-face with the man and spat on him.

'Funnily enough, I don't really believe in karma.' She waved her hand and her gang released the man and stepped back. The owner stood and tried to straighten his clothes.

'Who gave you permission to walk away from this mess? Have you no sense of civic duty? Clear away the plates and bowls before you move your ass. If you hadn't been punctual paying me protection money over the years, my boys would have pried you open and left you flopping on the floor like a skinned frog. One more thing. If I ever hear you undermining my business here, you can assume your wife and children have been cremated and their ashes flushed down the toilet.'

The man turned his back on us and started clearing up the plastic plates, bowls, spoons and chopsticks. He looked like a child drawing pictures on the sand, as the sea foamed up the shore, erasing the land under his feet.

'You've just made me unemployed,' Audrey Hepburn said.

'Nobody ever asked you to work. You know I can look after you,' Boss said with a cheeky grin.

Audrey Hepburn bent over and kissed her daughter on the cheek, who instantly rubbed it away.

Sitting by the roadside, my head was spinning. I tried to move my arm, but it was frozen. A rash had flared up where the needle had entered my flesh.

Boss popped two pills in my mouth and forced me to swallow them dry. 'Antibiotics, just in case.' She ordered the boys, 'Carry him back to my place and make sure he's alive.'

Propped up by two big lads, I tried to get my legs moving again. The flexible sinews in my body had been replaced by hard wires. Soon everything lost focus. The restaurant owner was now a block of meat and the plastic plates he was picking up crude brushstrokes of green and orange. All the details of the busy street seemed to have been washed away like watercolours dissolving after a shower of rain. I could no longer smell the distinctive star anise in the beef entrails broth, nor hear the hawkers' wagons rattling past. Smudgy silhouettes of children ran up and down the streets. A plane was reflected in the soapy water on the ground.

I found myself somewhere like England, wrapped in Boss's pink floral bed linen in her cast-iron Victorian bed. The afternoon sun came through a crack in the checkered curtains, splashing over the perfume bottles on the dressing table. The band of Dior caught the light and diffused a flash of gold. I had a splitting headache. The glare was torture.

'You slept for twenty-four hours, actually twenty-four

hours, twenty-two minutes and thirty-nine seconds, forty, forty-one, forty-two . . .' Boss was in bed next to me, with her eyes fixed on her gold LED watch.

I tried to speak but my throat was as dry as the Gobi Desert.

'I'll get you some water.' Audrey Hepburn rolled out of bed, fetched a glass and put it by my side. She crawled back under the duvet, next to Boss.

The water burned my throat but quenched the fire in my empty stomach.

'You drugged me.' I stared at Boss, as I tried to get out of bed. My legs were sore, and I had pins and needles all over.

'I saved you, you idiot. You should thank me.' Boss rolled over to my side. 'The needle was clean and it wasn't the real demon, Buddha. If I hadn't put you to sleep, your mind would have taken you back to the old dark places.' She prodded my head with her forefinger.

Those two little pills were stronger than any drugs I had ever taken. They had worked like an off-switch and shut down my whole system. Lying in the same bed with Boss and Audrey Hepburn, I could no longer distinguish between what was real and unreal. Though I knew those leather-bound books on Boss's bookshelf – Jane Austen, the Brontë sisters and George Eliot – weren't really books but a set of wooden props.

Audrey Hepburn started singing in Mandarin:

忘不了 忘不了
I can't forget I can't forget
忘不了你的錯 忘不了你的好
I can't forget your mistakes I can't forget your kindness
忘不了雨中的散步
I can't forget our walks in the rain
也忘不了那風裡的擁抱
and I can't forget our embrace in the wind

Her singing voice, though slightly out of tune, was tender and shy, as if she were undressing. I couldn't stop my tears. I hadn't heard the song for years, if not decades. It was one of those unforgettable tunes that resonated across Asia. It used to be on the radio, in taxis, on headphones, loudspeakers, on people's lips and everybody's mind. I turned to Boss and saw tears rain down her face too. She burrowed into my chest and hid her head there.

Audrey Hepburn hummed the melody and said, 'Do you know how many versions there are of this song? Hundreds. But I love the original version sung by 顧媚 (Koo Mei) best.'

She went on speaking to the ceiling. 'Do you remember the famous black-and-white Sixties film we watched together called 《不了情》 (*Love Without End*)? There was the famous scene when the charismatic 林黛 (Linda Lin Dai) sang this song in the nightclub and her drunken lover stormed in with two prostitutes on his arms. She was desperately trying to sing, but cracked up, left the stage, and fainted in the foyer.

Afterwards, she died of some mysterious illness. Nearly all female characters in those films died because of love.'

The song lingered in my head, though she'd stopped singing.

'I've got 鄧麗君 (Teresa Teng's) voice, haven't I? She had such a beautiful voice and I've always wanted to go to 寶島 (Treasure Island, meaning Taiwan) where she was born. Isn't it strange that Hong Kong, Britain and Taiwan are all islands? Japan is an island too. There are so many island countries in Asia. I've never thought of myself as an islander.'

She hummed the refrain again for a minute. 'Anyway, I could easily imagine having a bedroom like this in London. Every morning I'll wake up, open the curtains, smell the fresh air, make a cup of coffee, and say hello to my nice neighbours. I love those little red-brick houses in England with slanted roofs. I'll plant tulips and lavender in the front garden, and lots and lots of roses and fruit trees in the back. We'll have carpets, teapots, cups and saucers. We'll eat fish and chips, cucumber sandwiches, roast beef, Yorkshire pudding, and mushy peas. We'll drink Earl Grey, gin and tonic, and ginger ale. I'll feel like Julie Andrews – *raindrops on hoses and biscuits on kittens*.'

'*Roses and whiskers*, Mum!' Boss yelled and finally emerged from the duvet. 'You don't even drink coffee, you hate neighbours, and when was the last time you planted something? You're more likely to kill the roses. I can't imagine you in *The Sound of Music*. You would probably kill all the children. Maybe not on purpose but definitely by accident.'

Audrey Hepburn ignored Boss. She climbed over her daughter and made herself snug on my side of the bed. She whispered in my ear like a child sharing a secret. 'There's no hope for Hong Kong, Buddha. There's a rumour circulating in town that the Communist Army will march south with their tanks. What they've done over there with those tanks in the past, they'll do again here. We're so far away from Britain and the Queen won't be able to protect us. It's time to pack up and leave.'

'Most people don't have the choice to leave.' I said.

'But we have a choice!' Boss interjected. 'You must have heard that many rich people have acquired foreign citizenship in Canada, Australia and America. The most important people in the city have been handpicked by the British government. They've been offered permanent citizenship. You know what that means? Money and power can buy you anything, including a nationality.'

'Most people in Hong Kong don't have that option. Why do you think the British government is only offering citizenship to a select few?' I asked.

'Why shouldn't they? Britain is right to let only the best into the country. Doctors, lawyers, engineers, fashion designers, businessmen. Of course, they'll have to let in anybody who's rich and influential and who knows how to make money. People like me.' Boss sounded irritated.

'Buddha, why the hell do you support the Communist wolves? Don't forget we all have a British passport. We are British,' Audrey Hepburn said matter-of-factly.

'We are certainly not British. We are British Nationals (Overseas). And being BNO doesn't give us any right of abode in Britain. It's basically a fake passport.'

'It's not fake! It has the same crown, and what's that funny animal next to the lion? It's issued by the British government. We're British.' Audrey Hepburn raised her voice, searching for reassurance from Boss and me. 'We *are* British, aren't we?'

Boss gave me a knowing look and reached out to hold her mother's hands. 'Yes, of course, we are British.'

Sandwiched between mother and daughter who were comforting each other with lies, I couldn't find it in myself to contradict them. I sensed the turbulence in Audrey Hepburn's mind, and the way Boss tried to keep her mother's inner storms at bay.

Audrey Hepburn stretched her arms over her head. 'I'm pleased that our plan to go to Britain is shaping up. I can't wait to get the hell out of Diamond Hill, out of Hong Kong once and for all. Darling, do I really have to work in a Chinese restaurant? Can't I do something more glamorous?'

Boss blew her a kiss, reached over me to touch her mother's forehead. 'I'm afraid I need you to stay on the front line. You will be in charge of the till, not washing dishes. We'll take over one of the restaurants in Chinatown – I think it's called The Golden Palace – and use it as a base for cover. I'll play nice and cool at first, getting to know the gang, listening to their shit and complaints. After getting a handle on the situation, I'll set out the details of my reforms and the new management structure.'

'What if the people in Chinatown launch a counter-attack on us?'

'My boss here will be sending a backup team from Hong Kong ready for a hostile takeover and the Chinatown dumbos will have the devil to pay. Of course, that would only be the last resort. Nobody wants to go nuclear.'

Boss exhaled through her lips. Her hands rose as if gathering a mushroom cloud.

'Don't worry, Buddha. That's just standard practice. I'll make sure you stay out of trouble. The Triad likes the idea that I'm coming to London with an educated father. Your immaculate English will scare the shit out of those straw-heads in Chinatown. It'll give us *class*, which can't be bought for love or money.'

Without looking at the pair of them, I knew their eyes, like mine, were fixed on the empty ceiling, though I had no idea which country their mind had gone to. Chinese, Hong Kongese, British – they all sounded strange and transitory to me. I wondered how there could be a custody battle when Hong Kong was already a fully grown adult and all she wanted was exactly what her parents did, the wealth of the entire globe.

Boss's hand reached under the bed and fetched a camera. 'Stay there you two. This is a classic Polaroid family moment. This will be a great shot of the three of us lying here.'

Standing up and wobbling on the bed, Boss rearranged my head and her mother's hair, before tucking herself back under the duvet and holding a teddy bear to her chest. She passed the camera to me and positioned my arm in mid-air with the lens facing us.

'I'm going to count one to three, then you press the button, okay? One, two, three.'

'With one hand? I'm not sure I can manage.'

'Shut up and just get on with it. Again: one, two, three.'

I heard the flash, and then the mechanical whirr of the camera. A Polaroid film popped out. Boss started fanning it, shaking the image out of thin air.

'I love the smell of Polaroid. It's like a fine liqueur,' Audrey Hepburn said.

Boss held up the film. Slowly, I saw three blurry, overexposed figures appear on the glossy surface like an embarrassing out-take censored in a family album. Boss looked a lot younger in the picture, while Audrey Hepburn was posed like a supermodel with a mannequin's face that looked layered with the residue of decades of make-up. My oily shaved head reflected the flash as if a star had exploded on my forehead.

'I look like a fat ugly cow. Burn it.' Audrey Hepburn got

out of bed in a bad temper and opened the curtain, letting the sunlight flood into the Victorian bedroom.

'It's for you, Buddha. For the memory you lost because of my pills and for our future family life in London.' Boss shoved the photo in my pocket, took the camera, and started fiddling with it.

'Shit, no film! I never run of out film.'

Audrey Hepburn sat in front of the dressing table, painting her eyebrows in the mirror and humming the same song about forgetfulness. When I caught her eyes in the mirror, she stared back at me and said, 'Now with your memory loss, you and that malnourished nun can live like 一對喜雀 (a pair of happy magpies).'

'You mean Quartz?'

'You should ask the Iron Nun where the hell she's hidden Quartz's memory.' Audrey Hepburn got up without finishing her eyebrows and stormed out of the room.

'一個妒忌嘅女人係最靚嘅女人 (A jealous woman is the most beautiful woman),' Boss said, putting the camera under the bed. 'Have you fucked Quartz yet?'

I kicked the duvet off the bed.

'Good. I didn't think so. You wouldn't dare touch her under the Iron Nun's nose. Anyway, most men aren't keen on bony pussy. Me neither.'

She kept fiddling with her camera. 'Come on, don't be cross with me. I know my sixth sense might be annoying, but you should know my mum is the Goddess of Jealousy.

She'll do anything to get what she wants and you're her dream type, passive but educated. She'd do anything for love. She'll kill herself or kill you, if you don't go to London with us. I can't force you, but the door is open. You know you'll have no life in Hong Kong without us. We can be a family together. Think about that.'

She picked up my rucksack. 'It's getting late. You need to move your ass because I've a big business deal to take care of tonight. You witnessed how cocky and stupid my lads are. They cost me more than they're worth. I've got to spend so much time training them.

'*Chop-chop!*' she said in English and walked out of her room. 'I'll take you back to the nunnery.'

Shortcut after shortcut, Boss took me through secret meandering passages in the shanty town. She spoke in a calm and ruthlessly managerial style about her gang.

'Let me tell you how it works. The thing is my operation is getting too big and my lads are not mature and experienced enough to work independently. I have to hold it all together by myself, as there is no one I can trust.'

The alleyways twisted and turned like a cow's innards. Her lads stood on guard duty at random junctions, giving her the nod when she walked past, as if she were a queen in disguise, visiting her dwindling territory.

'Have you thought of working for me? You'd be able to save the shanty town.'

'How?'

'By turning off the life-support. After the landslide and with the rapid construction all around, people are living in a state of frenzy. Everyone is insecure, trapped, and trusts no one. The new town sounds an attractive option but sometimes opportunity is as scary as a death sentence.'

'What do you want me to do?'

'I am going to hike the drug prices soon. I want you to pretend to get hooked on drugs again and start spreading rumours about too little supply of the white powder. The lowlifes would really believe it if it comes from you, some-one who tried to resist its spell but failed in the end.'

'As you said, you have monopoly and are earning a lot anyway. Why do you need to add oil to a fire already raging? Is that what the Triad has asked you to do?'

'You have no idea how to run a successful business, have you? My kingdom in Diamond Hill is under threat because the poor families will soon be replaced by families with ovens and dishwashers. The more desperate people are, the more money I can make.'

'I don't want to be part of your business.'

'No problem. I can find somebody else.'

I thought she would hold a grudge against me for not helping her.

'You're right, Buddha. Mum wouldn't like me to put you in danger. I also don't want my dad to be a drug addict.'

The autumnal sky darkened quickly. The crushing noise

from the construction site cut through the sparse foliage on the uphill path to the nunnery. Although it was obvious that Boss wouldn't dream of coming back there with me, I thought I'd better ask the devil herself so that I could take the message back to Quartz.

'Quartz sent me out to look for you. She asked if you would like to come back to the nunnery.'

Boss laughed. 'Is she worried about me?'

She snapped a branch off a tree and threw it into the woods, in the direction of the construction site.

'She believes there is a better path for you than—'

'Being a gang leader and the daughter of a whore? She is a sweet person but so naive – and forgetful.'

The distant banging and drilling didn't stop Boss whistling the song Audrey Hepburn had sung in the bedroom. She walked ahead, and I quickened my pace to catch up with her.

'I've heard on the grapevine that Quartz's memory loss wasn't an accident. We lose something for a reason, and memory isn't the easiest thing to lose. After all, it's not like money, a house, a lover, or a set of keys, is it?'

'What does your mother know?'

Boss smiled mischievously. 'Who knows? She can't keep any secrets, so it's untypical of her not to have spilled the beans. It was a real shock to me when years ago Mum told me that the Iron Nun is her sister. Mum loses her soul whenever she sees something shiny but the Iron Nun is obsessed with her twisted doctrine of purity. They loathe each other but all the same have both landed up in this bomb site.'

'Is that why Audrey Hepburn is so desperate to leave Diamond Hill for London?'

'I'm no psychoanalyst, but it's obvious their sibling rivalry has been off the Richter scale since the beginning. Like you, they came from a good family. I can see why Mum's still attached to this place because of her Hollywood obsession, but I don't know anything about the ins and outs of how the Iron Nun got stuck here. They haven't seen or spoken to each other since Mum "found" me at the nunnery gate. You know what? Deep down, I think Mum is grateful to the Iron Nun.'

'Grateful for what?'

'For bringing me into her life. The Iron Nun could have given me to any foster parent. Instead she gave Audrey Hepburn an opportunity to be a mother, something precious that doesn't happen to every woman.'

The wind brushed through a row of white birches and leaves showered down from the fidgeting branches.

'What's wrong, Buddha? You look like shit.'

'Nothing.'

'Anyway, nobody can break the bond of blood. Why do you think the Iron Nun allows me to walk freely in and out of her forbidden city? 佢個心有鬼 (She has a ghost in her heart).'

'The Iron Nun is trying her best to save the nunnery.'

Boss stopped in her tracks, bending down, holding her

stomach with both hands and laughing her head off. She gasped for breath and leaned against a tree, trying to calm herself down, until another wave of laughter had her in stitches again.

'I've laughed so much I think I've peed myself. You don't believe me? Look, I'm wet.'

She finally stopped laughing. 'Don't you get it?'

'Get what?'

'Saving the nunnery is saving her own way of life.'

A quick wind ruffled up fallen leaves on the familiar track.

'Forget the shanty town, Buddha. It's finished. Life moves on.'

Boss hit the trunks with a stick as she rushed ahead. Her gold chain bounced up and down on her neck like a restless snake. Her girliness made me think of Little Red Riding Hood, except in Boss's version, she would be the little girl who managed to eat both her grandmother and the Big Bad Wolf.

'*Chop-chop*, Buddha! *Chop-chop!*'

She waited at the nunnery gate and contorted her arms and legs, pretending she was a prisoner.

'Do you think this is where your mother left you in a basket?' I said.

'Set me free, please! I'm innocent. I've done nothing wrong!'

She got bored and hit my head with the twig.

'Why don't you slip in to say hello to Quartz?'

She hit my head with the twig again, harder this time.

'What do you want me to tell her?' I asked.

She snapped the twig and threw the pieces inside the nunnery gate. She stood there like a child wanting a mother to take her home.

'Tell Quartz it's time to grow up. If I were her, I would have left the nunnery years ago and started a new life in the real world.'

Boss kissed my cheeks and said goodbye. 'Get ready, Daddy. Our flight to London is approaching fast.'

Only a faint line of red sun was left on the horizon. She ran downhill without looking back. The leaves at her feet rustled as she ran, and within ten seconds, she'd vanished. All I could hear was her whistling her song.

Standing on the steps of the Main Temple, I heard a knock on 木魚 (the wooden fish) and a ring on 法磬 (the Tibetan singing bowl). Another knock. Another ring.

I left my rucksack on the veranda, took off my shoes, and opened the screen door. The Iron Nun was chanting the heart sutra in the dark.

She invited me to join her and I kneeled down beside her.

She passed me the wooden mallet. I knocked gently on the wooden fish and started chanting.

The clear, hollow sound of wood striking wood helped me concentrate. Within a few seconds I'd forgotten the season, who I was, what I meant to do, where Hong Kong was heading, and why on earth I had entertained the possibility of starting a new life in London with Boss and Audrey Hepburn. The Iron Nun's lips moved like a fish breathing through its gills. Occasionally, without any premeditated rhythm, she struck a ring on the Tibetan singing bowl, and I could feel the sharp metallic call make all creeping things in the hills alert. After a while the words, the sutra, the chanting all disappeared, and what remained were the alternating sounds made from wood and metal. However hard I tried, the two instruments never harmonised. I couldn't help but think their stubborn attitudes towards each other reflected a lifelong conflict. They would not negotiate, nor would they yield. The wooden fish kept murmuring short hollow messages, while the Tibetan singing bowl gave long contradictory rings. The same ringing I'd heard in my father's metal shop on Hong Kong Island in the business I'd ruined.

I closed my eyes and listened to the wind stirring fallen leaves on the veranda. In the darkness of my mind, I imagined water dripping on a calm surface, and from the ripples the outline of a human figure started to dissolve, morphing into an octopus. Slowly, its tentacles spread out and its many powerful suckers squeezed my face, tightened around my neck, and tried to suffocate me like prey. Instead of fighting the powerful suckers, I let them take hold of me, and my head was slowly squeezed into its tight mouth. Quartz was right. The moment I let myself go and was ingested by the octopus, I couldn't see it anymore. I saw myself in the dark, as in an out-of-body experience.

Was Boss right to say that saving something dear to us was ultimately an act of selfishness?

A gust of evening wind toppled the plastic lilies on the altar. The Iron Nun got up and shut the screen door. I collected the flowers and put them back into the vase.

'Have you eaten yet?' she asked, lighting a lamp.

I shook my head and followed her to the back door of the Main Temple, an area forbidden to men. A thick curtain opened onto a sequestered inner courtyard with a covered wooden walkway. Everything was in disrepair. Floorboards were damaged and on one side the banisters had rotted away. Most of the delicate wooden carvings were battered beyond recognition. And yet, when the gaslight drew closer, lost details came alive. On one of the pillars there was a scene of two boys holding a big fish like a whale, one at its head and the other at its tail, while the Laughing Buddha lifted both his arms into the air, as if he was a cheerleader for them and their triumphant catch. I directed the lamp out towards the disused courtyard and found many dead potted plants and a dry well sealed off in a rusted cage. Three out of four rooms had been boarded up. The intricate carvings on the windowpanes and doorframes suggested this had once been a beautiful quarter of the nunnery.

The Iron Nun asked for the gaslight and invited me into her room.

It was smaller than my shed. Her narrow coffin-sized bed was tucked into a corner. There was no mattress, just a thin bamboo mat on a hard wooden board. Underneath the small pillow was a blanket folded into a perfect rectangle. She released a hook on the wall, and unfolded a half-desk secured by two makeshift legs. Having put the lamp on the narrow desk, she fetched a folding chair for me, before rummaging under her bed and taking out a portable gas stove, a clay pot, two bowls and two pairs of chopsticks. It was hard to find space to fit everything on the small desk. I turned on the gas stove and put the clay pot on. The heady smell of the gas filled the tiny room. She finally sat down and poured me a glass of hot tea from a flask.

It was only when I was seated in the wobbly folding chair that I saw the wall above her bed was covered by hundreds of postcards showing photographs of geographical landmarks from all over the world. Although I had visited so few, I was surprised I recognised so many – the Empire State Building, Mount Fuji, the Great Pyramids of Giza, Niagara Falls, the stone statues on Easter Island, the Forbidden City, the Eiffel Tower, Sydney Opera House, Christ the Redeemer in Rio, the Golden Gate Bridge, the Leaning Tower of Pisa, the Grand Canyon, the Colosseum in Rome, the Taj Mahal, the Statue of Liberty, the Great Wall of China, Big Ben, Mount Rushmore, Stonehenge . . . The postcards were neatly arranged and glued onto the wall, making a scenic quilt.

'This is a very impressive wall,' I said.

'It's my past, written up on the wall,' the Iron Nun said, lifting the clay pot lid and stirring the appetising ingredients inside. I saw silken and fried tofu, Chinese winter cabbages, shiitake mushrooms, black wooden fungi, glass noodles, carrots, turnips, bean sprouts and lotus roots.

'Have you been to all these places?'

'Not quite. These postcards are from my ex-colleagues.'

'Ex-colleagues? You mean other nuns?'

'No. I worked as a tour guide before I realised my vocation. I've kept in touch with some of them. Now and then they send me postcards just to tantalise me. Of course, in the heyday of the nunnery I used to travel abroad quite often on official business. Can you imagine this place was once full of energy? People came with big offerings and we did a great line in funerals. Well, I think the mushrooms are nearly ready. I don't like them overcooked.' She opened the lid and turned down the flames.

How could this emotionless person have led such an adventurous life?

The steam piped up from the pot and the savoury broth spilled over. Before helping herself, she served me a generous ladle of silken tofu, bean sprouts and shiitake mushrooms.

'You don't believe me, do you? You must wonder how someone who's travelled the world as I did ended up in exile in a dilapidated nunnery. The fact is I was an exile when I was a tour guide. Exotic places don't necessarily cheer you up if you've been born unhappy. Help yourself to more food. I think the carrots, turnips and lotus roots may need more cooking, but the rest should be ready now.'

She turned the gas to the lowest setting. The vegetables were boiling in the sweet amber-coloured broth of kelp and fermented soybeans.

'The mushrooms are delicious,' I said.

'Quartz picked them this morning.'

'What do you mean by exile?'

'Have you ever thought that you can't feel at home anywhere, that nowhere is home? You don't have a sense of belonging anywhere you go, and yet staying in one place isn't an option either.'

She stirred the contents of the pot once more. 'I grew up feeling deeply dissatisfied and unhappy, even though I was brought up in a well-to-do family like yours. I disliked everything about myself – my hands, my nose, my legs, my waist, even the way I breathed. I assumed that was what adolescence means – high expectations, continuous disappointments. Of course, it didn't help living with a sister obsessed with appearances and stardom.'

She gave me a knowing smile. 'You know Audrey Hepburn is my sister, don't you?'

I nodded.

'我同佢由細到大係火星撞地球 (Ever since we were kids we've clashed like Mars hitting Earth). I've often wondered if we were born from different wombs, but our parents were models of respectability.'

'You and Audrey Hepburn have certainly succeeded in breaking the mould.'

'You too. Truth be told: parents are the most tireless of ghosts. They haunt with a kind of searing legitimacy, and no season can remove the permanent burn marks they leave on our paths. There is no known exorcism for parents, or the lack of them.'

'Was that why you gave Boss away to Audrey Hepburn? To curse her with the burden of parenthood?'

The Iron Nun smiled. 'Unlike me, she was destined to be a mother. Undoubtedly she had a beautiful face and curvy figure, but her acting was atrocious. She was a classic case of unfulfilled dreams. It's taken her years to realise her complete lack of talent. Motherhood was a useful distraction. It gave her life some meaning.'

'So you do care about her.'

'You still don't get it, do you? My sister, you and I share the same path. We were never going to become the kind of woman or man our fathers wanted us to be.'

I tried to stop trembling.

The Iron Nun put down her bowl and chopsticks. 'Audrey Hepburn will never face the music, and you only did so reluctantly, but I realised that adulthood is a question of continual disappointment. Instead of not coming to terms with it like most people, I let a sense of failure take over my life. I became the epitome of an obedient, self-sacrificing elder sister.'

'That doesn't sound like the Iron Nun I know.'

She smiled sceptically. 'After my sister left home following her stupid Hollywood dream, broke Mum's heart and tore the family apart, I became more bitter and detached, but never showed my emotions to anyone. I smiled when a smile was needed, even during those embarrassing match-making lunches when my father introduced me to sons of his boring accountant friends. I hated being ordinary. And yet all my parents wanted was for me to marry a respectable professional man and produce two grandchildren, ideally a boy followed by a girl. I finished school and my father got me a job working as a secretary for the chief executive of Honda, instead of going into university, which I would have done if I had been his son. The office was in Central and very modern. Within a month of working at Honda, I met a young manager who fancied me and wanted to marry me. I was desperate to leave home. I was brought up in the era when marriage was the only opportunity for independence and sex without guilt, and I thought sex might be the missing ingredient for happiness. So I married him against my parents' wishes. He was Japanese, you know.'

'Japan was a forbidden word in my father's house too, even though he traded with Japanese companies,' I said.

'The Japanese did the most horrific things to my parents' generation. My grandfather died of hunger during the Japanese occupation. I was told he ate mud to keep his stomach from rumbling.'

'My grandparents had to surrender their metal shop to the Japanese at gunpoint. They lost everything overnight and became homeless. I heard the rations were terrible during 三年零八個月 (three years and eight months, the period of the occupation). They roamed further and further inland looking for food and had to make rice porridge with earthworms.'

'Did they survive?'

I nodded.

'They were lucky to be alive. Over a million people died in Hong Kong.' She closed her eyes and recited a short sutra. 'People forget the Second World War was brutally fought across Asia too, not only in Pearl Harbor. But I don't hold a grudge against the Japanese.'

'Why?'

'The Chinese and the British were not exactly saintly. What they called the Joint Declaration and the Basic Law are just another form of confusion and exploitation. There will be no peace in Hong Kong. An expiry date of 2047 is a curse.'

'I think it's easier to have a sense of an ending.'

'Yes, the past is like 千手觀音 (the Thousand Armed Avalokiteśvara), that Buddha who has an eye inside each of her palms. Her thousand arms are supposed to relieve the suffering of multitudes. Of course, the world has become much more populated since Buddha's time. I don't think a thousand arms would be enough now.'

The Iron Nun picked up the bowl, closed her eyes, and took a sip of the rich broth.

'I digress. I haven't told my story for a long time. In a way marrying a Japanese man changed the course of my entire life. One afternoon, about two weeks after our marriage, and while my husband was on a business trip in Shanghai and I was off sick at home, the doorbell rang. I wasn't going to get out of bed to answer it, but it went on ringing. When I opened the door, a quiet and well-dressed woman told me she had come from Nagasaki and was looking for her husband. She wore an emerald-coloured suit like the wife of a business executive. It was springtime and I remember the cherry-blossom brooch on her lapel. A little girl held her hand. A tiny thing. She couldn't be more than two years old. I presumed she was her daughter. The girl was polite, but her slightly open mouth showed that she was shocked to see me in my pyjamas. I didn't wear a bra, you know. The woman didn't move a single muscle on her face. I think the lotus roots are ready now. Do you want some?'

I nodded. The Iron Nun gave me two pieces. I bit into the brown crunchy root and a few strands of hair-like fibres got caught in my teeth.

'藕斷絲連 (A broken lotus root is connected by its silky fibres). Don't you think that's what memory is like? A series of broken images connected by unfulfilled desires?'

She wiped the soft fibres off her mouth.

'藕斷絲連 is a beautiful saying. Lotus root is my favourite vegetable too. Daishi couldn't live without it. What did you say to the woman from Nagasaki?'

The Iron Nun put the chopsticks down carefully on the bowl. 'I said I was the cleaner and invited them in. I knew Japanese etiquette: when in doubt, bow. So I bowed to her and apologised for wearing pyjamas. I told her I'd separated from my husband recently and had nowhere to stay. Her husband had kindly allowed me to stay in his apartment for a few days while he was away on business. The woman bowed in reply, before giving me a shy but knowing smile. I knew she knew. I offered her tea and the little girl a bar of chocolate. I told her I could ring a friend who would let me stay at her place. The woman didn't say anything. I excused myself and started packing my belongings into a suitcase – my clothes, books, jewellery, mug, photo album, and toothbrush. I said goodbye to her and the little girl. Before leaving, I gave them a deep bow, bending all the way down to waist level. In return, they bowed to me as respectfully as I'd done.'

She scooped a generous portion of glass noodles into my bowl with some broth. I saw Mount Fuji on a postcard through the savoury steam.

'I shut the door of my husband's apartment and walked all the way from Kennedy Town to the Excelsior Hotel in Causeway Bay. I checked in for a few nights into the most expensive suite overlooking Victoria Harbour. I called a male escort just for the thrill of it. I locked myself in the room for as long as I could, seeing no one except male escorts. After five days, I'd spent all my savings. I only had HKD$100 left in my purse. In the morning paper on the fifth day, I saw a job vacancy for a tour guide. On the spur of the moment I left the hotel and got myself a sexy low-cut dress showing my cleavage. I put on some expensive make-up and painted my lips cherry-red. The boss of the tour company was clearly a crook. He had a flashy office in Central and wore a gold Rolex. I told him that even though I had no experience of the tourism industry and had barely travelled abroad, I had no family ties and was happy to go wherever the company wanted. He raised his eyebrows and asked me what I thought about Cuba. I told him I liked cigars. He smiled and asked me if I believed in fortune telling. I said no, but he asked to read my palms. He read them very carefully without saying a word. A few minutes later, he shook my hand and took my passport to arrange a visa and the earliest flight to Havana.'

'It couldn't have been a very respectable business,' I said.

'Of course not. It was an interesting job and I was broke; I would have taken anything with a good salary. The excuse to leave Hong Kong and my parents was also tempting. I didn't mind accompanying a businessman to Havana to do whatever he needed to do. Leslie was his name. Of course, he was not as handsome as 張國榮 (Leslie Cheung), but not fat and ugly either, just dull and bespectacled. We had good sex, though I don't think sex meant a lot to him either. It was just something to kill time in somewhere exotic after a couple of mojitos. When I was there in Cuba, I realised it was almost a year after the missile crisis and that was why nobody in Hong Kong was willing to go. I stayed in a five-star hotel downtown while he had business meetings with important people. After work and sex, he would take me shopping and dining. I remember nothing about Havana, except the smell. Sweet and shitty, like a one-week-old baby. After my first trip, my boss said I'd done a sterling job and the client gave me a big bonus. That was how I started my career as a tour guide. I've never been back to Havana. I never saw Leslie again either. I sometimes wonder if he moved to Cuba for good.'

She turned off the gas stove, collected the last bits of fried tofu and carrots, and gave them to me.

'I'm full,' I said.

'One is *never* full. We don't waste food here.'

'Did you ever hear again from your husband?'

'Yes, of course. The answer to a lie is always another lie. I was just one tiny part of his lifetime of lies. He was desperate to get a divorce, but I was a nomad without an address. I heard he eventually went back to Japan. I felt for his poor wife and daughter.'

'Are you still married to him then?'

'Legally speaking. If the nunnery doesn't work out for me

in the end, I'll go to Nagasaki and claim half of his assets.'
She smiled wickedly.

'How did you become a nun and end up in Diamond Hill? Being a tour guide is definitely more lucrative.' She kept her mouth sealed. Then I said, 'I see a postcard of Wat Arun up there. Did you meet Daishi in Bangkok when you were a tour guide?'

She was about to clear the dirty dishes and I stopped her by touching her arm. She sat down.

'It's a long story. You could say I met Daishi too late. I met him when he was visiting Hong Kong and I was already a nun. If I had met him earlier, I mean before he became a monk, I would definitely have fallen for him. I gathered he had been a very sexy heroin addict.'

Her eyes reached out to mine for agreement.

'The truth is I didn't choose to be a nun. I got into serious trouble with a Russian client ten years ago. He owned a large area of land in Siberia where a special species of mink was abundant. Remember, it was the 1970s when any middle-aged woman felt naked without a fur coat in her wardrobe. I knew the man who owned the biggest fur-coat factory in Hong Kong, and the Russian wanted me to be the middlewoman, introducing him to the most powerful player in town. I accepted a smallish bribe from him but found out his money was dirtier than anything I'd ever imagined. The Hong Kong fur-coat client refused to meet him. I tried to return the money to the Russian, but it was too late. It's always too late in a story like this. Instead of getting at me, he started taunting my parents, breaking into their house, pouring dog's blood on their door: all the usual gangster threats.'

'Did the Russians bother Audrey Hepburn too?'

The Iron Nun froze. She stood up and I grabbed her hand. She stared at me with electric ferocity, then she sat down and poured herself a cup of tea from the flask. It was already cold, but she drank it anyway.

'Not at first. Mum was so frightened for my sister's safety that she forced her to move back home for a while. I think it was more than a year after Audrey Hepburn came to live in Diamond Hill. She finally moved back after being followed by strangers on the streets. One evening, I came home after work and found they had ransacked our apartment, smashed my parents' wedding china and torn their nice clothes into pieces. My parents held on to each other in bed, trembling like a tuning fork. Mum collapsed into my arms. Dad sat upright leaning against the wall with his eyes closed.'

'What exactly happened to Audrey Hepburn?'

'She locked herself in the bathroom and refused to let me in. I forced the door open and there she was in her floral dress, hiding her head under the steaming shower and rubbing her legs with a bar of soap.'

'Did they—'

'Whatever my sister told you, it is *not* true.'

'She didn't tell me anything.'

'They were debt collectors, not animals. They wouldn't have dared to touch her in front of my parents.'

'How can you be so sure? You weren't there.'

'Anyway, she was always a fragile flower in a green-house. The break-in probably did her good in the end. It toughened and opened her up. She was completely fine and returned to Diamond Hill to live out her dream of being a film extra. Whatever label you want to give her now, she is not mentally ill. She pretends to be crazy and hysterical, as we all pretend to be someone we're not. Not everyone deserves to be happy in this life. Aren't you also trying to pretend you could have a new life in London with my sister and her little teenage drug queen?'

'The same as you pretending not to be jealous of Audrey Hepburn having a daughter.'

'She could have raised a decent child, moved out of the shanty town, and made an honest living. Instead she let her self-indulgence ruin her daughter's life. Look at what Boss has done to this place with her white powder.'

'Your collaboration with the developers is equally destructive.'

'Don't ever compare me with my lowlife sister. Social cleansing is the only way to save Diamond Hill from moral filth.'

The Iron Nun stared at the clay pot. The residual heat had boiled the last mouthful of broth down to a black scab.

'Thank you for the dinner,' I said.

'Hang on. There's no free dinner here without giving something in return.' She lifted the desk, created an empty space between us, and asked, 'What happened the other night near the construction site? I hear you met the gentleman with the Bentley?'

I stood and took my leave, then waited for her to follow me onto the wooden walkway. The full moon had burned off the evening haze, casting a cold fluorescent light over the courtyard.

It didn't take her long to join me outside. She imitated my posture and rested her hand on the banisters as I said, 'I'm happy to give you the information you want.'

She took a deep breath and said, 'I'm listening.'

'Before I'll tell you anything about my encounter with the man in the Bentley, you need tell me what happened to Quartz when she first arrived in the nunnery.'

She smiled approvingly. 'You're really obsessed with her past, aren't you?'

'Yes.'

'Does she remind you of your wife – sorry – your ex-wife, who had a miscarriage? Your private life is none of my business. I know you're cross, but I didn't dig around. Daishi was desperate for me to take you in and he spilled the beans. It wasn't entirely your fault. Nobody would have thought she cared more about the money you lost than the baby inside her. Being depressed was one thing, but not eating—'

'Stop. I don't want to hear any more about it.'

'With respect, we all have our own pasts to take care of. Did Quartz tell you that like all the other poor souls in the nunnery, she came here because she wanted to forget what she'd done?'

I didn't know what to say.

'When she arrived, she was a classic case – broken, abandoned, and violated. Beyond repair. Her burning desire for a new life was so strong she would have killed herself if we hadn't given her what she wanted: forgetfulness. The images of her impure past could simply be washed away in the purifying river of Buddhism.'

'You must think I'm a three-year-old. You don't fool me with those lies about the white dew and water ritual. It's just your way of starving her to make her forget what she really needs to remember.'

She cackled and the whole courtyard reverberated.

'Your sister told me you've hidden Quartz's memory somewhere. What was all that about?'

'Even the most primitive torture has its own elaborate set of rituals,' she said, straightening her saffron robes. 'Look there. In the room opposite us there is a rosewood chair from the Qing dynasty. I was told a famous British politician sat on it when he signed the Treaty of Nanjing in 1842 and took Hong Kong. It's a beautiful chair with intricate carvings of a dragon and phoenix in communion on cloud nine. Before Kai Tak Airport was built, our

Founding Nun granted permission to have the flight path over Diamond Hill. As a token of gratitude, the British government donated the chair to the nunnery. The British are polite and diplomatic creatures. They only asked because they knew that the answer would be yes.'

The Iron Nun turned towards me, her face as brittle as bone china.

'Though it's hard to believe, this place was thriving back in the 1970s. By thriving, I mean there were more than twenty nuns.'

'Come on, it couldn't have been a coincidence that of all nunneries in Hong Kong, you chose the one closest to Audrey Hepburn.'

'You're right. I came here partly to remind my sister that she isn't the only casualty on this planet. I wanted to prove to everyone that I was better than Audrey Hepburn and could rise above any adversity.'

'By everyone, you mean your parents?'

The Iron Nun looked as if she'd been stung.

'Many people consider the Buddha's blessing is more precious than merely producing grandchildren.'

'I beg to differ.'

'You haven't done too well yourself in the offspring department.'

I bit my lip.

'Apart from wanting to gall your sister, why did you come to Diamond Hill?'

'I came because it had a good reputation of helping women start a new life and forget their wretched past. On the night of my arrival, some nuns talked about a haunted chair. They said whoever sat on it would have endless nightmares and their memories would eventually be wiped out. They called it 忘情椅 (the Chair of Forgetfulness).'

I looked at the room opposite, with its doors and windows all boarded up.

'Many people want to wipe out their memories. On my second night here, I was taken to see the chair. I thought, what an unimposing, commonplace chair. When I sat on it, the nuns asked, do you want to forget? I asked, forget what? They said, forget all the bad things that have happened to you. I said, yes, of course, I want to forget my husband, his Japanese wife and daughter, Cuba, Leslie, the Russians – that's why I'm here to purify myself and hide from the world. They said, there's no need to hide, and if you're willing, the chair will erase all your bad memories. What do you mean? I asked. They just told me to relax. They tied my arms, back, legs and head to the chair, and put two round metal rings on my wrists. Then I saw the wires, the many red and black wires connected to the metal rings, and how these wires were connected to a small generator, and the generator to a switch. I asked, what's going on? One nun said, a new life. Another, electricity.'

'I asked, what electricity? They said, *the* electricity, the power that makes the light bulbs glow, the power that makes you forget. I said, no, I don't want it. They said, don't be afraid, it's only for a few minutes. I shouted, no, I don't want it, let me go. I realised whatever I said and however much I resisted, they would not release me. So I played along and asked them to lower the power, as my bad memories were very recent and should be easily disposed of. They smiled and turned the power to the lowest setting. One nun said, the chair is gentle. The next thing I remembered was the colour black. Black hair. Black pupils. My black mouth. Nothing else, just solid, inflammable black, as if a full barrel of crude oil had been poured onto me.'

Abruptly she walked into the Main Temple. I heard the electric kettle boiling. I looked up at the moon utterly still, in contrast with the agitated water in the kettle.

She returned with two cups of jasmine tea.

'I finally woke up. I didn't know how long I'd been unconscious. I was in my bed, surrounded by all the nuns. The then Head Nun asked me how I felt. I was thirsty. She looked me in the eye and asked, do you remember why you came here? I said, what do you mean? She repeated the question and I gave the same answer. She smiled, and the other nuns smiled too. She said, that's good news, and now take some rest. When the door closed and I was left on my own, I cried for the first time in many years. There were so many tears I felt my eyes might dissolve. Real tears made of salt, not lies. I forced myself to remember every single bad memory. And there they all were, flooding back like the multiplying eyes on the hands of the Thousand Armed Avalokiteśvara. I swore to myself that the day I became Head Nun, I would destroy the Chair of Forgetfulness.'

'Why didn't you leave the nunnery?'

'I had nowhere to go. Just like you.' She stared hard into my face.

'Has it been destroyed?'

'I tried to destroy it. The chair is not the root of the problem, but instead our desire for such a thing. I made plans to burn it, but there's always a rotten apple in a place like this, and someone reported it to the Conservation Office. Ironically, the Office didn't even know it existed. They had no record of it. Without any official papers, they wouldn't acquire it for the museum, nor would they allow me to destroy it. I was ordered to lock it up in the room "pending further examination".'

'You could have destroyed it in secret. Why were you frightened of the Conservation Office?'

'I was frightened of the other nuns. There wouldn't be any nunnery without them.'

She paused and shrugged.

'Eventually, I locked it up. I knew I wasn't the one to blame. Once I had exiled the chair into obscurity, the nuns were overwhelmed by shame. It came as an epiphany. They must have realised the ritual they'd inflicted on themselves and others was the most shameful sin. Many of them left the nunnery, and the ones who stayed vowed the strictest secrecy. Years passed, and we forgot about the chair. Then one day a girl arrived at the gate who said she'd been raped by her father. She didn't come on her own. We could tell that there was a six-month-old heart throbbing inside her. We did everything to comfort her, look after her, reassure her, but she wanted to kill herself. We hid the knives, and she found the scissors. We hid the scissors, and she found the ropes. We hid the ropes, and she found the roof. We locked her up, and she started to starve herself. We kept telling her she was endangering her baby, but she took no notice. One of the old nuns couldn't bear it anymore and spilt the beans about the hidden chair. A few days later, I came back from town and found the girl sitting unconscious in the chair.

'I gathered nobody would help the girl and she must have broken into the room and tried to work the chair herself. Luckily the generator was still at the lowest setting, otherwise she and her baby would have been toast. When she came round two days later, she told me, "You only have two choices: save me from my past or let me die." Her face was drained white as a ghost, like the moon tonight. And her hands – her ten fingers were spread out like a raptor's claws, holding her belly. Somehow the baby survived. It was a miracle. I agreed to save her from her past on one condition: she mustn't hold her baby responsible for what had happened to her and she had to let the child live. She waited patiently for another three months. After I'd delivered the child to a foster parent, the girl spent another month on and off the chair. She forgot her father, her mother, even the existence of her child. She forgot everything about her childhood. She'd even forgotten her name – or at least so she told me. That was when I named her Quartz, a crystal that when electrified, tells the forward movement of time. I hoped that one day she would truly be free from her past.'

The Iron Nun ended her long answer to my simple question.

'Is Boss really Quartz's child?' I asked.

'No,' she replied unequivocally. 'She is just another orphan girl abandoned by some prostitute.'

She left me and went back to her room, where the quivering gaslight showed her profile against the postcard wall. I walked in and found her holding a postcard. She passed it to me.

I flipped it over and read the brief caption: 'Ben Bulben in County Sligo, seen from the north'. There was a sentence in English, handwritten in a rather shaky cursive: *Things fall apart; the centre cannot hold.* It must have been the Iron Nun's handwriting.

'It's a line from some famous Irish poet. That is the last postcard I sent to myself when I was a tour guide. I told myself when I received this postcard, I would leave my life behind. It's a beautiful view, isn't it?'

I nodded.

She sat on the folding chair sipping her tea, while she gestured with her hand for me to sit on her hard bed.

'Don't cry, young man.' The Iron Nun put her hand on my shoulder. 'Don't dwell on the past. It's a hovering ghost that's trying to suffocate us. Think about the future. That's all that matters.'

I took a deep breath and straightened my back. She gave me a knowing look and I remembered what I'd promised her. 'I didn't tell you what happened between me and the man with the Bentley. In fact, nothing happened. I barely met him. He threw me this out of his car window.'

I rummaged in my trousers and handed her the ten-pound note. Her face blossomed for a second, before she controlled herself.

'What does it mean?' I asked.

She turned it over, putting the Queen's face down. On the back a nurse tended two bandaged soldiers in a dark hospital ward.

'It's Florence Nightingale.'

'The famous nurse?'

'It means sickness and patience.'

The Iron Nun handed the banknote back to me and dimmed the gaslight. I wanted to leave her to her own devices, but my feet were heavy and tired. In the soft light, I felt her hand on my forehead like a nurse's, though it could have been a dream.

霜

Frost Descent

降

Quartz had disappeared from the nunnery. For two weeks I had failed to locate her in Diamond Hill. When not looking for her, I would sit under the banyan tree by the fenced-in concrete to watch the ants. They had created a vertical highway up the tree trunk, crawling up and down, touching each other's antennae and carrying scraps of food and raw materials to their underground nest. I was never a fan of insects, but ants annoyed me most. They move in such an orderly way and with such an obsessional group mentality: an unkillable species.

The ants were working as hard as if they too had been infected by the white powder. Would the banyan tree survive all the demolition around it? Was the Iron Nun right to say that social cleansing was the only way to remove the curse of drugs? Or was Boss right to assume that everything should die after serving its purpose?

There was a small shallow hole in the tree trunk, and whenever an ant stepped into it, I squashed the ant and left its tiny black carcass in the hole. I ate one to check what it tasted like. Citrusy, more lemon than orange, not what I expected at all.

Each day I woke up at the crack of dawn and walked

around the shanty town looking for any sign of Quartz. After lunch on my own in the nunnery, I headed out again until nightfall. The routine became an existential task, as if my life depended on it, as if it was a game of hide-and-seek, and the searching more important than the finding.

Quartz wasn't the only missing person. The Iron Nun hadn't spoken to me since our late-night conversation. There were rumours in the nunnery that she'd gone to visit a sister-temple in 佛山 (Foshan, Buddha Mountain). All the nuns had retreated into their private quarters and kept themselves to themselves. Sometimes they didn't even stick to the chanting routine. They skipped meals too, eating sparingly.

The north-westerly wind was biting hard, and brought nights cold enough to send shivers down my spine. Nowhere in my shed or bed was warm. I found a tin flask and used it as a hot water bottle. It leaked and wet my bed. In desperation, I boarded up the window, but drafts still whistled through the cracks in the thatched roof. Against nunnery regulations, I discreetly burned charcoal in a bucket just to help me sleep. One night a sudden wind dislodged some of my roof and a few reeds fell into the bucket. The nuns must have seen or smelt the smoke. Next morning they left me a note with four stern words on it: 無炭無火 (No charcoal, no fire).

More ants sleepwalked into my territory. Sometimes I pressed too hard and their corpses were too squashed to retrieve. Occasionally, if I was lucky, I could harvest more than ten ants in a minute, but when luck sided with them, I could only kill one or two. Of course, there were days when the ants went somewhere else. I could make an occupation of exterminating ants. How many ants would I need to fill up this small grave on the tree trunk?

But they would always find a way to survive.

In my search for Quartz, I noticed that many residents had already left the shanty town and whole houses had been boarded up or left vacant to be battered by the wintery elements. There was no sign of any schoolkids. All the hawkers had gone, except one selling piping hot congee. If only more people had decided to stay in Diamond Hill, many of the once-popular grocery shops wouldn't have had to close. Shopfronts had been vandalised, with one insult superimposed on another, written in pig's blood: 走狗 (traitors), 英國奴隸 (British slaves), 共產雞 (Communist whores), 香港馬伕 (Hong Kong pimps). I didn't know which group of the damned I belonged to. If I were to move to London with Boss and Audrey Hepburn, which of these would they call me?

I didn't know if Audrey Hepburn and Boss had been avoiding me or whether they had lost interest in me too. The morning that Quartz disappeared, I had rushed to their house to find their door triple-locked. I'd waited until sundown, but they never showed up. I went back the morning after and found Audrey Hepburn in a new outfit – a navy-blue blouse, dark tight jeans, and a stylish juniper-coloured jacket with sharp shoulder pads. She looked like a business executive dressed down for a stroll in the park. Unusually, she didn't invite me in, and from where I stood I could see her mountains of cardboard and shoe-boxes had all been cleared away. Her formerly messy room full of cobwebs, cockroaches and the occasional rat had been transformed into a bare shell, with only a bed, lamp and a metal clothes rack hung with a few monochrome T-shirts and skirts. It looked like a hospital ward, except that her house was just a flimsy tin shack. Even the kitchen had been pared down. The hazardous relay of electric extensions was gone. No wooden shelves, soup bowls, chopsticks or frying pans. No porn magazines or old newspapers. The gas-ring burner had been removed. The remaining canister at the far end of the room seemed out of place.

'Wow, you look so different,' Buddha said.

'I'm trying the latest look on the streets of London. What do you think?'

'You look good. Can I come in?' I asked, pushing my luck.

'Not now. Can't you see I'm busy packing up?' She looked impatient, though obviously there wasn't much left to pack.

'Where's all your stuff?'

'I'm doing an end-of-year spring clean. I'm only keeping a few nice things ready to be shipped to London. You're out of luck if you've come for the porn magazines. I found out they're collectables, so I sold the lot to a dirty bastard who travelled all the way from Causeway Bay to buy them. Men and porn are identical twins.'

'No, I don't want the magazines. I'm looking for Quartz.'
I put one hand on the door and another on her waist, trying
to sneak in.

'Sorry, handsome. My pussy is dry.'

I gave a quick glance up the stairs and saw that Boss's
room was padlocked.

'What are you hiding?'

'If you're looking for my girl, she's been invited to meet
油尖旺大佬 (the Big Brother in Yau Tsim Mong District).
She's getting promoted. My clever girl!'

'Shall I pop open a bottle of champagne?'

She gave me the middle finger.

'Can you let Boss know I'm looking for her?'

She nodded quarter-heartedly.

'Are you coming to London with us? You just need to say
yes and everything will be sorted by the company.'

I turned away and she kept shouting, '倫敦打嚟 你想唔想
接 (London's calling you. Will you answer?)'

Three days later I finally managed to pin Boss down in a
new store on the main street. I couldn't describe what kind
of a store it was, because it seemed to sell a vast array of
small random gifts – glass snow globes with Santa Claus
inside, a box of plastic hourglasses, a set of keyrings with
beer-bottle pendants, plastic toy cameras, fake Hello Kitty
and Mickey Mouse purses ... I spotted Boss at the back
of the store giving instructions to a group of middle-aged

deliverymen. Despite the cheap, incongruous gifts, the store was heaving with unfamiliar shoppers. Without browsing, people chose their items and queued with cash in hand, heading to the cashier, where five teenage boys lined up like factory workers helped customers put their purchases in nice boxes and carrier bags. I couldn't see a price tag on any of the products in the store, though people seemed to know the prices and paid the right amount without any need for change. They grabbed their well-wrapped gifts and dashed out. A seamless operation.

I played with one of the glass globes. The snow swirled, and as I fiddled with it, the plastic base fell apart. I picked up one of the beer-bottle key rings also filled with the white powder.

A teenage boy wearing a pair of aviators spotted me and whistled.

Alert as a lioness, Boss picked up the signal, stared at me, and waved her hand minimally.

I jostled my way through the busy shoppers to reach her. She was engrossed in a complicated logistical conversation with a van driver. Her eyes signed to me to step back, so I walked to the far side of the street. It had once been a thriving thoroughfare. Now there was only one grocery store left, selling necessities such as fresh vegetables, nylon bras, plastic stools, synthetic blankets, wooden ladders, charcoal and rat traps. The shopkeeper coughed, as she went on frantically wiping the surfaces covered with grey dust from the construction site.

After the delivery van had driven off, Boss approached me with her signature swagger, adjusting her groin in her oversized jeans, as if something big between her legs was slowing her down. She wore a tacky gold outfit – gold chain, gold rings, gold watch, gold earrings. Even her bra straps were gold.

'Stop staring you dirty bastard. It's the latest Gucci. I could charge you just for looking.'

She lit a Camel Mint with her gold lighter. 'Mum said you were looking for Quartz. Have you found her yet?'

'I wouldn't be here if I had.'

'You don't need to be so tetchy. I'm as concerned as you are.' She put a cigarette in my mouth. 'Hong Kong is a dangerous place these days, especially when an innocent, malnourished nun is freed from her Buddhist prison.'

'You're more concerned about your store than a missing person.' I handed the cigarette back to her.

'Sexy women are good at multi-tasking.' Her gold lighter made a sharp clink like a wind chime. She put the fag back in my mouth. 'Take it, it won't kill you. It'll calm you down.'

I'd never been a smoker, but I did like the white, minty smoke swirling around my head like a snake.

She took a new packet from her back pocket and handed it to me. 'Cigarettes are healthier than the white powder.'

'Your store seems to be attracting a different crowd. Selling it undercover isn't your usual style, is it?'

'Remind me which charity you work for. Don't roll your eyes. You nearly got me into trouble when you lied to the lawyer. He really believed what you said. I had to convince the Big Brother in Yau Tsim Mong District you're a harmless, insignificant ant, otherwise—'

'Otherwise what?'

'Nothing.' She fiddled with her hair, looking shifty. 'Anyway, back to business. Many of my customers are either dead or have already moved miles away to the fucking new town in Tin Shui Wai. The most sacred thing in my line of business is respect for borders and territory. I don't want to start a turf war with the rival gang in Wong Tai Sin. If I can't reach my customers, I can at least lure them to me. I've manipulated the goods a little bit and am selling them at a cut-throat price.'

'Manipulated?'

'Come on, Buddha, I'm not interested in the details. Mixing the stuff with other stuff. I learned this English word yesterday. *A-dul-te-rat-ed*. Is that right? Not *a-dul-tery*.' She gave me a dirty smile.

'How many people do you want to kill with your *adulterated* drugs?'

'Zero trouble and zero effort, Dad. A little bit of another illegal substance won't do anyone any harm. As long as they are inhaling and not injecting, everyone's happy. My lads have followed the professional recipe very carefully. If my stuff was below standard, it wouldn't have attracted all these loyal customers. Some have come all the way from the new town.'

She slid over and held my arm. Her perfume smelt of bubblegum.

'Dad, did you know I've been promoted?'

'Audrey Hepburn told me.'

'Once I get this massive cargo shifted, we can get our arses out of this shithole. London's calling, Buddha. I'm told a nice house is waiting for us in *E-a-ling*. Do you know where *E-a-ling* is? Apparently it is a very nice neighbourhood in zone 3 on the Tube, so about ten stops away from Leicester Square on the Piccadilly Line.'

She took out a *London A to Z* and showed me where South Ealing was. 'See the navy-blue Tube line there? Mum and I will work – I mean pretend to work – in the Golden Palace in Chinatown, just while we're getting settled. Once I'm used to London life, I'll venture into the gambling business. I've heard a lot of good things about it. It's so much more glamorous than drugs. I'll look like an undercover Bond girl in the London Triad.'

She adjusted her low-hung jeans and carefully put away the *London A to Z* like a pocket bible. 'Don't worry, Dad, I haven't forgotten you. You can work upstairs as the manager and you'll be properly paid in sterling. I reckon it will take me a year to get the Chinatown gang under control and another three or four years to get the gambling business shipshape. Once I've earned enough money, I will 金盆洗手

(wash my hands in a golden bowl and quit the Triad). After that, I'll sign up for a film-directing course.'

I finished the cigarette.

'Don't go all silent on me. I'm serious. Are you joining us? You know Diamond Hill has no future. Everything, I mean literally *everything* here, will be flattened. These streets, these dusty old shops, these smelly slums will all be gone. I know they are history, but definitely not the kind of history people like to remember. Life is so fucked up.'

She lit another cigarette for herself. 'You can't stay in the nunnery for ever. Even if the nuns tolerated you in the long term, which is unlikely, the nunnery will never be home to you.'

She pointed at the hills; the Main Temple's roof was just visible through the bare winter trees.

'Nothing is for ever, Buddha. Not even these fucking trees and hills. They've an expiry date like everything else. This city was once a tiny fishing port and look what's happened. A tax haven? Free port? Shoppers' paradise? Fuck them all! Hong Kong is just a big lawless casino for property developers. People are being tossed from one country to another like bargaining chips.'

She threw her cigarette to the ground.

'I know you're torn, but you have to remember Quartz is a nun. She'll never be your girlfriend or your wife. Now she's gone, you're free. I'm not forcing you to marry Mum, I just want you to play along. We'll move in together in a three-bedroom house in South Ealing so that we'll have our own space. Once Mum leaves Diamond Hill and is thousands of miles away from her controlling Iron Sister, she will feel better, more grounded and focused on starting a new life in Britain. She can finally act out her fantasy of being someone somewhere else. I know you've feelings for her and the gentle British air will bring magic to romance. I'm not going to wait for ever for you to make up your mind. We'll take off when the frost descends.'

I could sense that Boss's mind was already elsewhere. She blew a sharp, high-pitched whistle and her teenage herd responded with practised discipline. Whatever she was doing, she clearly had a talent for managing people in chaotic situations.

Boss's store closed down the following day. People on the streets said the stock had sold out in one day.

I didn't see Boss or Audrey Hepburn for days after its closure. Their tin shack was padlocked, and the two of them had evaporated.

It must have been a month after Quartz disappeared that I found myself sitting under the banyan tree, staring at the ants preparing for winter. Time seemed to have lost any sense for me, and my arms cast a long shadow on the concrete like the hands of a broken clock.

Would it make any difference to Diamond Hill or anything else if I were to spare this ant? It seemed to be hesitating, waving its antennae and licking its forearm, sensing danger ahead.

A new family with Audrey Hepburn? A manager in a Chinese supermarket? In London? If Boss could imagine it, she could pull it off.

A dog licked my hand, and the beggar was looking at me from the other side of the fence, standing on the white concrete like a malnourished cormorant.

'How did you get in there?'

He pointed to the far side, at the new path where the Chinese man had fallen. Someone had used wire-cutters to make a hole the size of a small child. I followed the dog rushing ahead and crawled through the fence.

The beggar gave me a hug. There was no whiff of rubbish, rotten fish or athlete's foot, but instead the smell of a river.

'石英! 石英! (Quartz! Quartz!)' He said, pointing to the far end of the fence where the concrete had created a perfectly levelled white horizon.

The dog ran off and the beggar followed her. I looked back at what survived of the shanty town and realised how decrepit it had grown. The winter sun shone harshly on the bare bones of the battered wooden houses and tin shacks. The only thing standing between the dying town and the brand-new concrete was the banyan tree. The tree wasn't an oasis but like a stranded monument – too old and too much trouble to get rid of.

The beggar came back and pulled my sleeves. We walked along the fence, skirting the ghostly, barely inhabited part of the town. I heard another dog barking from one of the remaining wooden houses. The beggar's dog stopped in her tracks and listened intently with cocked ears but did not respond.

The fence ran on and on until it hit a rock face. The dog slipped through an unlocked but well-maintained metal gate. The beggar signalled me to follow.

I trailed behind him through the dense rhododendrons. The light, humidity and temperature changed gradually, and we were inside a greenhouse. I could smell moist soil and a tropical fragrance, which I'd once smelt in Bangkok.

In front of me there were at least two hundred orchids of different species and colours, all neatly arranged on rows of three-tiered metal shelves. I was astounded by the firework display of vibrant pinks, whites, yellows and purples. But there was also a mass of other complicated colours on the petals. Lilacs with white freckles? Blue veiny pale yellow? The blossoms on their bare stems were carefully trained on thin bamboo sticks. I noticed that not a single plant touched any other. Each plant lived in isolation on its own small island of soil, sustained by only a few broad waxy leaves. I had not seen so many colours since arriving in Diamond Hill.

The dog barked and rushed back to her master.

An unfamiliar old man with a hunchback stepped inside

the greenhouse. Although he could barely raise his head high enough to greet us properly, he seemed to know who we were. He gave the dog an apple, and me and the beggar 菠蘿包 (a pineapple bun) each. The beggar retreated to a corner and devoured it hungrily. The old man's clothes looked respectable, but they were worn and old-fashioned. His heavy traditional Mao-style cotton jacket was frayed and full of holes, and he wore plastic slippers with thick white socks. His cloud of white hair and thick glasses were both greasy.

'後生仔 (Young man),' the old man said in Cantonese, with a strong Shanghainese accent, 'can you help me with something?'

'Of course.'

The old man led me out of the greenhouse and towards a nice brick house built in the colonial style with two floors, window shutters and balconies. It might have been a house in suburban London. It was a bit run down, but nonetheless the grandest house I'd seen in Diamond Hill.

'My grandfather built it with the help of a British architect from London. There were several colonial-style houses in this area. When Diamond Hill was our Hollywood, some of the film stars lived in mansions here with beautiful gardens and manicured lawns. It's all gone now. Nobody cares about the past here.'

The large front garden had been completely dug up. There were two flowerbeds – more like trenches, at least three feet deep, full of orchids, hundreds, even thousands, with their petals still radiant and their white twisted roots stuck in the yellow soil like baby fingers. A mass grave.

Sitting down in a wicker chair by the front door, the old man held on to his walking stick, panting as if his heart might stop any minute.

'What's wrong with these orchids? Do they have a disease?'

It took the old man another minute before he caught up with his breath.

'They're dead, young man. I'm burying them.'

'They don't look dead to me.' My eyes fixed on a particularly beautiful one at my feet, with dark purple flowers, the colour of dried blood. Each petal had a white maze-like webbing.

'I won't live much longer, but I don't want my orchids to fade because of my neglect. I'm too old to look after them, so I want my children to die with dignity.'

'Can't you employ someone to help keep the business running? Your orchids look rare and special.'

'This is – I beg your pardon – this was the biggest orchid library in Hong Kong. My grandfather passed it on to my father, and he passed it on to me. I handed it on to my only son.'

'Where is he?'

'Underground. He was one of the landslide victims. I gather you cut his hair.'

The old man's face was devoid of any emotion, but I could see the family resemblance.

The old man invited me to sit down beside him: '白頭人送黑頭人 (A white-haired person says farewell to a black-haired person). I thought that was the worst thing that could happen to any parent, but I was wrong. I lost a son, and everyone in Diamond Hill has lost their home. I might have been able to survive my bereavement, but it's heart-breaking to see the whole community being bereaved. I was in the Second World War and only narrowly escaped the grave, thanks to the kindness of a Japanese soldier. On the battlefield, I tripped over a dead man on Hoi Ha beach in Sai Kung and an enemy soldier pressed his gun to my forehead. I looked him in the eye and said, *Dōzo*.'

I waited for the old man to catch his breath, but he was lost in his thoughts.

'What did you say to the soldier?'

'*Dōzo*. 請隨便 (Please help yourself). I learned the phrase from my captain. He could have shot me on the spot. For some reason he didn't. He nodded and walked past. Whenever I told people this story, they thought it was bravery that saved me but I knew it was kindness, nothing else. All my life I've tried to be kind to my family, friends, neighbours, and my orchids. Obviously, it isn't enough just to be kind. Losing my son to a pile of mud was unbearable, but now I realise my son's death was just a prelude to losing my home, my ancestral home and business, to some people who don't even have the guts to show their faces.'

His breathing was too fast, too impatient, but I couldn't slow him down.

'After the mudslide, I received a letter from a lawyer offering me a large sum of money as compensation for my son's death. When I rang up and asked who had offered the payment, the lawyer wouldn't disclose their client's identity. What dirty tricks. They tried to shut me up and turn me into them by seducing me with money. I would never have thought we'd be wiped out by people without faces. Even the Japanese had the guts to look us in the eye when raising their rifles.'

He paused. He threw the walking stick away in a fit of anger.

'Young man, remember this: I'm not killed by old age or grief, but by the forces of anonymity.'

I kneeled and picked up the blood-orchid from the trench. The old man was right. Although the rare orchid still looked vibrant, the stem was weak and the leaves brown and shrivelled.

'They still want to live even though they're dying,' the old man said. 'They channel all their remaining energy to the flower hoping to make it seed. It's courageous but doomed.'

He got up from the chair. 'I've been waiting for you to help me out. Quartz said you'd come, but I wasn't convinced. I wondered how a young nun could meet a young man.'

He tried hard to get his footing and I hurried over to help him back into the chair.

'Do you know Quartz? Did she come here? When was the last time you saw her?'

The old man regained his focus and said, 'Every year on the Buddha's birthday I send the best orchid to the nunnery as an offering. I'd never met any of the nuns until a few days ago. It was *Ah Sir* who brought her here.'

The beggar reappeared, one hand rubbing his belly and the other empty, without a crumb of the pineapple bun to be seen. I gave him my bun and he disappeared with a big grin back into the greenhouse.

'*Ah Sir*? You mean the beggar?'

'Yes. He's never told me his name. When I started calling him *Ah Sir* years ago, he smiled and responded.'

'Did he bring Quartz here?'

'It must have been ten days ago. *Ah Sir* appeared with a young nun who looked thin and bony like a skeleton. She wouldn't speak to me at all. I reckoned she was in hiding and *Ah Sir* must have been feeding her, with whatever he managed to find in the streets. They would have struggled to find anything substantial these days as so many families have already left. The only nutritious food I had was a soy-sauce chicken I'd bought the night before to offer to 灶君 (the Kitchen God). It was the new moon, you know, time to worship the god. The two of them polished off the chicken at the speed of lightning and could hardly let go of the bones. That was quite a sight. I'd never seen a nun eating meat. Though she was skeletal, she had a beautiful face and petite mouth, as if she'd barely spoken or eaten anything since she was born.

'石英 (Quartz) is an unusual name for a nun, isn't it? I asked her the origin of her name, why she was with *Ah Sir*, what she wanted, and many other things. She wouldn't say a word and stayed as quiet as a frightened cat. When *Ah Sir* was leaving, she was desperate to leave with him. Luckily, he dragged her back into my house and forced her to stay. I told her *Ah Sir* would be back the next day, and she could stay in my house as long as she wanted. She shook her head and tears ran down her face. I did everything to make her stay, and it wasn't until I mentioned needing someone to help bury the orchids that she relented. She stared at me with those wide eyes of hers and asked, '葬蘭花 (Burying the orchids)?' When I explained why I needed to bury them, she agreed to help. I offered her my bed, but she insisted on sleeping on the floor with nothing underneath. No cushion, no pillow, not even a bamboo mat. It hurt to see her sleep there on the icy floor, using her bare hands as a pillow. What a stubborn, wounded soul.

'She stayed for three days. She dug up the two trenches and buried more than two-thirds of my orchids. I was amazed by how tough she was. You see how deep these trenches are. It was very physically demanding, and she was nothing but bones. She woke up at dawn each day, started working without breakfast, and only paused for water or a cup of jasmine tea. I offered her a pineapple bun for lunch, but she didn't touch any food during the day, so I bought her and *Ah Sir* a soy-sauce chicken every night and gave the bones to the dog. Even though I was burying the children my father and grandfather had raised for decades, the three days with Quartz and *Ah Sir* were the happiest since my son died.'

'Why did Quartz leave?'

'When I woke up on the third day, I couldn't find her in the house, the garden or the greenhouse. I was too frail to go to town and hoped *Ah Sir* would turn up. I waited and waited until sunset. It was a cold night with an icy wind, so I went to bed early. I left the lights on, the soy-sauce chicken on the kitchen table, and the door unlocked just in case they appeared. I fell deep asleep but was woken by Quartz in the middle of the night. The moon was out, and her naked face was like Quartz's face. What's happened? I asked. She held my hand and said, I'm sorry I have to leave. Where are you going? I asked. She said, I need to find my daughter. Where is she? I asked. Tin Shui Wai, she said. Where is Tin Shui Wai? I asked. The new town, she answered.'

Running out of breath, the old man coughed, and I rubbed his back to clear the rattle in his chest.

'She was just about to rush out of the house when I got

up and gave her some money. She refused it. I said it was
her wages and a reward for her kindness in helping me bury
the orchids. I wouldn't have been able to do it without her.
She said the work was unfinished, so she wouldn't touch
the money, shaking her head like a tree resisting a storm.
She hurried away but then I heard her footsteps stop outside. When I managed to find my walking stick and venture
out, I saw her looking up at the sky, as if frozen in the bright
moonlight. She was crying but smiling. They were happy
tears, I told myself. I handed the money to her again and
said, Little Mouth, you'll need it; the moon wants you to
have it. She smiled and kissed my forehead. She said a man
called Buddha would come and help me finish the work.
She took the money and disappeared. That was the last I
saw of her. I hadn't a clue what she was talking about until
you showed up. You are Buddha?'

I nodded.

'You should put the orchid down, Buddha. It's done for,'
the old man said, and the orchid dropped to the ground.
'人有悲歡離合 月有陰晴圓缺 (Human beings have happi-
ness, sadness, separation, and reunion. The Moon can be
clouded, sunny, full, and eclipsed). Please help me finish
burying them.'

He took hold of the stick, and with fierce determination
walked shakily into the greenhouse.

I looked at the colourful orchids in their mass grave.
Some of the reds screamed at me like tongues and genitals.

I was determined to help the old man, but desperate to set off for the new town to find Quartz as soon as I could.

My mind went blank.

'Can you bring the chair over here? If you don't mind fetching the orchids, I'd like to throw them into the grave.'

It took us more than three hours to shift all the orchids. By then the old man was dead tired and the sun was low on the horizon. He went inside and took a nap while I shovelled the earth into the graves to cover the flowers. The crumbly yellow soil got into my sleeves, inside my shoes, under my trousers, and into my eyes, nose and mouth, as if I was either digging myself out of the grave or burying myself inside it – I didn't know which.

By the time I had carefully flattened the graves with the rake and made sure that the ground was level for the old man's safe passage, the sun had partly disappeared over the horizon. He emerged in a freshly laundered black suit, white shirt, black tie and hat. If he had been wearing a pair of sunglasses, he would have looked perfect as a Hollywood film star or an Italian mafioso.

The day's labour had made his feet less steady. He struggled down the steps by the front door. 'It's just my old bones complaining about winter. Can you fetch the tray on the kitchen table for me?'

There was a fine mix of Chinese and British décor in his house: parquet wooden floors, lots of faded wallpaper, soft leather sofas and armchairs, nice lampshades, and hanging scrolls of Chinese paintings of mountains and rivers. There was also a poignant smell of old age: talcum powder, White Flower Oil, mothballs, musky clothes, black tea, and faded winter chrysanthemums. He must have had a cleaner, as the house was immaculate. On the kitchen table, I found a tray with three glasses of rice wine in red offering cups, six incense sticks, two candles, a lighter, and four oranges carefully arranged on a plate.

The sky had darkened much quicker than I expected. The old man had turned on the garden lights outside. He lit the two candles and asked me to place them by the graves, before handing me the incense sticks. While he prayed for the safe passage of his orchids to the underworld, I prayed for Quartz.

'我而家就心安理得 (Now I've peace of mind),' the old man said, holding on to my arm. His hand was icy. 'Why don't you come in and have dinner with me?'

'I must go and look for Quartz.'

'You won't be able to find her in the dark. Come on, Buddha, have a shower and change your clothes. I ordered 金針雲耳蒸雞 (Steamed chicken with golden pins and cloud ears) and 芥蘭 (Gai lan, or Chinese broccoli) from a good restaurant. I'll put the rice on.'

I did as he said, and when I appeared at the dinner table wearing his son's clothes, his face brightened.

'Do you believe in second chances, Buddha?' The old man gave me a bowl of fragrant rice.

'Do you mean a second life after this one?'

'Life or chance, it's the same thing. Lately, I've been pre-occupied by the idea of once-ness, the sense that because we only have one go in this life, there is an unbearable pressure to make good use of it. So we often mess it up. What if there's a special dispensation and we're allowed to have a second chance, not as a form of redemption, but like the start of a new cycle? What do you think?' He gave himself a bird's portion of rice.

'It sounds like Buddhism to me,' I said, helping him sit down.

'Not necessarily. One can reincarnate outside the confines of religion.'

I smiled. 'I'm one of those cowards who learn a foreign language but don't have the courage to live abroad.'

The old man smiled, offered me a glass of rice wine, and replied, 'Sometimes, nowhere is more foreign than home.'

'You mean Diamond Hill?'

'I mean Hong Kong, now.'

'What about the Handover? It's ten years away. Should we be frightened?'

'I'm too old to be frightened of the Motherland. After all, we are all Chinese, whatever that means. If my son were still alive, perhaps my feelings would be different.'

He poured me another glass of rice wine. I politely refused.

'Would you have asked your son to leave Hong Kong and start a new life somewhere else like Australia or Canada?'

'Who knows?' He finished his dinner, though he'd

hardly eaten. 'My late wife spoke fondly of New Zealand, though we never visited the country. She liked the idea of mountains full of sheep and had a fantasy about buying a farm there. I used to call her a dreamy sceptic and she called me a sceptical dreamer. All immigrants are dreamers, I suppose, and nearly everyone in Hong Kong is an immigrant one way or another. When I was ten my father fled Mainland China during the 1911 Revolution, the same year my only brother died of chickenpox. We were supposed to embark on a boat to Taipei, but at the last minute my father changed his mind and we boarded the ferry to Hong Kong. You could argue his decision completely changed the course of my life, but it would also have changed drastically if we had taken the boat to Taipei.'

'You'd be speaking Mandarin, not Cantonese, if you'd gone to Taipei.'

'That's true. After the Revolution, Sun Yat-sen and the other revolutionary leaders got around the table to decide which language should be the official language of the new China. Did you know Cantonese only lost to Mandarin by one vote? Imagine if Cantonese had won. Everyone in China would now be speaking Cantonese.'

'I'm not sure the government would agree with your proposition.'

'Which government are you talking about? Hong Kong, the British, or the Chinese?'

'None of them would like the idea.'

'You're probably right. Anything that disrupts the slogan of 安定繁榮 (Stability and Prosperity) is perceived as hazardous to the people and government.'

I smiled. The old man raised his glass and I poured him more wine. He emptied it in one mouthful.

'My son didn't like me babbling on about politics in public. It's good to get it all off one's chest from time to time,' he said, rummaging in his pocket and handing me a 金牛 (Golden Cow, or HKD $1,000). 'You shake your head like Quartz did.' He stood up and shoved the money into my shirt pocket.

'It's too much. I can't possibly take it,' I said, giving the Golden Cow back.

'Trust me, you'll need the money. Take a taxi to the new town first thing tomorrow and look for Quartz.' He said good night and thanked me for the day's work.

As he walked out of the room, he turned back, straightened his hunchback as much as he could, and bowed to me. He then smiled and said, '啲錢擺唔到入棺材 (There's no point keeping money in my coffin).'

I barely got any sleep on the old man's sofa. Instead of waiting for daybreak, I decided to get up and head for the new town, but first I tiptoed into his bedroom to see if he was awake. He looked fast asleep, though I couldn't hear any breathing. I panicked and reached out to touch his shoulder, but then he took a long, slow, chesty breath. I departed without saying goodbye.

I left the shanty town, following the newly paved concrete road until it joined Hammer Hill Road. It must have been about four in the morning and the sodium street lamps felt sharper and yellower in the cutting wind. I tried to hail a taxi, but they all swooshed past as if I didn't exist. I continued walking down Hammer Hill Road, which merged into Choi Hung Road, a dual carriageway which looked dangerous to cross. I tried to cross it anyway but was greeted by the blare of horns. There were at least four intercrossing flyovers in different directions. It was equally confusing at ground level where I was surrounded by a baffling, convoluted web of lanes, traffic lights and roundabouts. Skyscrapers shot up everywhere.

Unable to cross the dual carriageway, I walked back up Hammer Hill Road, holding my arm out and hoping a taxi would stop.

One driver pulled over and wound down his window.

'With your weird old-fashioned clothes and bald head, at this godawful hour I thought you were one of the dead.'

'Can you take me to Tin Shui Wai, the new town?'

'Why on earth do you want to go there? It's a big construction site, and there won't be a living soul there at night.'

'Can you take me there?' I showed him the money. 'I'll give you a good tip.'

'Okay, jump in.'

The outside world looked completely different from inside the taxi, as the roads flowed into bridges and bridges into tunnels. The city had changed so much, so fast.

The radio news channel was broadcasting continuous coverage of Black Monday. The newsreader in her deadpan voice announced, 'Yesterday morning, the Heng Sang Index, influenced by the weakening Nasdaq, fell 120 points. By noon, it dropped 235 points and finally closed 420 points down, losing more than 10 per cent of its entire value. The crash has spread all around the world, with the FTSE 100 down 11 per cent and the Dow Jones down 22.6 per cent, wiping out an estimated $500 billion. It is anticipated that losses will deepen when the Sydney Stock Exchange and New Zealand Stock Exchange open in a few hours' time. Analysts described yesterday as Black Monday, and the extent of the crash, they fear, may be as drastic as the Stock Market Crash of 1929. There are signs that the Hong Kong Exchanges and Clearing Limited may suspend trading today. Further confirmation will be announced as soon as—'

'屌你老母冚家鏟乜屎嘢都輸撚晒 (You motherfucker, I wish all your family were dead. Lots of people have lost everything)!' The taxi driver switched to the popular music channel. 'Sorry, I'm not cursing you. I'm just fed up to the back teeth with the markets. It's like the end of the world.'

'Is Ronald Reagan dead?'

'No. Why?'

'I thought that was the cause of Black Monday.'

'The analysts are blaming the trade deficit. The dollar is dropping down a bottomless pit and interest rates are soaring. No wonder the stock prices are nosediving.'

'Have you lost a lot of money?'

'What do you think? Everyone loses when the curve goes down. This looks like the biggest crash in my lifetime.'

I thought we were up on a bridge, but within seconds we glided down into a tunnel, with no cars in front of us.

'I don't even know the number of zeros in $500 billion.' I said, to make conversation.

He laughed. 'Me neither. You're a new boy, aren't you? I'm only a small fish in the pond and in it for the long game. Ironically, I bought quite a lot of shares at cut-throat prices yesterday just before the market closed. It won't flatline for long, I bet.'

I lost interest. He babbled on and gave me a series of amateurish, overexcited predictions about the bear market maintaining its position for the next few months, before the return of a bull market. The taxi glided along an empty flyover. The lights bleached all colour from the life of the city. The moon hung low over the harbour like a spaceship. A dozen or so cargo ships were unloading. I felt sleepy and everything went in and out of focus. I started counting the lights of ships in Victoria Harbour ... yellow ones, orange ones ...

I dozed off, but my window was rolled down automatically, and a chilly tree-scented wind blew into the taxi.

'Sorry to wake you.'

'What's all that construction over there in the harbour for?'

'你喺外國返嚟 (Have you been abroad)? They're building the Tsing Ma Bridge and the new airport on Lantau Island for the Handover.'

'What will happen to Kai Tak Airport?'

'It will be ancient history in ten years' time. Anyway, I woke you up as there are roadworks on the main road, so I have to take this detour. A lot of my colleagues say this road is haunted.'

He closed my window again and I could hear a familiar voice singing on the radio.

'Is it 張國榮 (Leslie Cheung)? Can you turn the volume up?' I asked.

The Japanese-sounding melody gave way to a single guitar. Just a few simple chords and his refined, unsentimental voice. The taxi driver turned the volume higher and started singing along:

I believe in my sore hands not fate

I've no strength left to stop the contradiction

My heart is tired and my eyes blurry you know

Hush, night is that you echo

'It's 有誰共鳴 ('Echo, Is That You'), his greatest hit last year. You don't know it? It's my absolute favourite.' The taxi driver tapped the mournful rhythm on the steering wheel.

The only echo I could hear was of Leslie Cheung's voice trapped inside the cab windows, while outside the vicious wind was punishing the trees. Was it raining, or could I hear the sea?

'I nearly didn't stop for you in Diamond Hill. With your shaved head, you looked like a nun. I was wondering why on earth a nun would be walking on her own in the middle of the night. I saw in my rear-view mirror that you were a man, and a chill ran down my spine. Your old-world clothes are creepy. You looked as if you'd just walked out of some period drama set in the Qing dynasty.'

The song had nearly ended, and the DJ faded it out. The next was a disco number and the driver turned the volume down.

'It's particularly spooky here because of Shek Kong Barracks nearby. A lot of British soldiers died there during the Japanese occupation. Some of my colleagues have seen British soldiers walking along here with missing limbs and Japanese soldiers lying in the middle of the road with their guts hanging out. There's also a little boy who begs by the roadside. People say he runs into the traffic and gets crushed on windscreens. When the driver stops the car, there is a pool of blood and the boy is nowhere to be seen. People drive off, but after a time they see the boy sitting in their car, one hand pointing at his head, which has a big gunshot wound, and the other holding a hand grenade.'

'Is the barracks still in use?'

'I think so, though I don't know what will happen to the Gurkha soldiers when the Chinese Army takes over in 1997.'

The taxi driver calmed down and asked, 'Why're you going to Tin Shui Wai in the middle of the night?'

'I'm looking for a friend who has moved to the new town.'

'Do you have an address? I'm telling you the place is just a massive construction site.'

'Can you drive around the area so I can look for her?'

'You mean like a chauffeur? I'll have to charge you extra.'

'That's fine.'

The radio was playing some classic Cantonese pop songs of the 1970s and the taxi driver turned the volume up. To kill time, I rolled the window up and down. The poorly lit road was now a series of bottleneck turns and it felt we were finally descending after a long climb. I understood why the driver thought this road was haunted. The dark hills looked restless, as if the wind had brought something else to the woods. I kept my eyes peeled, looking out for any sign of the limbless and the disembowelled, but turn after turn all I could see were rocks and trees and the village lights scattered down below. Secretly, I would have liked to meet the begging boy. Why would he repeat dying just to catch the attention of some random night driver?

'Where are we?'

'Tin Shui Wai.'

'I don't see any high-rise buildings.'

He pointed his cigarette at the dark silhouettes of high-rise structures, caged inside bamboo scaffolding. 'I told you. They're still under construction. Can't you see the big slogan there? They expect to complete in nine months and the estate will house 270,000 people.'

'These buildings look very cramped.'

'They're not going to be luxury apartments like the ones being built in Diamond Hill. Tin Shui Wai hasn't got the glamour of the Hollywood of the Orient. Haven't you heard of high-density "barrier-style" housing? They're not the free-standing posh skyscrapers like you see on Hong Kong Island, but like concrete cliffs that go on for ever. This area is very close to the Chinese border. The government must be preparing for immigrants coming over from the Mainland after the Handover.'

Tossing the cigarette butt away, he said, 'It's always chillier up here in the north near the Shenzhen border.'

The wind was howling from the north. I could hear it whistle through the skeletal high-rises, rattling the plastic sheets and making the bamboo scaffolding creak.

'How far are we from the border?' I asked.

'About a twenty-minute drive if there's no traffic. Why?'

'I wonder if my friend has crossed the border.'

'你朋友做雞呀 (Is your friend a whore)?'

'No, she's a nun.'

He caught my eyes in the rear-view mirror, 'I can see you're not joking. Is she from the nunnery in Diamond Hill? Why would she be in this godforsaken place in the dead of night?'

'That's what I'm trying to find out. Can you drive me around the nearby villages?'

'Villages?' He laughed. 'You'll be lucky to find one here.'

He drove slowly, stopping at junctions where there were makeshift tents built by homeless people, but the tents were empty. He called the place a ghost town, but I couldn't see even the shadow of a ghost.

After driving around for ten minutes, we saw some temporary housing fenced off from the rest of the high-rise development. They were box-like prefabs, all neatly lined up in a grid, like army barracks or refugee camps. Each prefab had an outside light by the front door and each door a three-digit number and a letter of the alphabet: 265a, 266b. It felt soulless and punitive.

I rolled down the window and heard people speaking Vietnamese.

'These boat people are so annoying. I know their country persecuted them because they're Chinese and we should give them a hand, but Hong Kong is smaller than a piece of tofu. I've nothing against immigrants – my father and mother were immigrants from the Mainland – but don't you think the city is already overloaded? There's barely space for anyone to breathe.'

The taxi driver stopped moaning and continued driving around the fringes of the temporary housing. The blinds were down, and most people must have been asleep. Perhaps the noodle-shop owner was living in one of these prefabs.

Out of nowhere we saw a few rowdy people sitting outside drinking beer and gathering around open fires. We stopped and I asked if they had seen a nun anywhere, but they misunderstood me, thinking that 'nun' was innuendo for 'whore'. A teenage girl with fishnet tights was sitting on a man's lap. The taxi driver drove us off before I had the chance to explain. They looked wilder and worldlier than Boss's gang.

'I don't think your nun friend is likely to be sauntering around here enjoying the scenery,' he said, and suggested that we drove back towards the construction site where there were a few makeshift tents we hadn't investigated.

When the taxi came close to a pedestrian bridge, I saw a girl in a red baseball cap and loose tracksuit kneeling next to a young homeless man, who was handing her some cash. She shoved something inside the man's pocket, and he disappeared into the bushes.

I remembered that baseball cap.

I rushed out of the taxi. The girl saw me and ran up the stairs. The taxi driver jumped out of the car and crossed the road.

'Stop, Boss, it's me!'

I couldn't keep up with her. She had already crossed the

bridge and was scampering down the stairs on the far side, like a young deer being hunted.

Then I saw her tumble down the stairs, as if she'd been shot or was falling off a cliff.

'Don't worry, I've got her!' I heard a man shouting.

The stairs were steeper than I'd thought. From high above the bridge, I could see the taxi driver at the bottom holding Boss in his arms. The red baseball cap had fallen and landed on the roadside. The driver was rubbing his hands on the girl's bald head. It was Quartz, wearing Boss's signature outfit.

'Are you okay? Did you hurt yourself?' I tried to hold her in my arms, but she wouldn't let me near her.

'She was very lucky,' the taxi driver said. 'I was going to catch her and was just a few feet away when she tripped. I don't think she's hurt.'

Quartz pushed him away.

There were a dozen plastic beer-bottle keyrings scattered around the staircase. One or two were broken and the white powder had spilled everywhere. She ran to the roadside, frantically looking for her baseball cap.

'I've never seen a nun selling the white powder before. This is so fucked up,' the taxi driver said, looking half-stunned, half-amused.

I started picking up the keyrings and putting them in my pockets. Quartz came back, hiding her face under the cap.

She swore at me. 'What the fuck are you doing? These keyrings are mine.'

'They're not fucking yours!'

She tried to get her hands on them, but I clenched my fists. The taxi driver restrained her.

A magpie flew over us and perched on the railings of the bridge looking at me curiously. Its husky call was interrupted by the noise of another taxi zooming past.

The sun must have risen, but the clouds were so thick and low that they blocked the light.

'You both need to calm down. It's getting brighter and there'll soon be lots of people around.' He loosened his hold on Quartz.

'Let's go,' I said.

'Don't boss me around. You do not own me. I am going nowhere with you.'

'What are you doing here?'

She laughed sarcastically.

'Will you come back to Diamond Hill with me?'

'I'm not leaving till I've sold all my keyrings.'

'You have already. I've bought them all.'

She laughed again. This time more alarmingly, like Boss's laugh.

'How much do they cost?'

'Five hundred dollars.'

'How much is the return fare to Diamond Hill?' I asked the taxi driver.

'I'm not sure I want drugs in my car. I don't want any hassle.'

'Is five hundred dollars enough?'

'Hmm . . . I don't like to get involved in . . .'

I handed him the $1,000 banknote and said, 'I will let you both split it.'

The taxi driver took it without further complaint.

'I'm giving you a free ride, Quartz. You need to get back to base and restock anyway,' I said, and crossed the road to head back to the taxi.

Nobody spoke. When the driver turned on the radio, the newsreader had just started the six o'clock news and was reporting the shock crash of the Sydney Stock Market. Quartz covered her ears with both hands. The taxi driver tuned the radio to the classical music channel. A bland piano melody filled the car.

Quartz had become a living ghost; her gaunt face was weighed down by black bags under her eyes, as if she hadn't slept properly for days. She had stopped shaving her head and couldn't hide the stubbly hair under Boss's baseball cap. She hadn't lost weight, though hadn't gained any either. Her battered trainers suggested that she must have done a lot of walking. Judging from the smell of deep-fried food coming from her tracksuit, she must have been eating more than her daily twenty-three drops of white dew.

Her head leant feebly against the car window, her legs

were bunched up in a knot, and her empty hands seemed to be looking for something solid to hold on to. Every few seconds, her body shivered involuntarily, but when I tried to comfort her she shrank away and refused to be touched. She clenched her jaw trying to control her fits, and yet the harder she tried, the more erratic the seizures became. When she calmed down at last, she turned her head not to me, but to the jacket pockets where I had put the keyrings with the white powder. She knew I knew she was defence-less without a dose of heroin.

I asked the taxi driver to stop the car near the nunnery. He gave me change of $500, which I handed to Quartz. She folded the banknote carefully into a small rectangle and hid it in her bra, as so many addicts do.

I thanked the driver and wished him good luck with his investments. 'It's all in the lap of the gods.' He closed the window and did a sharp U-turn, before disappearing round the bend of the road.

Quartz ran up the hill and I chased after her. She got a stitch after less than a minute, bent down and fought to regain her breath.

'You obviously wanted me to look for you in Tin Shui Wai. Otherwise you wouldn't have told the orchid man where you were going.'

'Did you help him bury the orchids?'

'They had a proper burial and have probably been reincarnated as something or someone else by now.'

She smiled. There was still tenderness in her face.

Instead of taking the left turn to the nunnery, she turned right down the fenced concrete path towards the shanty town. It must have been about seven in the morning, but the planes had already started landing. I found it unimaginable that Kai Tak would soon vanish, and Diamond Hill be freed from the curse of sky engines.

The morning air was bitterly cold, and Quartz's thin tracksuit couldn't really have kept her warm. I handed her my jumper, the one she'd given me when she took me to feed the bats in the cave. She refused it. The northern wind hadn't stopped weeds spreading around the edges of the concrete path. Dandelions festooned in the narrow gaps. Some had flowered and some had finished seeding.

I tried hard to keep the conversation going but she blanked me. The silence was painful.

'Why did you leave the nunnery?'

'The safety of the nunnery is a mirage. If I really care about the suffering of others, I have to open my eyes and experience the world first hand. I can't just stand aside like you while everything is being torn down.'

'Did Boss ask you to sell drugs for her?'

'No, I volunteered. She wouldn't come back to the nunnery with me, so I'm helping her out and staying at her house. After all these years, I'm finally getting to know her.'

'You're a nun—'

'I've quit and I'm making a living like other people in

Diamond Hill. Of course, you've forgotten what work is.'

'You must be aware that selling drugs only adds to the suffering of others – and your own.'

I grabbed her by the arms, forcing her to confront her shaky hands by holding them out in front of her. Her arms were full of needle marks.

She flung me off, turned away and chortled. 'We can't escape suffering, so we might as well get on with it.'

'Why are you torturing yourself like this? Is it your way of getting closer to Boss?'

Through the fence, a bulldozer drove into a row of tin shacks and wooden houses. Two pigeons darted up into the air and landed on a lamppost.

'That's you, a bulldozer.'

'What?'

'That's your wife.' She pointed at the wooden house smashed by the blade of the bulldozer. 'And that's your little boy.' The small tin shack from the top of the wooden house fell under the wide tracks.

She remained motionless. All I could hear was a mechanical beeping from the construction site.

'You lied to me. You didn't just leave Hong Kong because you were ashamed of losing the family business. It was because you ruined your wife's life and killed your own son.'

'If that's what the Iron Nun told you, it's not true. My wife had a miscarriage.'

'It wasn't just a miscarriage, was it?'

'I told you, she had a miscarriage. I ruined my father's business and she got depressed. She was upset that we had to start again from scratch. It was very tough for her. She was born with a silver spoon in her mouth.'

'貧富患難 同床共枕 (For richer, for poorer, in sickness and in health, you shared the same bed and pillows with her).'

'You're right. We did have a good show for a year or two when the business was booming. She loved decorating our apartment in Causeway Bay and filled the rooms with orchids and lilies. You might find it hard to imagine, but we had Italian sofas and a gleaming rosewood table from London. She adored music and I bought her a little Steinway and found her one of the best piano teachers around. But when the money ran out, we lost everything.'

'That's tough, but in a good marriage people stick together through thick and thin.'

'You don't know her. She had her own manservant until the age of thirteen. She had never stepped into a kitchen or even touched a wok in her life until we were married. Me losing the business was a perfect excuse for her to leave me. Our marriage was never—'

'You're wrong. 一日夫妻百日恩 (One day of marriage is a hundred days of intimacy). Your wife must have loved you, otherwise she wouldn't have carried your baby.'

I bit my lip. The bulldozer left a trail of debris – dining tables, crushed wardrobes, bed frames.

'You say she had a miscarriage. What caused it?'

'She was depressed and didn't eat enough for herself, let alone the baby.'

Quartz wiped her cheeks. 'She must have really hated you to sacrifice her own child. Where were you when she most needed you?'

'We were already separated when that happened.'

'You think that lets you off the hook?'

'My parents sided with her and I rented a single room in Mong Kok and left her the apartment in Causeway Bay. It was worth quite a lot of money. They tried to look after her, but she distanced herself from everybody. A month later when they found their grandchild was gone, they cut me off and refused to see me again. I lost everything overnight and had nowhere to go. A friend said that before the creditors came, I should 早啲着草 (pick up the grass sandals and flee Hong Kong as soon as possible). He knew a businessman who had relocated a garment factory to the outskirts of Bangkok. The next day, I travelled across the South China Sea on a cargo ship full of plastic flowers.'

'How could you have left your wife when she'd just lost her baby, *your* baby?'

'She blamed me for the miscarriage and for being a total failure in business. She didn't want to see me again. Night and day I tried reaching out to her, but she bolted the door and wouldn't answer my calls. In the end, her lawyer threatened me with a court order and stopped me contacting her.'

'So, you gave up just like that? She was bereaved and must have been in a state of real shock. And you abandoned her.'

I lowered my head. The dandelion between my feet had lost its parachute.

'And your beautiful new life in Bangkok, why did that go wrong?'

'That was my own fault. I got an administrative job in the garment factory and was soon bored out of my mind. I spent my salary on women and brandy. I couldn't sleep and needed to kill time. It kept ticking in my brain like a bomb. Sometimes when I was drunk, I passed out on the streets and got robbed. I often didn't turn up to work. Within three months I'd lost my job. After that, I couldn't pay rent. All my friends gave up on me. The landlord said I could stay on if I helped him shift the white powder on the streets. I needed a roof over my head and he gave me some of his best stuff to take the edge off the pain. It stopped the ticking bomb like magic, but the magic soon wore off, and I needed a stronger dose. You can guess the rest.'

'You mean you became a drug dealer like Boss.'

'You overestimate me. I was at the bottom of the food chain. Anyway, I'd no chance of earning a living once I'd touched the white powder. A serious dealer never takes the goods he sells. Boss is a good example and she shouldn't have let you take drugs—'

Quartz turned towards me and sneered. 'You're so naive. It was my own decision; it had nothing to do with Boss.'

'If Boss really cared about you, she would have stopped you from the outset.'

'So, did Daishi stop *you* the first time he met you?'

'No ... but he did in the end, after I'd spent months on my own on the streets.'

'You should have known that starting is always easier than finishing. I'm surprised you didn't die on the streets in Thailand.' Quartz squeezed her hands through the fence and placed her palms together as if she was praying.

'Bangkok was a hospitable place. Monks always fed me. When people saw the monks feeding me, they started feeding me too. There was no need for shelter in the tropical night, except when it rained torrentially. Anyway, most people didn't want to refuse a ghost fostered by the monks and let me stay in their front porch for the odd night. If that failed, I had trees. And if that failed, I had temples.'

'What did you do when you were living on the streets?'

'I've no idea. Perhaps I wanted to disappear, to be a nobody. Hong Kong was the last place on earth I wanted to see again. I really thought the white powder would kill me before I had time to sort my life out. It would have been an easy exit.'

'Did you try reaching out to your parents?'

'No.'

'Are they still living in Hong Kong?'

I didn't say a word.

'Don't you want to see them again? They must be getting old. After all, you're their son and 血濃於水 (blood is thicker than water).'

'They must be in their late eighties by now, and I wonder if they're still alive. They thought I was worse than trash. I sent them letters when I first arrived in Bangkok but they never replied. I'd brought too much shame to the family. It must have been a relief to them that I'd disappeared and let them off the hook. Even if they are still alive, what good news can I tell them? That I live in a decrepit nunnery with no job and no prospects? It will only add more sadness to their old bones.'

Quartz hesitated, and finally asked, 'How about your wife? Where is she? Did she get remarried?'

'I don't know. We were never divorced.'

Quartz separated her palms and clenched her hands into fists too big to pass through the fence.

'Does she know you are back in Hong Kong?'

'I imagine that would be the last thing she wants to know.'

'So, you are still married to her. Do you miss her?'

'We should never have got married in the first place. We came from different worlds. As the saying goes: 我哋竹門對木門 (my bamboo door is inferior to her wooden door).'

Quartz smiled disparagingly.

'Do you ever think about your boy?'

'I don't know. Not often.'

'You could have been a father if it wasn't for your cow-ardice and carelessness. You've got blood on your hands.'

'What are you banging on about? He was never born.'

'You talk about your own son as if he was a lifeless stone. Don't you know that a six-month-old foetus has eyelashes, nails and teeth? They can even suck their thumb and yawn.'

'What do you want from me? Yes, I neglected my wife and lost my boy. But what's done cannot be undone. You think I don't carry an anchor of shame round my neck every day? You reckon it was easy for me to set foot in this damn city again?'

'You can still atone for your sins and forgive yourself. You could still look after your parents if they're alive ... and try to be a proper husband to your wife a second time. You need to take responsibility for what you have done and make peace with yourself.'

I laughed. 'Don't give me lessons on how to be a decent human being. You sat on the Chair of Forgetfulness when you were pregnant. Don't tell me you don't remember. Isn't that what this is really about?'

Quartz turned away abruptly, as if stung.

'We all have things we try to erase,' I said, and reached out to touch her shoulder but didn't dare to.

Boss stood near the banyan tree. The second she caught my eye, she walked towards me with her boyish prance, constantly adjusting her gold chain, gold bra straps, floppy low-hanging jeans. She nodded coolly at Quartz and put her arm around her. In response, Quartz rested her head on the teenager's shoulder. They ignored me and walked off. I followed them, not knowing what else I could do. By the banyan tree, Boss kissed Quartz on both cheeks and handed her some drugs and fresh needles. Then they said goodbye to each other. Quartz treated me as if I didn't exist.

I didn't go after Quartz and snatch the drugs from her. She would just have gone back for more. When I was an addict, the more resistance I'd encountered, the more determined I became.

'You look tense, Buddha. Did Quartz upset you? Or did *you* upset her?'

I ignored her.

'I know you're angry with me, Dad. To be honest, I didn't kidnap Quartz and force her to do anything. She came to me saying she wanted a job. She knows perfectly well what I do for a living. I think she must have run away from the nunnery because she'd really had enough of it. You should have seen the state of her when she came to see me. If I hadn't looked after her, she would have starved to death.'

'How on earth can you say you're looking after her when you're supplying her with drugs? You're killing her.'

'Come on. Everyone takes the stuff here. You took it and you're okay. She just wants to be free, to be an independent woman like me.'

'Don't fool yourself. You've made her into one of your

slaves. And you're no different, you are a slave too, living off the Triad like a flea.'

'What's wrong with getting a little bit of help?' She popped a bubblegum in her mouth and started chewing angrily. 'Let me tell you the truth, Buddha. I'm gifted, and I can see into the future. There it is right in front of us, across this fence, on the bare grey concrete. What are people most frightened of? Independence. Look, the new land is full of possibilities. All that emptiness gives people space to contemplate and *that* is dangerous. The government doesn't want us to think. That's why they build these jam-packed high-rises like a dam to keep back the flood.'

'What a load of rubbish.' I turned towards her and saw that Boss was right. The white concrete had turned grey. There were two pigeons pecking at the battered dandelions.

She took the chewing gum out of her mouth, moulded it with her fingers, and stuffed it into the small hole in the banyan tree. The ants quickly detected the sugary saliva and swarmed all over it.

'I know you've spent hours playing with that hole, like a child. What's it feel like now it's gone?' She smiled slyly.

I felt a sense of relief, but I didn't tell her. All I could think of was Quartz's addiction and how she was probably in some alley now, squatting in the shadows and fumbling with a syringe.

'Did it occur to you that Quartz came to you because she thinks you're her daughter?'

Boss laughed her fake laugh and wiped her face with a new $1,000 banknote, looking very pleased with herself.

She rolled her eyes. 'In normal circumstances, I would have taken her under my wing as one of my trusted troopers. She is a sweet woman and was a mother to me when I was ill. She was doing all right in the new town until she crossed the line and started taking the white powder. That's just fucking weak.'

'Or outright exploitation on your part.'

'Say what you like, Buddha. You know the poor nun is a troubled soul without any childhood memories.'

'Don't forget we all have a troubled past. Look at Audrey—'

'Don't compare Quartz to Mum. I know Audrey Hepburn is far from perfect, but she is strong. She never touches the nasty stuff, not even for a quick sniff. Quartz became dead to me the moment she started on the white powder. I can't trust her anymore.'

'She might be your mother.'

'Between you and me, Buddha, I am fed up playing this game of who is my mother and who isn't. Do you think it's easy not being an orphan? When I was young, I hated the idea of having a mother. I felt ashamed that Audrey Hepburn was not my *real* mother. I wanted her to be someone less embarrassing like an aunt. All the same, after growing up in this dump I've realised I would never have survived without Audrey Hepburn. With all those fantasies about being a famous actor, I know she isn't right in the head. But you know what? Her madness has fed me, brought me up, got me out of trouble.'

Boss wiped her eyes before they got damp.

A fierce wind shook the banyan and a cloud of yellow sand engulfed the construction site. I shielded Boss, who held on to me until the sandstorm subsided.

'Thank you, Buddha.'

She patted my back as I coughed some sand out.

Patches of sand had stuck on the tear marks running down her face. She turned towards the fence and said, 'Do you know why the Triad is so successful? They are like the nunnery. They promote a twisted version of family values and all these broken kids are desperate to be adopted. Like the nunnery, the Triad feeds on broken hearts. And do you know why I am so successful? The new Hong Kong will be based on business values. I'm here to do business, for things like my career, not some fucked-up family-replacement shit.'

I gave her a tissue.

'Mothers are a necessary evil, like disposable plastic cups. They're useful for a while but you chuck them in the bin when the party is over. I don't give a fuck about my *heritage*, my *origin*, my *family*. I'm only interested in making something of my life, earning lots of money, and becoming a famous film director.'

I knew not everything she said was true.

'What about Quartz?' I asked.

She ignored me and glanced towards the banyan tree tossing in a gust of dusty wind. 'Your poor tree. I am a hundred per cent certain it will be chopped down in no time and hacked into a hundred pieces. Like the rest of Hong Kong.'

She tilted her head skywards and circled around the banyan tree like a criminal measuring the prison yard in preparation for an escape. 'I know your heart clings to Quartz's, but you can see she has now replaced religion with another drug.'

'If someone knocks on your door begging for drugs, it doesn't mean you have to supply them.'

'Cut it, Buddha! Stop nagging me. Do you pity her? Or are you pitying yourself? I never force anybody to take my goodies. She is lucky to have direct access to me. I've only given her the premium, unadulterated stuff. Imagine if she had bought the stuff in the streets; she would have been a real mess by now. She's working hard to pay me back, but I'm making a loss all the same.'

She handed me a receipt from the gas company, and said, 'I've asked for two new canisters and some heaters to be delivered to the nunnery. The weather forecast says a massive cold front is coming all the way down from Siberia. The temperature will drop below five degrees. The nuns are used to the cold, but you will freeze to death. The delivery arrives this afternoon, so look out for it.'

'Where's Quartz?' I grabbed her arm.

'Calm down, Buddha, she's staying at my place. My lads think she is the Virgin Mary and they're obsessed with her. You can pop by and say hello any time you want, though I can't guarantee she'll see you.'

She walked away, brushing her shoulder against mine.

'Forget Quartz. She is a dead end. You should concentrate on my mum and preparing for London.'

When I returned to the nunnery, the gas company had already delivered the two canisters and four heaters. It took me an hour to carry them up the steep steps.

The sun set more quickly in the hills. It was five in the afternoon and the light was fast disappearing. The icy wind cut through my jacket, and I couldn't see any lights from the side hall by the nuns' private chambers. Normally they would have started the first round of night chanting. The silence made the place even chillier.

Nobody except me had looked after the hens since Quartz's departure. Though I was only away for a day, they had laid nearly a dozen eggs, as if they wanted to offload them as quickly as possible to increase their own chance of survival during the coming winter monsoon. Some eggs had fallen out of the wooden coop, cracked, and been eaten by the hens. The whole place was a mess. The hay was encrusted with droppings, feathers, dried egg whites and yolks. The hens were lethargic and mean-spirited towards each other. Nearly all of them had yolk on their beaks and patches of dried egg white in their feathers. What could I do to save Quartz from drugs? She was deep in it, so any resistance from the outside world would only harden her resolve. No drug addict manages to quit because they're forced to do so. That I knew.

The courtyard was deserted. The pond had dried up and the thick yellowy algae filled the bottom with sludge. Even the plastic grass on the lawn had faded to a pale sickly green. The mock-stone mountain was full of bird droppings and cobwebs, the garden tap was broken, and I couldn't find the hose. The only thing still growing in the vegetable patch was a pumpkin. I came closer to pick it up and a rat, its hair as thick as a wig, darted out of the pumpkin's orange flesh and scurried away down a hole. With Quartz gone, I felt responsible for the whole place getting so run-down.

The candles in the side temple were still flickering. The nuns must have forgotten to blow them out. In the candle-light, the dark mahogany wood panels depicting the life of the Buddha made the hall look like a cave. The Buddha's facial expression remained almost unchanged throughout his life. His tight lips never showed his teeth, his posture stayed straight as a lamppost, and his almond-shaped eyes were unmoved, as if the whole world was spinning around them. My favourite panel showed him as a boy running around his father's opulent palace. He was almost laughing, darting around like a bird. It all began with a happy child playing hide-and-seek among the austere faces in the royal court. Like Boss before she became Boss, before she'd stabbed someone to fill her empty stomach.

The sun dropped below the horizon and the wind started whistling. I switched on the gas heater in my shed. Within a few minutes, my bed was warm.

I woke to a loud bang. It sounded like a plane crashing in the hills. I was drenched in night sweats as I must have left the heater on. Someone was kicking my shed door in, breaking its hinges as it finally came open. I screamed, and it wasn't a nightmare.

Boss grabbed my arm. She held a gas lamp in her free hand. 'What's going on?'

'Something has happened, and I don't know what to do.' She dragged me out of bed.

The Main Temple was fully lit. Boss ran ahead yelling, 'Quick! Quick!' as if she'd lost her marbles.

I ran after her and couldn't see any sign of clouds or moon in the icy sky. The stone steps were covered with a light dusting of frost. As I climbed them, I could see three thin shadows stretched across the screens. The longest shadow spilled out and zigzagged down the stairs.

The Iron Nun stood facing the seated golden Buddha. The candles wavered erratically as the wind wailed. Everything inside the Main Temple was out of focus. Audrey Hepburn was kneeling on the floor. The two sisters refused to look each other in the eyes. Despite all their differences, for the first time I could now see the unmistakable family resemblance between them.

Boss reached out and pulled me into the Temple. Handing me the gas lamp, she rushed back to close the screen door. The body on the ground was dressed in a pair of thick white socks, saffron robes and a necklace of wooden rosary beads. A cleanly shaved head rested on a pillow. It was Quartz.

'What's happened to her?' I asked Audrey Hepburn, but she shook her head robotically.

'She's passed out. I think she's had an overdose.' Boss came over and took the gaslight from me. She sat gingerly at Quartz's feet, touching them.

'How long has she been unconscious?' I asked.

'We don't know,' Boss muttered.

'What do you mean you don't know? Where did you find her?' My voice echoed through the hall.

The Iron Nun hushed me, still sternly facing the golden Buddha.

Boss said, 'The Iron Nun wanted her to look decent, so we changed her clothes.'

'How long has she been unconscious?'

Boss raised her voice. 'I said I don't know! Don't blame me! I came back home after midnight and asked Mum where Quartz was, as I hadn't seen her in town all afternoon. Mum said she hadn't either and assumed she was with me . . . I went upstairs and when I saw Quartz sleeping in my bed, I thought I'd just let her rest, so I got myself a cup noodle. Later, when I headed up to bed, I discovered she was stone cold and unconscious—'

'Why didn't you call an ambulance?' I tried to keep my voice down.

'Are you fucking stupid?' Boss shouted. 'I don't want to get arrested.' I sensed that despite her anger, she was out of her depth. 'She'll be fine. People pass out all the time when they're high, you should know that. Mum said the nunnery was the safest place for her to rest. I've checked her pulse and she is alive, that's the most important thing. She looks a lot better than a few minutes ago. Look at the colour on her cheeks. She just needs to sleep it off.'

'It's three in the morning,' Audrey Hepburn muttered. 'I doubt the ambulance will come if you call them. Nobody from the outside world cares about this shithole anyway.'

With some difficulty, I found Quartz's pulse on her neck. It was slow and faint, but definitely there.

'I'm calling the ambulance now.' I was about to rush out to get to the telephone in the side hall.

'Stop!' The Iron Nun turned around. 'Stay where you are. We don't need an ambulance or any interference from the outside world. She's breathing well and will recover soon. This is a private matter for the nunnery. She will be taken to her room and looked after.'

'Shouldn't you be caring for the sick? She is one of your own.'

She stared back at me. 'She is *not* sick. She has had an

overdose and just needs to sleep it off. This pathetic episode of hers is disgraceful. She deserved to be punished, after sneaking out of the nunnery—'

'Don't pretend she was ever coming back. You knew she'd left for good.'

The Iron Nun groaned. 'All nuns have qualms about their vocation once in a blue moon. It's only natural. She left all her belongings here and there is no question that her heart is deeply rooted in this place. Look what you have done to her. You're an expert in overdoses. She is soiled like a piece of used toilet paper with your filth. I should never have let you stay here.'

'You can blame me for many things, but not this. Why did you tell her about my wife and her miscarriage? You persuaded Quartz to give her own baby away—'

'Are you afraid people will find out who you really are, Buddha?'

The Iron Nun took Quartz's prayer beads from her neck and started praying for her. Audrey Hepburn joined in. Boss rolled her eyes and yawned.

'It's you who's scared of the past. Do you really think you can let people electrocute themselves and their past will disappear for ever?'

'Listen to yourself. You are out of your mind. I want you to leave. Now.' The Iron Nun pointed at the door.

'I'm not going anywhere. Are *you* afraid people will find out who you really are?'

The Iron Nun sneered.

'What the hell are you talking about, you crazy man?' Audrey Hepburn interrupted.

'I'm not crazy. You may have forgotten things too. Did your sister also sit you on the Chair of Forgetfulness?'

Audrey Hepburn and Boss looked puzzled.

The Iron Nun yelled at Audrey Hepburn, 'You are good for nothing. You always bring me trouble.'

Audrey Hepburn muttered, '江山易改 稟性難移 (It's easy to move a mountain but difficult to change one's personality). One thing I haven't forgotten is your embittered selfishness. Obviously years of Buddhist teaching haven't done you any good.' She ignored her sister and started caressing Quartz's forehead.

I ran to the back of the Main Temple, through the secret courtyard to the locked room where the Iron Nun had hidden the Chair. I yanked off the mouldy wooden boards easily, but the metal gate proved trickier. I shook it, kicked it, and banged it with my shoulder, though the four rusted Yale locks were stronger than they looked. I tried to prise the locks open with a wooden broomstick, but it snapped and cut my hand. Where were the keys hidden? Under a stone, tiles or a flowerpot? I searched everywhere, leaving bloody handprints on everything I touched.

When I got back into the Main Temple, the Iron Nun had put a white cloth over Quartz's face. There were three new incense sticks burning at the altar. She hit the Tibetan singing bowl once, and with closed eyes, started chanting a sutra I had not heard before. Boss was scratching at the floorboards with a thick gold bracelet wrapped around her fist, peeling the wood off and making noises like a rat chewing through a cage. Audrey Hepburn, self-possessed and wooden, stared at the floor.

I sat next to Quartz and lifted the white cloth off her face. She looked very much like the nun I'd first encountered. I pressed up and down on her chest and touched her small mouth for the first time, filling her cheeks with air. I had often puzzled over her tiny mouth. It was like a mistake, a minor defect. I continued trying for a minute but there was no pulse. She lay there unmoving, her eyes shut. I gently closed her lips.

'She just stopped breathing. I tried to resuscitate her, but she was beyond it,' Boss said, still scarring the floorboards.

I covered up Quartz's face again with the white cloth. I trembled when the Iron Nun hit the Tibetan singing bowl again.

'We need to move her body out of the Main Temple immediately. I don't want the other nuns to see her. Some of them are young and won't be able to cope with this.' The Iron Nun's voice was cold.

She walked off to the storeroom at the back of the Temple and came back with a big cardboard box, the old packaging for the television. 'Can you both help me put her inside?'

Incredulously, I interrupted, 'I am not letting you put Quartz inside that bloody box. Show her some respect.'

'Her body must be hidden from the nuns.'

Boss tapped on Audrey Hepburn's shoulder and signalled for her to leave. 'As you say, this is a private nunnery matter. We don't want any trouble.' She avoided my eye and wrapped her mother's arm over her shoulders, hoisting her up and heading towards the screen door.

The Iron Nun was clumsily trying to lift Quartz's body, as if folding a mannequin. She pulled the arms up and propped up the body with one knee. The white cloth fell off Quartz's face. One of her arms flopped and banged the floor. Her mouth fell open.

My mind ran blank as I grabbed mechanically at her frosty feet, the Iron Nun held her armpits, and we lifted the body over the side. I had never thought a dead body as slim as Quartz's could be so heavy. I disentangled her arms and placed them on her lap. I copied the Iron Nun but didn't register what I was doing. Everything blurred.

The Iron Nun laid Quartz's prayer beads carefully inside the box. She sealed it up with duct tape before I had a chance to protest and signalled that we were to carry the box into the secret courtyard. Quartz seemed a lot lighter now that she was inside the box. I could hear her body wobbling about as we moved it. The Iron Nun wanted the box in her bedroom, but there wasn't space. We could have put it on her bed, but she hesitated. Noticing that I had trashed the courtyard and tried to break into the locked room, she gave me an accusing look. In the end, we put the box behind the caged well. She placed a plastic bucket, a couple of unbroken flowerpots and other objects around it, trying to make it less conspicuous.

'The nuns will soon be up for morning prayers. We will deal with this later.'

'The nuns haven't been praying at all while you were away.'

'They certainly will, now I am back.' She went into her room and shut the door.

The night sky was empty.

The cardboard box blended discreetly into the disused courtyard. It was as if it had been there for years gathering dust.

I stood on the veranda and gave the Main Temple one last look. The candlelight wavered on the golden Buddha and the Tibetan singing bowl. I fixed my eyes on the spot where Quartz's body had lain and thought if I looked hard enough, she could rematerialise, stand up, walk towards me, tell me, 'Everything is fine, Buddha. You're in a dream. Wake up.' The wind sliced my bones. There was no Quartz, nothing except the fidgeting reflections of the light on shiny objects. I closed the screen door without blowing the candles out, hoping the flames would keep Quartz company.

When I walked past the nuns' private chambers, there

was no sign of them. The hens were sound asleep in the coop and the sky was shadowy. The light pollution from the city made it hard to see the stars. One conspicuous light due north was high up over my shed. Was it a satellite or another plane?

I had left the gas heater on by mistake, but the shed was still freezing. I tried to fix the broken door in the dark without success. To keep warm, I curled up in bed and wrapped myself as tightly as I could. I stuffed my hands in my jacket pockets and found the beer-bottle keyrings filled with the white powder. It was only yesterday I'd bought them from Quartz.

I could have opened one of the keyrings for relief. If I wanted to accompany Quartz to the underworld, I could have taken them all in one go. I pictured her walking down the dark passage on her own. Soon she would meet the Taoist figure of 孟婆 (Meng Po), the Lady of Forgetfulness by the Narakade Bridge. Meng Po would give Quartz the Tea of Oblivion, made from herbs she'd gathered on the banks of the Dark River. The complex brew had eight flavours: sour, sweet, bitter, spicy, salty, astringent, fishy and hot. Once the tea touched Quartz's tongue, she would finally forget the past, and all memories of previous lives would also be erased. There would be no need for the electric chair, just a cup of tea. Would she drink it? Or would she trick Meng Po and pour the tea into the river when she crossed the bridge, as it is claimed many dead people have done? After all, she had spent most of her life trying to forget. Would she prefer to remember in the afterlife?

I closed my eyes and fell asleep. I dreamed that I was sitting by the Dark River near the Narakade Bridge, washing my hands in black bone-cold water. About a hundred yards downstream, a long queue of heads waited to cross the arched wooden bridge. An old woman – she must be Meng Po – was ladling tea into a small cup and handing it out to the crowds. Some drank it without thinking. Some pretended to drink and threw it discreetly into the river. Meng Po didn't make a fuss about those who refused to drink her tea but went on ladling. I scanned the crowds, hoping to find Quartz's face, only to realise that no one in the queue had a face at all. I thought I heard myself screaming but it was a loud bell ringing.

I woke to an acrid burning smell and a sizzling noise in my thatched roof. A bunch of reeds at the corner had caught fire and smoke was pouring down into the shed. I jumped out of bed and found the hens calling hysterically, flapping their wings, trying to escape. A tower of red smoke welled up from the side temple. Sparks, lifted by the high wind, rained down all over the nunnery. Some went out before landing, but others ignited small fires on the wooden beams and banisters. Like a hungry animal, the blaze roared and guzzled the dry air. Ash clouds soared up above the surrounding hills. Smoke clogged into my eyes and lungs.

Ducking down to get some air, I crawled along the stone

path looking for the water tap in the vegetable plot. I turned the tap on, and the hose jumped out of my hand, dancing like a snake. I drenched myself from head to toe in ice-cold water, before hosing the hens and coop down, praying that they would survive. I didn't know whether to free them or keep them in their cage. When I finally managed to extinguish the fire on the thatch, half of the roof was destroyed. There were burn marks on the oak door.

The bell from the Main Temple rang out like a siren. Running towards it with the hose in my hand, I saw the fire had engulfed nearly all the side temple and the wind was now blowing the flames towards the Main Temple. The nuns' private quarters were smothered in dense smoke. The hose wasn't long enough, so I took my T-shirt off, wetted it, and wrapped it around my face. I climbed the steps into the nuns' private quarters. Suddenly something exploded at the heart of the nunnery. The red flames turned blue and yellow, before reddening again. I smelt gas. The entire roof structure on the veranda collapsed in front of me. I fell over and grabbed the hose, pouring more water over myself.

I could barely see through the choking smoke, so I kept running away from the scorching flames until I could see the roof of the Main Temple. The screen doors had all burned down, but the golden Buddha seated on his lotus was untouched. At the top of the steps, the Iron Nun was striking a gong. Her ashen face was lit up by the flames. She rushed down the stairs and collapsed in my arms.

'Here! We are down here!' Voices were shouting from below, behind me, in the direction of the nunnery gate.

I held on to the Iron Nun's shoulders and shook her hard. Her eyes rolled backwards. She was gasping for breath. I wrapped my wet T-shirt over her mouth and helped her up. Her feet wobbled at first but then regained their stance. I put an arm around her shoulders and dragged her down the stone steps towards the gate.

As we descended, fresh air whooshed upwards and was sucked into the fire, fanning the blaze. Through the smoke, I saw a big crowd of people outside the gate. The other nuns had escaped. They were holding on to the wooden panels from the side temple. They seemed to have salvaged all the panels – the Buddha's smiling face was undeterred by the catastrophe around him. When they saw the Iron Nun, they dashed across to help her down.

My body was numb, hot and cold. My eyes were streaming, my mouth sandpapery. Two planes appeared in the sky and dropped water and yellowish pink powder into the blazing nunnery.

Suddenly I remembered the cardboard box hidden by the dry well.

'Quartz!' I screamed. 'Quartz is still inside!' I found myself pinned down to the ground by a gang of teenage boys. Boss was standing there, throwing a bucket of freezing water over me. My entire body tingled, as if pricked by a thousand needles.

'Get off me. I need to take Quartz's body out.'

'Did he say Quartz?' a nun cried out.

One of the boys shoved his fist in my mouth and whispered, 'Nobody is interested in a dead nun.' I tasted blood that could have been his or mine. He smiled at me like a clown without its make-up.

The crowd gathered around me. With his fist in my mouth, I couldn't breathe and was getting dizzy.

'Ignore him,' the Iron Nun shouted to the crowd.

People were turning into grotesque blurs around me. The boy finally removed his fist and Boss waved her boys away.

Audrey Hepburn kneeled beside me and placed a white flannel gently over my mouth to stop the bleeding.

'Hush, Buddha. Not a single word from now on.'

I moved my tongue. The open wound touched the ridge of my mouth and an electric shock went down my spine. Another plane dropped a bucket of powder over the burning nunnery.

'Mummy, what's that?' In the crowd, I saw a mother holding her daughter, whose hand was pointing at the red smoky sky.

'It's just sand.'

'Why are they using sand?'

'I don't know. We've seen enough. Let's go home.'

The girl hid her face in her mother's chest. As they were leaving, she caught my eye. Her tiny forefinger touched her mouth as if to hush me.

冬

Winter Solstice

至

I returned to the old man's house, and for two weeks I slept in the same room Quartz had slept in after burying the orchids. Night after night, I lay there wide awake staring at the ceiling. At first I insisted on sleeping on the cold floor, as Quartz had done, but woke up each morning with a splitting headache. After that, the old man ignored my stubbornness, made up a bed on the sofa and kept the electric heater on. Since the fire, I'd grown sensitive to light and everything seemed too bright. I lay in the pitch-dark living room with my eyes open and brain empty, listening to the grandfather clock. Night after night, the mechanical movement spoke to me in the same code – tick-tock, tick-tock – and if I held my breath I could hear the pendulum swinging in the chest. In the dead of night I tried to stop my bitten tongue from healing. I pressed the wound against the sharp edge of my teeth, but despite my best efforts it was healing much faster than I expected.

The old man said there had been no report about the nunnery fire on the radio. There were rumours in the shanty town that the nunnery had been cordoned off and was being guarded round the clock by the police. He was afraid I would be an easy target and a potential suspect for arson. I had distributed the gas heaters for the nuns and left the candles burning in the Main Temple after putting Quartz in the cardboard box.

'Feel free to read any of the books in the house.'

'I'm in no mood to read.'

'I know you're blaming yourself for Quartz's death. But it's not your fault.'

'If I hadn't come to Diamond Hill, Quartz would not be dead.'

'How can you be certain? A broken vase might look perfect after careful repairs, but when you pour water in, it leaks and you see all the cracks.'

'Are you saying I am the water?'

'You might be as clueless as water, but you're certainly not the reason the vase broke in the first place.'

He walked towards the window and sighed.

Despite the cold, every few days one or two orchids managed to break the surface of their graves. The old man couldn't bear it and asked me to beat them down with a spade. Whenever I saw an orchid, I remembered Quartz in the Sony cardboard box and wondered if her body had survived the fire. I also found two earthworms tied together in a knot. The old man said it was 蚯蚓結 (an earthworm knot), something which often happened around the winter solstice when the ground was almost frozen and earthworms huddled to keep warm.

The old man looked exhausted and I thought he had

drifted off in the middle of our conversation. He struggled into his bed and drew the covers over himself.

'Don't close the curtains,' he said. 'I'm enjoying the sun.' He turned his face towards the window and soaked up the warm light like a child on a beach in summer. He lay there, breathing huskily.

Massaging his shoulder, he said, 'Buddha, my old bones need looking after and I'm moving into a nursing home. For the moment I want to give the house to you, but it'll be knocked down before long, like everything else around here.' He held my hand. 'You cannot hide from the sun. Go to the nunnery and get Quartz's body back. You need to bury her.'

His breathing slowed down, and at last he let go of my hand and curled up like a caterpillar. It was as if, any minute, he would start secreting silk and wrap himself in a cocoon. Would he emerge as a hawk moth? He dropped off and started to snore. When I saw he was settled for a nap, I put on my jacket and left the house.

There were three yellow bulldozers parked at the edge of the shanty town, though no sign of any construction workers. I wandered through the ghost-like streets and guessed there were no more than a dozen families left. Dotted right and left, I could see removal trucks, cardboard boxes and metal trolleys, as well as a handful of people who stared at me as I walked past. A couple of boys – the last remaining – stuck out their tongues, made funny faces, and gave me the middle finger. Were they the same boys who'd heckled me when I first arrived in Diamond Hill? I tried to look as unsuspicious as I could and sneaked off into an alley. The needles, metal spoons, leather belts, toilet paper, shit and blood had all been cleared away. Pink powder was scattered along the edges. It looked like rat poison, though there were no warning notices on the walls.

I couldn't see a cordon or policeman at the nunnery gate, so I walked up the stone path now littered with ash, charred wood and plastic bottles. The firefighters had left big blackened boot-prints on the paving stones, like those iconic footprints of the first Moon landing. A row of trees up the hill had scorch marks on their trunks. The wind carried an acrid smell from the woods like snuffed-out cigars left burning on ashtrays. Usually, midway up the steps I would see the carved dragon at the highest point of the roof, but now there was just empty sky. The nunnery was deserted, and every surface coated with the fine brownish sand the fire brigade had used to extinguish the blaze.

The side temple had been burned to the ground. Nothing remained, not a single piece of wood or furniture. Weighed down by piles of white ash, rubble and blackened sand, it resembled a bomb site. I couldn't stop myself reconstructing the whole side temple in my mind, from the low-hanging door that humbled everyone as they entered, to the small figurine of the Goddess of Mercy in the middle, and the mahogany panels depicting the Buddha's life. Of all the sacred places in the nunnery the side temple was the most intimate and moving.

A crow took off, heading to the hills. It cawed as it flew over the roof of the Main Temple. Half of the building had been destroyed, though the other half was intact, almost in pristine condition. I had to brace myself as I approached the charred doors. He wore some minor dents, ash, and burn scars, but the golden Buddha was otherwise largely unharmed. He sat there matter-of-factly among the fallen beams. A scroll with fine calligraphy had somehow survived the blaze and read: 宇世虛空如系漣漪 (The world is nothing but a series of ripples). As I approached the seated Buddha, my feet felt heavier and heavier. I looked for the exact spot where Quartz had died but could no longer find it.

I sensed a sudden movement in the temple and slipped behind the statue. It was the Iron Nun, looking like a cleaner with her sleeves rolled up. She scrubbed away with a bucket of soapy water and frantically removed the burn marks on the Buddha.

She noticed me but didn't raise her head.

'People believe it's a miracle the Buddha survived. The fire brigade said the flames had encircled him, but he remained unscathed.' She rinsed the towel in the bucket and asked, 'What are you doing here?'

'I've come for Quartz's body.'

'You're the last person she would have wanted to see.'

'You killed her. You knew she was vulnerable and then spilt the beans about the shipwreck of my marriage.'

She faked a laugh. 'That night, I know I blamed you for her death, but we both know full well it was her own fault. There is no happy ending for those who choose the path of the white powder.'

'You could at least show some remorse. Quartz always treated you with respect.'

'I saved her numerous times, but even salvation has a quota. 前世債 今世還 (I can only hope the suffering she endured in this life will repay the terrible debts she must have accumulated in her previous life).'

I walked towards her private quarters at the back of the Main Temple. The entire area had been burned to the ground. The wooden veranda with its intricate carved banisters, her bedroom, the locked room where the Chair of Forgetfulness had been hidden, the flowerpots, the Sony cardboard box and Quartz's body were all gone. It was a scene of total devastation. The only thing left standing were the charred stones of the old well. I thought I could hear someone in the well, but it was only the wind whistling.

'Apparently it was a furnace next door, and yet the Buddha was barely touched by the fire. The statue is older than you and me combined. It was made at the turn of the century using the famous incense wood from Hong Kong. Whoever crafted it was a master.'

She gave me a quick stare. 'It's a bit too late for tears now, isn't it? It's lucky that some of the unwanted objects in this place were burned to nothing. As the old saying goes: 人算不如天算 不幸中之大幸 (human calculation can never match fate, and there is luck in being unlucky).'

'You have blood on your hands.' I kicked the bucket and splashed the black water all over the floor, soaking her robes.

'Your hands are not squeaky clean either. Even if her body had survived the fire, the post-mortem would have shown she'd died of an overdose. You should thank the fire. A man with your troubled past might come out badly in a criminal investigation.'

'Where are the other nuns?'

'We all need a fresh start.'

'Did they abandon you because they realised you're a monster? Are you pleased you've now got Diamond Hill all to yourself?'

'They will beg me to take them back when the nunnery is rebuilt. The fire will breathe new life into this sad old place. Like a phoenix from the ashes, it will emerge as a much grander modern nunnery. It'll be featured in tourist guidebooks in many languages and people from all over the world will flock to pay tribute to the famous Buddha who survived the great fire.'

'So this is all part of your plan.'

'Accidents are accidents.'

The Iron Nun stiffened her face and went into the

storeroom. She came out and handed me a brown paper envelope stuffed with what looked like money.

'Now Quartz is dead, there is no reason for you to stick around. It isn't like your wife or parents are going to forgive you for what you have done to them. This should be enough for you to disappear for good. Bangkok, London or Tin Shui Wai – I don't care where. I should never have listened to Daishi and agreed to take you under my roof. I owed him, but it was a moment of weakness. Now we're even. I don't ever want to see you again.'

She threw the envelope at me. 'Oh, one more thing. Do you remember when you first arrived here in spring, I asked you whether, though Daishi had forgiven you, you could actually forgive yourself? You don't need to answer me now. Your baby boy might not have had any consciousness when he died, and so can't haunt you. But Quartz will no doubt follow you to the grave.'

She walked away.

That was it. She brought out another side of me that I'd never known existed. I let her walk a few paces, before catching up with her. I whistled, and she looked back. I don't understand what came over me, but I found myself grabbing her throat. I considered pinning her to the wall, but it seemed easier just to throw her to the floor next to the Tibetan singing bowl. She must have screamed but all I could hear was the roar of an airplane touching down. Her face had never looked so animated. Her muscles moved like those of a fish out of water and I could feel her neck sweating. I didn't grab her throat very hard; I had no intention of suffocating her. I lay on top of her to stop her getting away. I didn't know why she looked so frightened. Perhaps I said something like, 'Is this what you want? Is this what you want?' But I really couldn't hear anything except the deafening engines in my head. I was simply mouthing words. To reassure her, I restrained her busy arms with one hand and sandwiched her strong legs with my thighs. Her eyes blinked erratically. What was I looking for in them? Tears ran down her face and over the big awkward mole near her mouth. Finally, her eyes rolled back into her head as a plane took off and headed somewhere faraway. Then there were only echoes. When she stopped struggling I let her go. She lay there like a block of rusted iron.

I got up and dusted the ashes off my trousers.

A roaring cough finally opened up her chest and her windpipe gave an eerie, high-pitched call. Her lungs seemed desperate to suck in as much oxygen as possible in a few short breaths. When she came round, she punched me in the face and my nose broke with a crunch. She ran out of the Main Temple without glancing back.

My hands and legs were sore, my nose bleeding, and my left cheek as bruised as a steamed bun. I'd always known she was a tough woman. If she had grabbed the Tibetan singing bowl, no doubt she would have split my skull. I dashed out to track her down, but she had disappeared like a ghost.

The blaze had melted the hose I'd left outside. It now looked like a flattened black snake encrusted on the paving stones. The vegetable plot had survived, and the ash must have provided fresh nutrients, as two new pumpkins had fattened up among the weeds. The hen coop had been spared. Either the Iron Nun had let the hens out or they had somehow escaped. Two had gone astray, but the remaining four looked well, pecking happily at the weeds. Soon they would discover the sweet pumpkins. The Iron Nun had obviously moved into my shed and removed all my stuff. I retrieved two things I'd hidden under the mattress: the old newspaper with the picture of the falling British Prime Minister and the official letter from the clerk of Wat Arun. The Iron Nun had repaired the thatched roof and the door hinges. She'd made a small shrine on the desk, with a burning incense stick and three oranges as offerings, in front of a porcelain figurine of the Goddess of Mercy. Next to the goddess lay her worn-out prayer beads.

I went into the kitchen and fetched an empty jar, then walked back to the Main Temple but could find no trace of the Iron Nun. Behind the dried-up well there were a few shards of charred terracotta, though nothing resembling human bones or teeth. I went on repeating Quartz's name as I scooped up the black ash and bits and pieces of unidentified objects on the ground. The jar was filled to the brim and looked like a souvenir from an active volcano. My stomach tightened, as if a strong weather system was passing through my body. Though I wanted to cry, my eyes seemed to have run out of tears. I mopped up the dirty water in the Main Temple. It was the last time I saw the nunnery or the Iron Nun.

On automatic pilot, I walked to Boss and Audrey Hepburn's tin shack. It was one of the very last shacks left, standing alone, rubble filled with weeds on either side of it. The gate was padlocked with four Yale locks and covered with obscene graffiti and demolition notices. It stank, as if someone had smeared it with dog shit. The windows were boarded up. Perhaps they'd already left.

The door opened, and Boss popped her head out sheepishly. '屌你老母你去撚咗邊 (You motherfucker, where have you been)?'

'I've been staying at the orchid man's house.'

'Who?'

'The old man who grows all the orchids.'

She rolled her eyes. 'I can't believe he's still alive. Wealthy people always live longer. Are you in mourning? You look miserable.'

'I don't understand how you and Audrey Hepburn could leave the Main Temple that night after what happened.'

'It was a terrible accident, Buddha. We mustn't blame ourselves.'

'She is your biological mother.'

'As I told you, one mother is more than enough for me. I

barely knew Quartz. Audrey Hepburn is my only mother. Anyway, we can't unfuck the past, but let's try and not fuck up our future.'

'You've no morals.'

She laughed. 'Neither do you, Buddha. Unlike the nuns, I don't judge you for leaving your wife and her miscarriage behind. Shit happens and we move on. That's how the world functions. Feel it, it's spinning on regardless. Don't let the past drag you down. You'll soon forget what happened.'

She turned back, leaving the door slightly ajar. I glanced inside, but she quickly reappeared and handed me a red, only slightly bruised passport, with the gold crest of the lion and the unicorn.

'This will cheer you up.'

'What's this? I've got my own.'

'Look closer, Dumbo.'

I turned to the photograph page that showed my mug-shot and date of birth. In the nationality field, instead of British National (Overseas), I had become a British Citizen.

'Do you like the upgrade?'

'Why would I need a fake passport.' I handed it back to her.

'It's not fake. Well, strictly speaking, it's unofficial, but it's definitely not a counterfeit.'

She smelt my suspicions. 'I won't get you into any trouble, Buddha. They've guaranteed, and I quote, that *it's as authentic as the Union Jack.*'

She showed me Audrey Hepburn's passport and her own, both of which had also been upgraded. 'Look, we're family now – I swear it's not a trick. We're some of the lucky ones hand-picked for the upgrade.'

'I'm a nobody, why on earth would anyone upgrade me?'

Boss's face relaxed into a smile. 'Grow up, Buddha, everything has a price tag. Let's just say you're lucky to have met me, and that from now on, you're no longer a nobody. You're my father and the manager of the Golden Palace in London Chinatown.'

She slipped the passport into my pocket. 'Listen, we'll meet you at the airport on Thursday. I've got everything sorted in London, so travel light and just bring the essentials. We only have thirty-two kilos per person and I would love you to bits if you can spare ten kilos for me. I had no idea my collection of Gucci handbags was so heavy.'

'Where's Audrey Hepburn?'

'Mum doesn't want to see you.'

'Why?'

'She is worried you won't go to London with us and can't bear seeing you again. Save your innocent face for another day. You know what women are like. You disappeared, and she thought Quartz had fucked up your head so badly you'd gone back to Bangkok.'

'I never said I'd go to London with you.'

'你條撚樣佢對你有感情 (You dickhead, my mum has real feelings for you).'

'You know better than anybody she lives in a fantasy world.'

'Life is make-believe but you're not a fantasy. If you stay here, it's game over.' She carefully checked all the Yale locks on the gate. 'Remember, it's a lot colder in London. It might even be snowing now. Get yourself a down jacket. Have you got some cash?'

I didn't answer.

'Thursday, nine p.m., Cathay Pacific check-in counter. Our flight's at midnight. It won't wait for you.'

Before shutting the door, she winked and said, 'Lie low and don't come back here. See you on Thursday night. As they say in Britain, *Cheerio!*'

All the houses on the outskirts of the shanty town had been flattened, leaving a trail of debris circling Diamond Hill. Among the broken roofs and bent lampposts stood a shattered brick wall covered with black graffiti: 走狗 (Traitors running like stray dogs) and 狗官 (Corrupt officers governing like hungry dogs). The wind whistled as it cut through the cracks. I strolled on without any sense of direction. Not a shadow of a living thing around.

I found *Ah Sir*'s dog nestled against the banyan tree in the sun, but the beggar was nowhere to be seen.

'Where's *Ah Sir*?' I asked, but the dog was too lazy to even twitch her ears.

The old man was right: the wind had changed direction

and it felt milder. A couple of ants climbed onto the dog's moist nose and she sneezed. I took my jacket off and realised I was still carrying the beer-bottle keyrings. The white powder was fluorescent in the sun. I opened the tiny bottles and poured the heroin out. The fine powder blew away into the air like pollen. I attached the keyrings to the metal fence and said goodbye to the dog. She wagged her tail in the green shade and gazed at me idly with her tongue out.

When I returned to the old man's house, someone had already packed his clothes and essentials into a few cardboard boxes. The bookcases had all been emptied, except for a copy of 《紅樓夢》 (*Dream of the Red Chamber*) left on the middle shelf. The grandfather clock had been packed in bubble-wrap and nearly all the furniture was tagged with an antique label ready for auction. I shivered when I saw the boxes. The old man came out of his bedroom.

'That's for you.' He pointed at the book on the shelf.

'I thought you'd already left,' I said.

'How is the nunnery?' He tottered as he walked, and sat down at last in his favourite wicker chair.

'The golden Buddha in the Main Temple has survived the fire. I've been told the nunnery will be rebuilt on a grand scale.'

'There has been too much destruction around here.'

He looked out of the window.

'My father told me orchids are stubborn plants. Look.' It

irked him that a white orchid had somehow taken root in the icy soil. I helped him to his chair.

'This poor chair must be fed up of me by now. I'm glad the old Buddha has survived. It's not surprising the nunnery will be rebuilt. It's the spirit of Diamond Hill. People are bound to travel miles to visit a miraculous Buddha. Perhaps the area will flourish again, in time.'

He looked tired and short of breath. 'Did you find Quartz's remains?'

I showed him the jar and he raised his eyebrows. Though his hands were shaky, he wanted to hold it. 'I am more frightened by this wretched shakiness than by death itself.' He closed his eyes. 'Never mind. What are you going to do with her remains?'

'These are not her remains. I just scooped up what was left on the ground.'

'I see.' He paused. 'What matters is that part of her was there on the ground, and you've got some of her in your hands now.'

'I suppose I should bury her somewhere.'

'Or you can carry her around, wherever you are, as a keepsake. What are you going to do with yourself?' His eyes were slow but inquisitive.

'I don't know. I'm not good with the future.'

'I don't blame you; me neither. I'll take it one step at a time. Now, I'm going to rest.' He grabbed his walking stick, gathered up all his energy, and tried to stand on his own feet. He did it finally, after three goes. Instead of returning to his bedroom, he came towards me with open arms. His hunched back made any embrace difficult, but we did manage to hold each other, and I understood what he meant by his wretched shakiness.

'I can see my orchids in you.'

'What?'

'Don't expect a second chance, Buddha. One is enough,' he whispered, as he held me firmly in his arms.

That night, with the grandfather clock wrapped and ready to go, I couldn't sleep. There was a high-pitched silence in the house, similar to the call the Iron Nun made when she was gasping for air. In the dark, among the boxes, I held on to the ashes of Quartz in the jar and Daishi in the bamboo container. Would I have felt better if I had eaten his ashes? Should I eat her ashes too? I turned on the lamp and leafed through the heavy *Dream of the Red Chamber*, but my mind was too numb to read anything.

In the distance, I could hear a plane landing at Kai Tak Airport at this godforsaken hour. I'd always thought that the invention of flight was as miraculous as the discovery of gravity, and yet, in order to fly we have to accept our fear and vulnerability – the clunky mechanical noise of the wheels lowering in preparation for landing, the precarious contact when the wheels touch the tarmac, the smell of burnt plastic, and the unstoppable forward movement pulling at the seatbelt until the brakes take hold. A flurry of reddish signal light came through the curtain, and I could picture thousands of aeroplanes climbing up cloud towers and cruising through the different time zones. Beijing, Tokyo, San Francisco. New Delhi, Istanbul, London. I couldn't remember the last time I flew.

A pair of wings fluttered in the lampshade. They were big shadowy wings, like a butterfly's. I went over, and it came towards my nose, before settling on the windowpane. It was a moth with three alternating black and yellow stripes on its wings. Strangely, it gravitated to the dark window rather than the lamp, so I lifted the latch and helped it escape. The half-moon looked like a paper cut-out pasted to the sky. The moth circled round the orchid trenches, before flying back to the window ledge beside me. It stretched its wings, as if it had just woken in springtime. Outside I could see Quartz clearly reflected in the windowpane, fully robed, standing between the orchid trenches. Her small mouth moved, beckoning me. I changed quickly, put on my jacket, and grabbed the ashes and a torch and hurried over towards her, but she was gone before I could get there. The moth took off towards the hills, and disappeared.

I knew where I needed to go. I ran through the familiar streets of Diamond Hill until I was breathless. Instead of taking the path to the nunnery, I followed the narrow uphill path along the stream. The moon, though not full, was blindingly bright in the clear sky. The wind had calmed, and the stream smelt sweet in the unseasonal warm air. I turned off the torch to let my eyes readjust to the dark. Through the branches, the shanty town was a pitch-black pool, surrounded by a web of yellow lights mapping the new concrete paths. The construction site had encroached upon and flattened the dilapidated houses under a cement sheet.

I followed the stream, anxious that I would get lost, then turned the torch on again and hurried ahead, desperate to locate the waterfall. I closed my eyes for a moment, and between the sounds of the insects going about their business and the calls of monkeys, I could hear gushing water.

I followed my ears, then my nose, and after a few minutes found the waterfall behind a thick screen of trees. The water was as crisp and fresh as when I'd tasted it with Quartz back in autumn. I waited to see if the beggar would emerge from his bathing place, but he wasn't there. Further along the pool, I found the uphill stony path to the clearing and my torch revealed the mesmerising shadows and crevices of the gigantic rock face. It was hard to find the entrance to the cave, so I felt my way along the rock with my hands. A rush of warm air hit me and I entered the narrow passageway, holding the torch in my mouth and feeling the rock corridor opening out overhead.

The hibernating bats were sound asleep, some hanging from the ceiling and some in funny vertiginous positions in rock crevices. I saw an odd one fly out, and others come in. The pile of eggshells gleamed on the carpet of bat shit.

There I was, all on my own in the cave. Hundreds of little hearts beat slowly above me. I was envious of these bats, able to turn their bodies to sleep in the toughest months and re-emerge when the hills were green and insects abundant.

I opened the jar and scattered Quartz's remains. Once the black ash landed, it became indistinguishable from the bat shit. She had dreamed of becoming a bat in her next life, and there she was, lying in the cave, among her friends.

I opened the bamboo container and tipped Daishi's ashes into my mouth. The complex taste was bitter, chalky, salty, sweet. Perhaps it tasted like the eight-flavoured herbal tea that Meng Po, the Lady of Forgetfulness, offers the returning souls by the river. What was the name of the river?

I switched off the torch and lay in the dark, imitating the position of the reclining Buddha from the famous temple in Bangkok. I imagined Daishi, cut off from the outside world in Doi Pui Mountain, finding shelter in some moist shady spot under a tree and letting his final moments pass. It was warm among the sleeping bats. Everywhere I looked I was greeted by darkness, so it didn't matter whether my eyes were open or closed.

I had learned how to breathe when I came out of my mother's womb, but for the first time in my life, I gained a new awareness of my own breathing, which started to regulate itself, establishing a slow rhythm I'd never known before.

I've heard people say that at the end of everything, there is a tunnel, and at the end of the tunnel there will be light, and I will just need to follow it. Others say that fragments of our life will flash in front of our eyes, and I'll have no choice but to decipher those old images, as if on a roll of Kodak film on which the people and places I've known will gradually dissolve. According to some, the soul will make its escape at the last minute, and I'll witness myself here among the bat shit, eggshells, and Quartz's remains, pretending to be the sleeping Buddha.

My eyes were heavy, and I drifted off, but I saw no tunnel, no light, no fragments, and no Kodak films.

Daishi once told me a good thing happens when someone dies. Or had I made that up?

Quartz wanted to be nothing but a chrysalis by the time she died. Like hers, my body now seemed like a shell.

No two lives are identical, but even if I shared my name with the real Buddha, I found myself hoping that a good thing would happen when I died. Instead of the tender pork or truffles the real Buddha tasted before his death, I could taste the ashes I had eaten. Instead of lying between a pair of sal trees, I was lying in the cave, with my head pointing roughly north and my left foot over the right foot, as depicted in the last mahogany panel in the side temple.

I could hear Daishi's voice telling me that whether I

believed in anything or not, I still had to let go. My rest was long and deep, and the bats remained quiet, as if they'd got used to my company.

Sharing a place with me made no difference to them one way or the other.

驚

The Awakening of Insects

蟄

The unexpectedly warm weather had lasted three days, and afterwards, even though the wind got colder, winter failed to wrest back control. Now that all the people had left, pests and vermin had nowhere to hide. The use of rat poison in the shanty town had had a great effect and the streets stood empty. The rats had been wiped out.

Underground, though, the mini-heatwave had excited the maggots, who were eating their way out of the rats' intestines and into their skin and hair. Despite their insatiable appetite, the maggots would never see the light of day, trapped beneath tons of rubble.

It didn't stop the flies, though.

Against all the obstacles, the flies found their way through the slightest of cracks, feasting on the rotting rats, before laying millions of eggs in the disused pipes. Confined in all that heat, the eggs hatched and the well-fed larvae grew into adults within four days.

One day construction workers noticed a buzzing swarm during lunch and reported it to the site manager, who called a special environmental unit to get the infestation under control. Toxic gas was pumped out over the site, and all the construction workers were given three days off.

Millions of flies found refuge in the hills. Without human waste, food was scarce, and many flies died of hunger. The more adventurous ones left Diamond Hill and migrated to other neighbourhoods. Many found their way to Kai Tak Airport. Some of the lucky ones ended up in departure lounges where passengers rushing to catch planes left uneaten food.

'I hate flies. Why are there so many in this airport?' a young teenage girl in an all-gold outfit asked. 'Do you like Mum's black dress? With the Chanel sunglasses, she looks like Audrey in *Breakfast at Tiffany's*, doesn't she? Don't we look like the owners of the Golden Palace in Chinatown?'

Her mother lowered the oversized sunglasses down to the tip of her nose, just like the Hollywood star. She shook her head. 'You are a shame to the family. Look at your baggy trousers and shapeless down jacket!'

'Don't worry, Mum. He isn't sitting next to you. I've arranged separate seats for us in different parts of the plane. I'm in the front row. Mum, you're at the back. Buddha, you're in the middle. It's an old trick to cover our backs in case someone gets suspicious.'

They queued at the boarding gate and the girl struck out at one of the flies, which dodged, sensing her murderous intention.

'Of course, there are other added benefits. If, and it's a big *if*, we have an accident, there is a better chance that one or more of us might survive.'

The girl walked out over the tarmac towards the plane, swaggering like a boy.

The fly swirled around the girl's head. Her mother tried to hit it, whacking the girl instead. They laughed and climbed the stairs to the waiting cabin crew.

The threatened fly flew on into the cabin of the aircraft. The thunderous engine noise and sudden atmospheric change unsettled it, forcing it to swish up and down frantically.

After a few minutes, the fly found a landing place on the plastic ceiling and steadied itself above the girl. She was glued to the jewellery adverts in the in-flight magazine. It flew to the back of the plane where the mother was rouging her cheeks with the help of a hand mirror, before settling in the middle where the bald man seemed to be fast asleep. The temperature dropped drastically with the air-con, and the insect landed on the man's shoulder and crawled beneath his soft jacket collar.

The man woke suddenly from a shallow sleep and checked his watch. 9:58 Hong Kong time, which meant the plane had been airborne for nearly ten hours. He pulled up the plastic window screen. The sky was still dark. There were no lights outside.

Breakfast was being served.

'This is disgusting. The scrambled eggs taste like plastic, the tomatoes are soggy and the sausages are disinfectant,' the girl shouted, and made a scene in front of a flight attendant.

The man barely touched the food. He finished the bread roll with margarine and strawberry jam but left everything else. The fly feasted on the scrambled eggs, but the man didn't seem bothered. He closed his eyes and pretended to sleep.

Once the plane landed at Heathrow, the passengers bustled around impatiently, desperate to get out into the open air.

The man put on his jacket, checked his passport and a big brown envelope stuffed with cash. From the cabin windows he saw a grey overcast sky, almost drizzly and snowy. The in-flight announcement welcomed all the passengers to London and reported that the temperature in the capital was sub-zero.

As passengers made their way onto the sealed walkway, the fly escaped.

The airport was packed. The man headed briskly in the direction of the yellow ARRIVALS sign.

At the Immigration Desk, the officer in the glass box checked the man's passport and examined his face carefully twice. The man gave him a polite smile. The officer smiled back in a British way.

'Welcome back, Mr Bu.'

Once past Immigration, the bald man found himself among hundreds of people in the luggage-collection area. There were two exits. He walked quickly across to Exit B, straight through the custom checks with nothing to declare.

At the arrival hall outside Exit A, the mother and daughter were already waiting for the man. The girl was eating a sandwich and sipping Fanta. The woman in the classy black dress was still hiding under big sunglasses that covered half her face.

Meanwhile, the man carried on past colourful adverts, cigarette smoke, placards with passenger names written on them, families embracing and reunited lovers kissing. As the crowds around him gathered and dispersed, thinned and thickened, he spotted the woman wearing her ridiculous sunglasses in the middle of winter and the girl in gold-trimmed trainers, belt, top, necklace, earrings and hairband. He turned away and moved in the opposite direction, camouflaged by a group of airport cleaners going about their business.

The automatic sliding door opened, and a gust of icy air hit him in the face. He zipped up his jacket and pulled the hood over his head, bracing himself as he strode into the unfamiliar, grey world.

Outside the terminal, a bus to the city centre pulled in and the man jumped on like a local. Most of the seats were already taken. More people squeezed in and kept saying sorry to each other. He finally found an empty seat at the back. All the windows were steamed up and nearly everyone was smoking. He wiped the condensation off the glass with his sleeve. Smudged faces walked in and out of the arrival and departure halls.

He picked out the figures of the mother and child in the crowd, ten feet or so away. They were both staring straight at him, and he stared back.

The bus pulled out.

The man waved at them through the smeared windows.

The woman looked bereaved, with her parted lips and knotted brows. The girl's face remained expressionless. She waved back at the man as the bus turned a corner and joined the traffic, following the signs to Central London.

Note on Cantonese slang and profanities

The novel uses two forms of Chinese written characters: the formal characters widely recognised as the standard form of writing and the colloquial Cantonese slang words. Cantonese is a spoken language, the lingua franca of Hong Kong and the province of Guangdong. Although spoken throughout the city, Cantonese is not taught as a written language in the school curriculum, and until recently has not figured in official writing.

Cantonese slang is full of profanities that were common in daily conversations in the 1980s, some of which have survived. Like profanities in other languages, vulgar Cantonese words mostly refer to sexual organs. However, Cantonese swear words are particularly agile, allowing the speaker to conjugate inventive insults through puns and metaphors. Although forbidden in mainstream media, Cantonese swear words loom large in local speakers' imaginations and sense of humour, transcending social boundaries and taboo.

Recent reports suggest that the number of Cantonese

speakers in Hong Kong is decreasing. The reasons for this are multiple, including demographic change, new educational policies, and the increasing political and economic power of Mainland China. With its subversive power, Cantonese profanities reflect a pervasive creativity integral to the vitality of the language. Though it might not mean a lot to non-Cantonese speakers, it is hoped that citing it in both Chinese and English will give a culturally distinctive inflection to a language that is under threat, not unlike the shanty town in the novel.

Acknowledgements

I am grateful to the judges of the Northern Writers' Awards – Kerry Hudson and Jonathan Ruppin – for their encouragement, and staff at New Writing North, especially Will Mackie and Claire Malcolm for their support. I thank Mimi Ching, my teacher and friend, who spent time with the book during the recent troubles in Hong Kong and shared an old photograph of Diamond Hill with me. I thank Adam Phillips and David Nicholls for reading the manuscript and encouraging me. Thanks to Kate Weaver and Michelle Kelly who also read the draft and helped me with humour and insight. Thank you to Matt Turner, my agent, for championing the manuscript from the word go and helping me polish and re-polish a rough diamond. I am grateful to Sharmaine Lovegrove, my publisher in the UK, for believing in me and teaching me how to listen to the characters and their stories, and to the wonderful team, especially David Bamford, at Dialogue Books and Little, Brown for bringing the book to light. I thank Judith Uyterlinde, my publisher in the US, for believing in the novel, and to the amazing team at World Editions, especially Lydia Unsworth whose meticulous editing kept me on the right path. I am indebted to my parents 林瑞貞 (Lam Shui Ching) and 范上中 (Fan Sheung Chung), and my sister 范進欣 (Fan Chun Yan). Thank you to my friends for conversations and being there: Anna Armstrong, John Barnard, Emily Berry, Judith Clark, Brian Cummings, Ziad Elmarsafy, Michael Fend, Teresa Kittler, Hermione Lee, Hélène Lecossois, Lam Ling, Amanda Lillie, Lorraine Ng, Kabbie Ngo, Caitríona O'Reilly, Lionel Pilkington, Freya Sierhuis, Cyrus Tse, Geoffrey Weaver, Polly Yuen Throntveit, and Elizabeth Tyler. Above all, I thank Hugh Haughton who has accompanied me on every page.

Thank you, Hong Kong, for your stories and spirits.

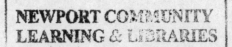

Bringing a book from manuscript to what you are reading is a team effort.

Dialogue Books would like to thank everyone at Little, Brown who helped to publish *Diamond Hill* in the UK.

Editorial
Sharmaine Lovegrove
David Bamford
Amy Baxter

Contracts
Stephanie Cockburn

Sales
Andrew Cattanach
Hannah Methuen
Caitriona Row
Sinead White
Jack Hallam

Design
Sophie Harris
Jo Taylor

Production
Narges Nojoumi

Operations
Natasha Allen
Sanjeev Braich

Publicity
Millie Seaward

Marketing
Emily Moran
Celeste Ward-Best

Copy Editor
Steve Cox

Proof Reader
Saxon Bullock